LIBERATED SPACE

By
Johnny Dolphin

sp
SYNERGETIC PRESS
Santa Fe, New Mexico

All characters are fictional.
Public events described occurred.

Cover design by Elemental Graphics
Cover photo © by Lisa Law.

ISBN 0 907791 33 6

TO ALL THOSE WHO MADE "1967"

Time's Operator

That clear chill invigorating leafless day in late November, 1965, at the official age of 36, I had escaped Time by becoming a ten year old at the great round of seats on the fountain in Washington Square below Washington's Arch, freed by a word of truth to eat my chocolate ice cream in a wonderful peace that left my physiology noiselessly concentrating energy. In this silence, I knew that, just as I had discovered eternity in the meditative Kief Café above the Zocco Chico in Tangier where tick-tock time had disappeared into an afternoon of communion with Tangier's being, I had discovered the third dimension of Time, Time's Operator, on this boyish day in Manhattan. Beyond tick-tock time lay multileveled fullnesses of time, and beyond the fullnesses of time crouched Time's Operator which could decide destinies, by creating time lines.

In that decisive moment, I knew I could also escape my spatial fate, avant-garde inventor laden with mauve dangers and glamours of India and Vietnam and redolent traditions and precision of mining and Harvard, with physiological microminiaturizations from theaters of cruelty and opening doors of herbal perceptions and wild and painful romances and ambitions, with Popperian, Marxist, Nietszchean, and Godellien manipulations of truth propositions. But I did not know how, when, and where to use my powers. I was properly afeared, and sought for knowledge.

Knowledge I found in two headwaters. The meeting where I had heard the word of truth from Jason the black man in Prince's cool steak place on Sullivan Street near the Park led me to a breakaway metaphysical group in a Village loft where, after a late meeting a month after my discovery of Time's Operator, I discovered in a corner, closed but not locked, a wooden chest. While the others were occupied with a ping-pong interlude in another room, I opened that chest and quickly found books by the two men from whom this leader of the breakaway group had stolen what knowledge he had, two men never mentioned to us.

These two books, clues to my first headwater, led me to two mansions in green, stream-filled, oak-landscaped Southern England. One man, with piercing eyes and a trim beard, had access to and practiced with mastery the ancient knowledge that Anil Thakkar had exemplified to me in India. The other man, tall, imperial, had access to and practiced with creativity the new knowledge of multi-dimensional mathematics and world history. I made my contacts with them, masters of past wisdom and eternities, and masters of future wisdoms and Time's Operator. The one was half-Scottish and half-Central Asian, the other half-British and half-American.

The master of the new had met me, by appointment by letter, at his door, wordlessly tossed a match packet at me without warning, and upon my catching it, indicated I should make a fire in the living room. When he returned, he nodded in approval at the crackling flame, and began to talk. "There are three dimensions of Time to match the three dimensions of Space . . . These can be called the Three Domains."

Finding out from a student of that master of futures where the master of eternities lived, I waited until this something inside I had called Time's Operator made its move, and then walked to this man's mansion. He opened the door; no one else was in the house or on the extensive grounds. We had fullness of time, an eternity to talk, interrupted by two phone calls he dealt with incisively. "I don't need the paraphernalia. Real knowledge resides in a school called supercession of ephemeral phenomena." I could see 'ephemeral phenomena,' kingdoms, empires, religions, family lives, languages, forms of teaching knowledge, arts and sciences appearing and disappearing. "This knowledge is not a grocery store, money and wanting it do you no good here."

For me, leaving micro-skirted swinging London two days later, in October, 1966, after seeing my writing buddy, Terry, from Tangier, in Portobello, living with his hip callgirl friend, and after an afternoon's meditation in Saint James Park, my next step seemed clear. With access to real knowledge from future and past, I needed now to contact access to knowledge of right now. I decided to take a full LSD voyage on my own in the middle of Manhattan. Even after my experiences with Bill Layton in our laboratory south of Houston Street with DMT, mescaline, and ibogaine, under controlled conditions, I knew this experiment would push me past my limit. And that's what I needed to contact, the infinite in the present to balance contact with infinite in the past and future.

Securing 200 micrograms from a special stash Bill Layton located of the discontinued pure Sandoz Albert Hofmann product, I put the sugar cube in my mouth at five o-clock in the afternoon. I intended to use Time's Operator to jump from time-line to time-line, fullness of time to fullness of time, until I could master sensing its arrival and how to ride it from now to now and then to then and fullness to fullness as opportunity and intention should coalesce.

I had called up my old friend Val, now a professor of Far Eastern History at Columbia, to meet me at five-thirty at the coffee shop on MacDougal and Bleeker where we had occasionally met to play Go before my journey around the planet. Val had stared at a leaf in Ryoanji until he became one with the leaf, married a daughter of one of the old families of Kyoto, and on occasion had advised the State Department. Years ago, he had tossed me around, demonstrating his judo prowess, at our yearly meetings at obscure parks in randomly picked cities such as Indianapolis. Val had specialized in emotional impenetrability and a specialist impeccability that had buried the brilliant young athlete versed in semiotics and aspiration I had met on the shores of Lake Michigan nearly twenty years earlier. Only in his Go game did he still reveal the skilled probing mercilessness toward weaknesses that had made me so fond of him.

I had also asked a slim beautiful dancer of adventurous sexuality to join us. Val and Jeannette were soon talking animatedly. I had given each a romantic portrait of the other and of their initiation into those two graceful skills of dance and sitting.

Jeannette soon stripped off Val's monogamous mask, deep-set though it had become. They both entered a contact high from my state. I stroked Jeannette's thigh every time she made a hit in Val's armor and brought a spark to his eye. I hung on every word of his that made her lean forward. I threw kindling on their fires.

Soon it was a replay of all the triangles of my life, including the Terry-Lita scene in Tangier as well as the primal one, and all those in between. Never had Jeannette seemed so desirable, never had Val seemed so quick and admirable. Never had all the possibilities in such an eternity attained such a common presence of life. Their wealth flooded my attention with delights, crimes, triplicities, and irreversible up and down gradings, all being enacted at the same time with equal reality.

I felt the Time Operator and decided to split this eternity glittering with its enchanted potentiality. With murmured apology I pretended to go to the toilet, but walked out of the café and around the block to the Kiwi bar on Houston Street. I knew my friendship with Val had ended. When I stood up to leave, a great freedom relaxed my body and I had stood a second too long inhaling the scene of the two. "You look like Zeus ready to hurl a thunderbolt at a rival admirer of Niobe," Val had said, an almost frightened look suddenly appearing on his still youthfully carved countenance. "Oh no," I had laughed. "Only Hermes winging messages around the night."

The Kiwi gave entrance into another eternity, as dense or denser with time lines. The little boy off the street that lived in the great cardboard box in the back room sat on his small carpet, watching. Bridget, the red-haired tall would-be Irish writer sitting at the bar over her scotch next to sloping shouldered Dan, who did write between his merchant seaman trips. They knew each other too well to sleep together, but each would have died defending the other from any attack in any form from whatever source including God himself.

My Iroquois buddy who worked on the high rise constructions had interested the newest East Side blonde who had heard of the Kiwi and patiently, craftily led her on by subtle alternations of attention to her body, her words, her emotions, her sex, her absences, her startings-up, to his seduction. By now, he knew every move in the repertoire of a young Ivy League lady living in a door watched East Sixties building. I waved to Bonnie, the glorious young Swedish blonde from Minnesota who had just moved into the neighborhood, and disappeared into her friendly lips so much more eloquent in their movements than in her words.

The Kiwi's fullness of time revealed Vermeer after Vermeer of motionless configurations. The sign again came and I decided to slip out toward Washington Park. Found myself pacing with a young brown man from some destroyed past. His eyes shone and we vibed synchronistically around the park before speaking a word. We both knew we were "on."

"I been on acid for three days," he said. "Ain't been outta the park. The cops ain't able to see me. I pick up food that's left. You're the first one that's seen me."

We glided on through the night, changing distances from each other, digging chess players, maker-outers, beggars, voyeurs, cops, isolates, groupies, and I could see him deliriously happy from breaking out of his time line, living with the entire full time of the Park. Like Tangier to me, the Park had breached his sandbags and spread over all his fertile lands, depositing a rich silt for future growths, its mysterious midnights, dangerous currents, and liquid musics refining his apperceptions. His grace, his skill, his art of camouflaged movement brought out my mimic. I also was skittering out of a destroyed past, more, out of several destroyed pasts, and I imitated his abilities to vibe in and out of scenes.

Once more the sign, and decisively off towards Slug's jazz joint on Avenue C. Dancing congealed to a tall slim woman in the freest space at that moment in Manhattan.

"We going South early in the morning," she said. "On the bus to Mississippi for the Resistance."

"Aren't you scared?"

"Yes, but I'm going. And just before going some of us always come to Slug's, take a line or two and live it up. I been down there before and it's hard. They hit you and insult you."

Slug's was dark and blues and cocaine and freedom and building action that night. Slug's was the Revolution In-being. Slug's was the America I loved. I knew why she was going South in the early morning.

"Come home with me."

"I gotta leave early at five, for our last strategy talk."

We never exchanged names. From Slug's we entered another fullness of time. Forever she lay silent on her back, her long lean legs straight up at exactly ninety degrees from the hips, alternately tightening and relaxing her sex, opening and closing her eyes, while I ramped in a hundred different lives and ways until my palimpsest of motion matched her ocean. We solved all the problems of bloody horrendous and ambiguous pasts in a future that will take at least a century of a hundred million conscious efforts to arrive in tick-tock time.

I scrambled eggs, she made toast and coffee, then she parted with the majestic presence of the Nile. I decided to leave Manhattan for the second time. The first time I had left from the top of a great skyscraper, the young provincial who had made it all and saw the horror of a dreary forty years of fighting through chills, thrills and spills for the propertied death of a member of the American ruling class. I had sought and found secrets of eternity in Tangier and then in the furthest East. This second time, I was leaving in the fullness of life, the eternity of Manhattan, but desperate to take part in the shaping of a new Reality. This lean girl with glorious eyes had shown me the third great headwater. One had to go to the point where the action was at. For her, Mississippi. For me, it would have to be San Francisco. It was July, 1967. Why had I waited so long? I knew that Haight Ashbury was where the battle for history now concentrated. In that liberated space the conscience of America was being created by dropping out, turned-on music, and tuned-in cunning, that conscience that had been corrupted almost inevitably in the devil's pact for Manifest Destiny with slavery, gold, and the destruction of the Indian tribes. That battle of consciousness needed to be won in San Francisco as well as her battle for freedom in Mississippi. I was damned if I would let her efforts exceed mine.

Jumping In

I arrived in San Francisco with two thousand dollars in travelers checks and a hundred in a wad of ones and fives thrust in my right front pocket, in blue jeans, boots, plaid shirt, T-shirt beneath, a corduroy jacket, a writer's notebook in each pocket, and a shoulder-slung canvas suitcase stuffed with a pair of tennis shoes, khaki pants, socks, T-shirts, yellow writing pads, toilet kit, and multi-vitamin supplement.

Getting on a bus outside the greyhound station for the Haight, I watched two girls jumping on behind me without paying. They gave a cheerful smile to the bus driver and each handed him a chocolate. Proceeding down the bus aisle they handed each passenger a chocolate, saying "Love", and got out the back door at the first stop. Everybody was smiling. They wore flowers in their hair.

Arriving at the already fabled intersection, I jumped down into the everflowing crowd of colorfully clad and calm faces whose expressions brought back faces at Berber markets, at Malakal in the Sudanic Nile, in Patan in Nepal. But this was different. Here, these faces not only in time and the fullness of time, but behind them, coalescing the varied movements, Time's operator. They were creating something decisively new, incorporating science, technics, and the contradictions of America and Western Europe into the state of consciousness produced by poets, transformational psychologists, and magicians of the will in Africa, Asia, and the American tribes for thousands of years and till two thousand years ago, in Europe itself in its mystery dramas. But "seeing" this was not enough for me. I determined to experience it all, to fight as a foot soldier in such moment-by-moment skirmishes as might occur in my area, my volume, my time line. I understood that a vision, no matter how true, would never become real without each cell in my body reaching the ability to incarnate that vision as best it could. If some of us could do that, and only then, the world could evolve. That's how I totally felt.

Reaching the liberated area of the park, I strolled by the watery throb of bongos and the sweet smell of grass, then through the underpass and the traffic. An archetypal entrance to a world so ineluctable in its modality, ensconced among the trees, upon the grassy plain, sitting on the sloping ridge, strolling the paths, that words left me. I wept with joy. I laughed with aching heart. My entire body relaxed. I now knew what I needed to know to start.

Sitting by a three-trunked tree, a guru from Harlem held forth to five acolytes, two blonde and three dark. I loosely dropped, cross-legged, into their circle. Admired the guru's well-shaped bare feet, dug the guru's mellow voice. Too high to make out his words, I bowed again, reached out, and stroked that guru's left foot into an entire world of blue rivers of blood, pink deserts, dark cliffs.

"The devil! He's the devil!" The guru jerked his heel from my caress, jumped up, and ran off shouting, followed by his devotees neither he nor they daring a single glance behind.

I saw a tight circle of bent heads silently standing above low bushes on a small rise. Sauntered over to catch their mantram. But they circled a mesomorphic strong-breasted blond fucking a slim quick-assed long hair. "She thinks people ought to have a chance to see a pure good fuck," a guy whispered in my ear. They all stood silent resonating with the soundless graceful ritual, her smooth legs draped over his thighs, her face, gazeless, in touch with the sky. I contemplated, breathed in and out with ten beautiful strokes, then, satiated, breath caught full in my chest, walked back through the tunnel and up onto Haight Street past benches of meditative smokers exchanging a glint or a glance with each pair of eyes.

Hungry, I wandered to the Diggers' stand, thick hot soup and chewy bread. Didn't want to learn about their riff or their anarchy, why they were doing it, anymore than I wanted to know why fog crept in or sun shone or cops and robbers played their games. Why dropped away. What and how came down. Why? Because it all fitted together like the girl and the guy. When I finished sopping the soup, set their undecorated bowl on the wash-off stand. Delicious. Filling. Beans that'd stick to your ribs. The Diggers' had a trip but they didn't lay it on you directly.

I poked around a couple of trash cans before I fished out a discarded Oracle newspaper, lazily plopped down on a curb, and crossing my legs, relaxed, hid between two cars to groove on the technicolor front-page designs and read aloud a few words of those fervent texts.

Then, I sat, spine slowly straightening, on the curb, its film of dirt transformed to sparkling little grit between a Ford and a Chevvie, each of which cost a lot more than I had lived on the past two years.

"If I can't do it here, I can't do it anywhere else," I lazily mouthed the slow appearing words. "The entire world has acquiesced for these few blocks to be it for now. I will take whatever happens, ready for anything, I hope. I refuse to move on until it all comes together in me, and if it doesn't, it undoubtedly never will for me, because I will never be more ready. 'Readiness is All' and what if Everything is Ready?" I grinned to myself. Who was I kidding? I knew this was the place and the time and I was lucky as hell to be here and also that it would be as tricky to do it here as in Mississippi for my Manhattan muse.

Moving on, fell into stride with a young girl, long straight dark hair. "Do you know anything beyond the theater of cruelty?" she asked. Not a note of a sex game in her voice or glance.

"Yes, The theater of recontouring impossibility."

"Where?"

"In my head, in life, and soon, I hope, right here."

We strolled on through costumes, traffic, eyes, vibrations. My body slid through cracks in the thick ambiance that my finger could feel as I moved it like an antenna ahead of me in the surround. She moved like an habitué through discontinuities I had only began to discover.

"I dance, but I want to do theater," she said.

"I travel, but I want to write theater."

We stopped to gaze into each other's eyes, trading energies and enigmas.

We resumed strolling between immense alternities, far-wandering crossroads. Nothing inevitable about a single one of our steps. If she broke the attention connection for a single one of them, I decided to disappear down the next opportunity I dug. But, if she could keep this up to her destination, she would be the first member of my karass, that circle of beings that recur throughout the generations all of whom it is necessary to meet and connect with for an individual to accomplish destiny in his lifetime. I knew myself well enough to know the discovery of my karass had to be my next step. One really travelled the world to grok the karass, although many would confuse the first grok with a single love, and sell transcendence short, reaping erotic profits but never gaining access to the cornucopia center. Two steps at a time up three flights of wooden stairs, bounding to a stop in a dancing workshop.

"Madison," the princess introduced me to a slim energetic glowing woman. "Ann Zalbin. He writes plays and wants to learn your approach."

After warm-up, "Find a partner. One of you lie on your back. The other kneel behind the head. Lift the head, then drop it, but catch it in your palms before it hits the floor. Trust, we must learn trust."

Ann herself knelt behind my head, lifted it as high as it would go, then dropped it. Distrust. I learned more about distrust in that brief time of my head dropping than ever before. Distrust of my motive for being there, for risking my head, of hers for putting out pabulum of trust in a world uncertain, shifting, full of conflicting motivations. I could clearly see the differences in a world of trust and a world of alertness and chose without hesitation. Anything can happen in either world but you're readier for it when you don't trust in the phenomena.

"Meet you tomorrow at the Park at ten."

If she doesn't kiss me good-bye, I'll know this is all delusion, and write it off. She brushed my lips, a microsecond after the thought.

In the chill star-bedazzled thinning fog finally found a car with an unlocked door. Sacked out in the rear seat till dawn. Let body crumple into what shape it finds, sweet sleep comes. My decision to be here rules my life, no more blame, no improvements, only tracking. The quiet tracker moved by turns through worlds of objects, thoughts, dreams, and sleep's pure self, in pursuit of powers to seek and to find what I could not quite make out but intuited must exist in flesh as well as vision.

Roy Howard, tall, broad shouldered, slouchy, thin-lipped smile, small paunch, consequence of his love and limitation to small indulgences, plaid shirt, jeans, blue farsighted quizzical eyes, sandy hair, skilled worker's square-fingered hands with double-jointed thumbs, standing in front of colorfully painted bus, "Hi."

Hadn't seen Roy since on the Yugoslav freighter heading for Tangier, November '63. He had introduced me to hashish, which stretched me out like a cat on the yawing, pitching, and rolling floor of his cabin. I had watched ever-changing mathematics of yellow light turning patterns on the concrete through the wicket wastebasket, entranced by the Euclidean transformations proceeding in direct perceptual meta-formulas. I had no interest left for the desk above and society's published books.

Roy had fled, soon after landing. The complex sexualities and subtle non-humanistic ways of Tangier Berbers, several of whom had entangled bisexually with Burroughs, inspired avant-garde efforts to relate physiology to perception without intervention of Platonic inventions such as Soul, Mind, and Essences, but scared Roy off.

"A mess isn't it?" Roy said. "The Haight. This street. I'm with the Jefferson Camp. Everyday I drive the bus in and we take out fifteen-twenty walking wounded for some good food, a night or two in the mountains by Sonoma, try to get them off the street."

"I like the street," I said. "This action's made my whole life worthwhile. I never knew what freedom meant before. As to T.J., my family was Jeffersonian with Jefferson himself. Reason, marketplace of ideas, sturdy farmers, wide-ranging scholarship, political process to ensure human rights. Roy, that's not how it is today. No yeoman farmers left now, scholarly presidents. That's all a lie now, not even a real myth like Shiva-Shakti or Shango-Ogun, just an indoctrination. You are against Haight Ashbury because it's too hot just like Tangier. Worse, here you're acting against it, you don't cool it, there you just fled back to Ibiza, pleasure, and the art market, plus a little DMT."

"Joe, come out and spend the night. Lucy's baking some good bread. Wood oven. Old log house. Fireplace. Breathe some sweet fresh air and clear your brain."

"Why the hell not?" Joe Madison always inclusive, synchrony symphony of opposites.

Shady and cool up in their wooded Sonoma hills. Lucy, a stripper who met Roy after becoming an artist's model, baked a crusty chewy loaf. The guy who bankrolled the project wheeled himself up in his chair, a thin furry animal's face, non-species specific.

"Roy told me about you. Roy's our foreman, but I could use someone to help structure the programs for the ones we're trying to rescue."

He and Roy and Lucy looked like they needed rescue. A mountain range of concepts protected their read-outs from their own sensations; their sure answers appeared before ambiguities arrived. As long as this funny guy could bankroll, this phony backwoods act would play.

I smiled, acted stupid and friendly.

Roy offered me a toke before he and Lucy turned in. "Is this Jeffersonian?" I asked.

"Probably. Washington grew hemp and it was in the pharmacopoeia till Roosevelt. We're not doctrinaire, Joe. Liberty. But hallucinations, free sex, schizos that call themselves gurus, bad sanitation, that's not freedom, Joe, that's anarchy and it'll end in a reaction, in a constitutionally masked dictatorship by the oligarchy claiming to save the youth. Save youth alright, for cannon fodder and dollar fodder."

We gazed at each other's suddenly carefully muscled masks, a long moon-mellowed gaze in the crisp night air. You can't lie to someone you've tripped with in old Tangier where anything went, and anything always went in the direction of strangest and strongest magic. "Abstractions have lost their power over me," I said. "Even abstractions the best of my family fought for, a few died for, and which occupied fifteen years of my life in work and thought. If it doesn't register with my physiology as life-enhancing, I won't touch it anymore. What you've got here is a rich man's imitation of my grandfather's ranch life, except he can't do anything, you're a hired flunky, Lucy's happy to have a suburban husband, and it's the ghost of a ghost of a frontier destroyed by the world market and the creations of artists and scientists working with shadows and quanta. Haight Street in San Francisco vibrates with future, including all futures that will die there, strangled in the cradle by remorseless selection. In the past it might have taken centuries for certain weaknesses to become apparent. Pick up who you can, Roy, and then watch them eat white bread as soon as Lucy's come-on baked bread has landed them back in their jobs. Withering into power-possessing simulacrums, ignored by those moving quickly. The quick and the dead."

Roy inhaled the last of the toke carefully placing the small remainder in the corner of the square right pocket on his jean copper studded jacket.

"You and I see things differently."

"We sure do."

We hugged each other and pounded each other on the back, he a Jeffersonian respecting dissent, I an opportunist figuring you never knew about a man until long after he was dead, if then. Roy would easily switch to something else when the money cut and ran.

In the morning Lucy and I hugged, but she didn't let her breasts engage and looked relieved when I left on the bus. Seeing that I caught it, she blushed and ran to get me a loaf of bread and a jar of apple butter "to keep yourself a day or so on the street."

"Lucy, I wish I'd seen you dance."

"Well, you saw me cook." Defiantly.

I jumped from the bus as soon as its door opened, headed for the liberated area.

Romance

The tall beautiful Cherokee young woman ran "the anthropological house". It was supported by the anthropology department of City University. She arranged to set up a commune, make the scene, and allow two of the anthropologists to crash from time to time and anonymously perform their specialized observations.

I met her strolling in the Panhandle, where we both had been brought to a stop by a red-haired mime actress hanging head bent back, over the ropes of a boxing ring like the sun going down in the west, screaming in a not unpleasant soprano, kicking, in desultory opposition, a milk-white calf and bare foot in the general direction of lean ugly lecherously moving pantaloon, while behind him brilliantly colored harlequin somersaulted toward the rescue. Cool sun barely held back fog just rising above the hills to the oceanside.

We followed the silent touchless and soon breathless procedure of vibing in. During a pause in the drama, with a glance, walked away together. At the India House, she ordered two teas, and broke out a tightly rolled joint. "Let me get them," she said. "I have some money because those anthropologists pay me to run a commune, two hundred and fifty a month, and cover my expenses there as well."

We gasped with as much laughter as Navajos or Polynesians at her description of the antics of anthropologists who were the first chance many individuals in cultures around the planet had to study closely the doctrinaire behavior of academics from a Thirteenth Century religion based system of specialist categories, the university, that held the youth of the West by the throat, choking out submissive learned-by-rote answers to officially approved textbooks, "fables for sophomores". Of course, she said, missionaries, soldiers, and bosses all from the same European domination submission systems, had always showed up demanding behavioral and psychological secrets from the locals, but those power figures always kept their distance from interactions except at rituals, parades, executions, and fat-assed thin-lipped order-givings. Anthropologists actually had to live with the people and act non-judgmental for their own health while laying down in funded papers their judgment for the benefit of functionaries of the imperial world market. So anthropologists alone of Western officialdom could be studied at leisure by the locals who vied with each other to tell tantalizing lies to provoke the range of reactions possessed by "the investigator", the better to understand the range of these marauding world-transformers in order to use this knowledge to protect themselves. "So we study these guys who think they're studying us," she laughed, "just like the Navajo do."

"I'll see you after dinner," she said after we took a full minute to trail fingers. It wasn't a brush-off. Dinner, an especially important event at communes just as in all types of extended families, was mostly of interest only to its own members. Individual life came later.

At ten o'clock I showed up at her green Victorian house, whose parts, carefully crafted in New England factories, were sailed to San Francisco round Cape Horn. On arrival they were assembled much as automobiles and airplanes come together today. I admired the advanced notions of the Nineteenth Century that put organized industrial production at the service of making fine houses to last at least a century rather than stamping out metal widgets with a one year warranty and doubtful benefit. A boyish boisterous girl pointed me up the perfectly carpentered stairway bathed in faint lavender perfume. Multi-colored lights softly reflected in various mirrors, creating a dispassionate mood from subliminal subtle images on the edges of forms. "The room on the right at the front of the house," she said.

Knocking with deliciously foolish anticipation of enlightenment, of happiness, of trance and even of an ending of all my past life and a commencement of something gorgeously new, I heard her fig-shaped voice murmur "come in."

She danced with a black guy I knew from the one commune existing on Fillmore Street. Some parts of Fillmore you walked down the middle of the street. James' commune was OK, rehabilitation of "fallen" sisters, making out selling used clothes plus rhetoric coerced contributions from businessmen looking for alternatives to the Black Panthers and their rifles. I stood motionless trying to stay cool and groove while they glided hiplocked in rhythm, but a feeling I should leave, no right to be there, rose nearly to my throat. Could barely puff the joint she offered with her left hand as she slid by.

For the next two hours the guy and I alternated dances. Midnight. I'd finally felt a conclusion fill my body. Stay there until she asked me to leave or him, or he left on his own. Never done that before in my life. I'd always made the first move to leave. "Don't impose." That wonderful alchemy that occurs from intentionally breaking a habit seeped tastily through the mnemonic cellules stored throughout the muscles, ending my chemical structure of prematurely conceded defeat that, I realized, had stealthily limited a hundred of my wanderings through American nights and African days. Wanderings that turned all too often into fleeings.

Without a word, just after midnight, he left, quietly, politely, gently closing the door. We barely managed to pull ourselves apart to remove our clothing. Though I struggled to maintain minute observation of each change, the apex of sudden complete ecstasy that prolonged itself when over left no experience. I could not retrace my path. I still could not outwit that river of gorgeous forgetfulness. She slept. In the false dawn drifting through partings in the velvet purple curtains, I saw her suddenly groan, begin to heave, then run out the door to the bathroom where a series of racking vomits began. She returned. I pretended to sleep. When she fell off again, I tiptoed out, down the superbly carpentered stairway, quietly turned the old brass doorknob, backed out, bowing, turned in a whirl, and ran down the steps toward Haight.

Saw her again three weeks later at a party. A long blonde haired guy, grinning with happiness, surveyed the room, allowing anyone to gaze at him, sitting, broad shouldered, knees spread apart, hands relaxed between his thighs, on a black leather chair at least three feet wide between the arms. She sat at his left knee, drinking him in, seeing nothing else, her long legs neatly folded together.

Minute Particulars

Then I abandoned living for my autobiography, an ambition which had continued even after dropping living for my biography. Abandoned Saint Augustine, Benvenuto Cellini, and Frank Harris. Even abandoned living for memories. Abandoned Montaigne. Abandoned living for deeds. Abandoned my unacknowledged master, Plutarch. I escaped the debauched slavery of endeavoring by every means possible to live a life interesting enough to write about for others. I understood that a human could live many lives. That most of those lives were only for me, some for a few, and no more than a couple or so were for a public. A greater revelation than the one four years ago when I had left glitter gulch Manhattan for the neotonies and epiphanies of majoon bedazzled and Berber-eyed Tangier, and, on the way there in the pitching yawing Harvatska in the mid-Atlantic, realized I didn't want to be President of all those failed marriages. Entire worlds of personal and historic power moved far above and way to the side and behind and in front of the President. How right Jefferson had been to leave that temporary and local title off his tombstone and leave his private life and conversations hidden, hidden, deeply hidden.

Yes, I stopped living for my fantasy autobiography while gazing at that beautiful Cherokee gazing at that beautiful blond himself gazing at vacancy. I understood the meaning at last of that disappearance of time in that white-cloud islanded blue sky cut by those three black lines of the electric wire sitting that afternoon above the Tangier medina. The autobiographical form itself, the self-written life, that greatest work of fiction written, painted, and analyzed by the masters of Western Art and Psychology, Augustine, Rembrandt, Cellini, Freud, and James Joyce, and a host of lesser memoirs, had at last disappeared. Continued contact with the Haight's montaged multilevels revealed Asiatic reincarnation itself as a drawn-out boring way of doing many incarnations one after the other.

The secret of conquest of time, that merciless destroyer whenever opposed or cajoled in a single form flirted with me as I strolled down

Haight toward the liberated space in the park. Along the gentle ridge of the first hill in the park, a mounted policeman rode from time to time looking down on the colorful spectacle below, taking in the bongos, watching small groups pursuing enlightenment, pleasure, ecstasy, instinctive well-being, in short, pursuing happiness with their life and liberty, ready to arrest them the minute he was given the go-ahead to end the provocative spectacle. Each passing day aroused in the policeman a stronger impulse to destroy that scene in which he was forbidden to participate, not only by order but by conditioning, never to play a part. A destructive impulse continually regenerated by his own self-denied desire to join in, if only for once, to see what it was all about.

In the nearby streets, the Communications Company commune kept up the network of necessary public information that word-of-mouth might occasionally lack, and word-of-mouth kept Communication Company up on all that it should know, and word-of-mouth kept to itself what could not be entrusted to any Company whatsoever, even composed of those of kith and cool.

David Smith's Free Clinic kept vigilance over sex, liver, and epidemic disease, curing without spreading the crippling American epidemic of moral taxation.

Each commune an experimental center of intimate, dynamic, shaking, risky and profound experience looking for existential bridges to the meta-human. A seeker could crash wherever he or she found rapport. People took big chances because they could see big pay-offs. Losers could always make it one way or another by returning as prodigal sons to the society of habit from which they had emerged. A new commune could be founded for 300 dollars a month rent, one-month deposit paid with it, plus your life's investment in emotions, payable upon demand.

My dear Joe Madison had always loved oil and mining boom towns. Now I watched the Haight, a boom town of experience. A line of cars bumper-to-bumper down the street, windows open, the occupants astounded at clear voices and artistic costumes of freedom in action, just as I had seen people driving off the main highways to cruise Grand Junction to watch the prospectors with Geiger counters, geologists, claim buyers, and nightclub girls in the uranium boom. Each day a new storefront began. The sound of hammers like an old frontier town going up near a gold mine. Nearly every car bought an *Oracle* and the *Oracle* salesmen recycled their money to the community. The *Oracle* was a newspaper based on writing about this new boom, not the newest recurrence of old booms that was the staple of the *Chronicle* and the *Times*: war, crime, inventions, emigration, or stimulation, but about certain possibilities not yet quite here but how to get rich (in experience) while it was happening. Invest in the right trip!

I could buy anything, meet anyone, play any role, that my means, desire, perception, and ability allowed. Even a fast food and a supermarket remained on Haight for anyone experiencing too great a jolt of culture shock to make a temporary re-entry to bottom line, much as a ranch or two would persist next to a gold rush.

I saw the princess again walking with her long dance- trained stride. "I've been selling some of the two dollar jewelry we make, that's how we buy our food, but I'm on my way back to hear Bob talk about Prophets of the West. This evening, it's Blake. Want to come?"

"Who's we?"

"The people at the house I live in plus a few guests."

"Sure." We fell into synchronous loose lope. Someone just before had slipped me a two hundred and fifty microgram tab, "pure Owsley". Every trip is different and my trip about trips was not to use sacred substance on grooving, sex, or following the light and sound show of the inner worlds of colors, memories, gods, demons, messages, the chills, thrills, and spills of esoteric esoterica, but to pay attention more closely to movements, sensations, and conversation. I made many discoveries doing this that never seemed necessary or even possible or particularly useful to endeavor to share since they always related to contextual minute particulars, but each showed me some new way to work with my body.

And doubtless because this last phrase had just arrived to my contemplation and that minute particulars had been one of Blake's favorite phrases, my organism and I had so quickly responded to the princess's invitation to attend her seminar.

"Princess Precious Pearl," I murmured, "you are taking me to China and the Prophet has commanded to seek knowledge, even as far as China."

"Maybe I'm from beyond China. This is the space age, Joe."

The evening air becoming aqueous at that point from streetlights, clouds, stars, and a momentary gibbous moon, she changed before my eyes. "Of course, from Otter Mongolia."

We immediately rolled like otters over the broad green lawn adjacent to the sidewalk.

"That's where we're really from, Otter Mongolia."
"No one else need ever know."
"No one else could ever know."
"No one else would want to know."
"Because they're on the road to China."
"If they're on the road."
"They also sweat who stand and wait."
Silence.
"The Theater of Colliding Impossibilities," I said.
"That's the one the world can never see," she said.
"That's the only one I'm hot for."
"That's between you and me."

"Between you and me and this deco lamp post." I swung, one hand holding on, the other stretched around that serendipitous object, watching the volume of light shade exponentially to darkness while she stood in the penumbra, laughing, a richly melancholic, toothy, rococo Saturnine, eighteen year old brilliant laugh.

Camouflage

About twenty of us, sat on the pillowed floor in the bay window room of the two story plus basement classic Victorian wooden house. Princess and I had walked in past the window with the small sticker "Enterprise for Investigating Potentiality."

Bob was one of those guys whose basic masculinity reminded me of my own. He had grown up on a Montana ranch and I in the Western Oklahoma shortgrass country. Sanguine with a trace of choleric flaring-up, a mesomorph who had obviously played contact sports, worked at a primary industry or two, fishing, ranching, mining, or timber, for a living, with a scholarly rasp sharpening his otherwise bold and jovial tongue. Our movements synched and our vitalities morphed together. Very different from me, though, in the direction he had taken, or which had taken him. Clearly he had become one of those satirical masterful black comedy Moses types who had to lead a chosen people however small, to spread his accidentally and ecstatically acquired knowledge, an eye-on-the-ball, on-the-toes experimenter with magic, history, and social power. Some insinuations from a subtle world had caught his rapt mesomorphic attention, focused his gregarious frontier mind with purpose, attracted his passionate attention, and sent him forth crippled by and numinous with that didactic disease of talented members of this subcaste of humanity, "to transmit his understanding of the truth." I always preferred freedom, but I loved him immediately, seeing that he was one of those genuine nuts endeavoring "to show people." Since he was good at it in his own intense way I immediately saw at least twenty years of unimaginable sufferings ahead of him before he finished with this exalted mad enterprise if it didn't finish him first. Twenty years of karma-producing labor that I could not even imagine undertaking, nor could find any wish to do so. Myself, I could contemplate human ignorance cheerfully and extensively without feeling the slightest impulsion, much less compulsion, to risk my time, my health, my life, my digestion, in making a fore-doomed attempt to bestir another human. Hard enough to bestir myself. Humans, the most dangerous life-form on the planet, both to other species and to members of their own, envy, malice, suspicion, deceit, camouflage, betrayal and faction being among their primary instincts. No, I was no more tempted to arouse thought in another human who had not done it for itself than to wake up a sleeping attack dog or shout at a cliff of snow hanging loose above me.

However, these haughty-generous guys and ladies are often extremely instructive and useful to those of us interested in tracking certain exceptional experiences. The exultant intellectual-emotional juice that flows through them can be real as a rose or a lily or a peyote or a wolf pack or a cholera. They always produce a contact high and, often, an aphorism. Their personal poignancy lies mainly in that they extract so little for themselves from that induced flow. They can't eat the dinner that they prepare for themselves: the bitter tastes of transference and counter transference, the onslaughts of greed, hatred, and lust, and most disgusting of all, the abdication of critical thought and emotional discrimination amongst a percentage of those they attract. Following my own cautiously-feeling-my-way-forward approach, of course I said nothing to Bob, then or later about my views, but prepared to catch my cupful from his outpouring, his splendid sacrifice that I confidently thought to render a little less useless by taking some tasty morsels and chewing them with my own saliva. Maybe I could even help him if he ever lost his footing in a pack fight.

"Blake," he began as directly as Ornette Coleman blows his first note, "who helped rescue Thomas Paine, and who never once wavered in fighting for freedom, saw the inextricable links between desire, wrath,and minute particulars.This man, the first of the modern prophets of the West to speak directly to our experience, as, for example, Swedenburg, Mesmer, and John Dee don't, never compromised on the direct translation of his insights and created an aphoristic poetry surpassing in important aspects even Zen, Tao, and Sufi poets. 'Energy is eternal delight.' 'The tigers of wrath are wiser than the horses of instruction.' I want to comment on these two statements which can be considered part of a manual of instructions. . . ."

Suddenly, Bob had given me a whole new way to "get" poetry. Some of it, the lines that engraved themselves in mental space, recollectible light displays, actually instructions for attitude embedded in a poem like pecans in a pie. Blake, Baudelaire, Whitman, Dostoyevsky, the prophets Bob listed on his series had all done this. That explained their peculiar power that no literary criticism of style or amateur appreciation of content could dispel or explain. Literature as camouflage. *Camouflage*, my favorite US Army book. My favorite art in life. Camouflage. How else to disappear when looked at? Mimicry. When Bates had discovered mimicry of poisonous insects by sweet-tasting insects in Amazonia, Darwin jumped with excitement. Evolution by natural selection had been decisively proved. Lorenz considered mastery of imitation to be the key to humanity's unique biological status.

When the talk, flow rather, ended, we left. I shook hands with Bob and automatically both our hands went into the Old West testing mode. He, in a shy cowboy way, accepted my handing him three dollars, his price for the talk. Princess beckoned me to see their back garden. Banners hung in the air with symbols for the numbers from one to nine. The symbol for one looked like a zero to me.

"One contains everything inside its boundary," she answered, "and excludes everything outside its boundary, but since One on the inside is the product exclusively of your attention, it is nothing, or zero to anyone else, and since on the outside one is a product of someone else's attention, it is nothing, or zero to you." I felt the curtain drawback to reveal a stage on which a play new to me would commence. And this play was designed to occur in life and within myself. "I'll take you to hear some special music in a few days," she said.

The Cheetah

"I used to think the biggest game in the world was training tigers," Tommy Faraway grinned affably, blue eyes intentionally magnetic, set like deep cenotes in his sun-reddened face, vivid beneath pure white hair. Leashed next to his right leg, his cheetah sat alert on wide-spread haunches.

We faced each other over a nondescript white plastic table in the harshly lighted café at the corner of Haight and Ashbury. Tommy suddenly rose, limped to the door with his sleek cheetah, then limped back, dropping yogi-like on his chair without a trace of slack to his spine.

"I earned this limp during a circus. The big guy got me in his jaws and started walking around the cage with me. Crowd screaming, me bleeding. I stuck my leg between the bars to stop his build-up of energy pacing to and fro with me. He broke my leg trying to tug it out of the bars until my assistant drove him off.

"But the limp didn't drive me out of the wild animal taming business. I got out because I discovered the biggest and most dangerous predator. Woman! Concealed by the simple fact that she looks like a prey to us, and sometimes in some existential ways she is, which makes it even more confusing, but in essence, she's predator.

"So my specialty is training predators to obey by teaching them satisfying tricks as rewards. I learned to teach women tricks, just how I trained tigers, teaching them new tricks, like you know I found there's fifty seven spots to produce orgasm?"

His ice-blue eyes never left off watching me. I didn't react but waited. "Okay," he said, "so you studied something somewhere, or you would have got excited one way or the other. See these scars on my neck?" He bent forward to show six point scars around the jugular vein, fingering his shirt apart at the neck.

"That was my final examination in the world's toughest hatha yoga school, in Tibet, just before the Dalai Lama fled. You had to stand there, in the state where you don't move, you control your reactions no matter what happens, your back against a wall, while the master's assistant lunges at you with a pointed knife and pierces in about an eighth of an inch."

"Yeah," I said. This time I didn't react because my body sat there soaking it in. I found no disbelief. He weighed me, rolled me back and forth in the palms of his eyes, let me drop.

"Be sure you don't move this time either," he said, and stroked a finger at the cheetah, then towards me.

I could see the cheetah haunch down, rise, open jaws, charge, and snap within an inch of my face.

Tommy patted his cheetah. "Can't get bit if you don't move," he said, picking up the check, and limped toward the counter, clothed in the simple glamour of real knowledge.

Remaking History

However equally Bob tried to behave to everyone during a session, at other times it was clear that he had two favorites, Princess, and a tallish, lean green-eyed blonde, from a ranch in Wyoming, Pauline.

Pauline never lost a chance to exhibit her bony, elegant knees, or to extend her long-fingered palm in an open gesture. Those gestures worked quite effectively combined with an open green-eyed try-me gaze. They never became old with her, and I enjoyed watching them recur, like motifs in a great jam session.

While Princess occasionally shyly and sensually visited me in my small closet, and even added to its decor two rhinestoned Berber pillows together with an incense stand, nothing could shake her position with and feeling for Bob, nor did I really wish to try. Being in the action, not acting in the action much less directing the action, distilling in the end an alchemical-historical text for millennia of contemplatives who wished to "see" the world had become my leisurely new ambition, superseding writing the great American novel! Leisurely because first I wished to make sure that "I" could "see" the world, and second because of my certainty that I would live a long time, that I had decades to recollect my emotions, sensations, and shifts and displacements of perception, that I would have the time and eventually the material means to do it right. I had made a few enigmatic journal entries about certain discoveries since preparing to leave New York for Tangier in 1963 and this method of notes would serve as neuronic triggers in the future, if necessary, if memory should somehow, driven by fears as yet unconscious to me, lock away my incest with the cosmos.

Bob found me sitting in the back garden one cool, sunny afternoon studying the symbols of his structures of action sewed in gold cloth on green banners. "As you so well know from your work with Reich's psycho-physiology," he began immediately according to his undeviating policy of eliminating small talk, but with his disarming grin and twinkle, "we do not really see but only look or focus for too short and scattered periods to comprehend the mysteries that occasionally constellate themselves directly in phenomena.

"The causes of this blindness relate directly to the repression, then suppression, then forgetting of direct insights, then living the perceptually restricted life created by muscularly and hormonally displaced aims that sexual-creative energy seductively morphs. This energy, once called sacred, must find some desirous escape valve, however freaky, to avoid building up under this pressure to explode in ecstatic behavior that would be directly punished by our society, any society now existing, except a few tribal ones which have special dionysiac celebrations, faintly approximated by certain bars in North Beach and by Rock.

"I see that you have been able to move into my house, blend with the people here, almost unnoticed except by Elaine, the girl you call Princess, and that while exceptionally discreet, you are not a closet ascetic." He smiled and sat down by me, cross-legged and companionable for the first time, revealing a youthful sardonic side that I interpreted as "Let's cut the bullshit." Watching my eyes move, he said, "Yeah, let's cut the bullshit between us. You want to experiment with life. You don't believe anything without testing it and neither do I.

"I would like for you to attend a session tonight at ten o'clock in my room with myself, Elaine, and Pauline. They're pretty real, too, and I want to explore my idea of the history of sexuality. That's where the bullshit is. Don't you agree?"

Bob's room served also as library for the House, to which he had donated over five hundred specialist books expounding or at least hinting at practical discoveries in death, sex, transformations, truths, and powers. Its floor undulated with forms and colors from used rugs: a Turkish kelim, a Zapotec, a Navajo, a Bokhara, a Tibetan, and a Persian. He unrolled a double-size sleeping bag to retire at night, so he said. In the day and evening, rolled up, it reclined against a wall acting as an extra cushion or pillow.

At ten o'clock, the three of us, without speaking, first gathered outside then glided in Bob's door, one after the other, Pauline, Princess, and then myself. Bob cancelled a meeting if anyone came in late by even a minute. No one was to enter his chamber after dinner, or until after breakfast. This absolute rule meant that no one even knocked at the door. Undoubtedly, except for Princess and Pauline, I was the first to enter silently at night.

At his gesture, we arranged ourselves, cross-legged, around the interior of the Zapotecan rug, he facing me, Princess facing Pauline, about four feet between the facing pairs of eyes. Two candles rendered the only light.

"You wish to write, at least eventually," he said to me, "you to dance," to Princess, "and you to make jewelry and prepare perfumes," to Pauline. "You are artists, certainly in potential, and I wish for these sessions, should you agree to them, to release your energies to enable your intelligence to contact powerful and enlightening forms, while for myself I wish to understand how sexual history might not have became a nightmare and once and for all release my life from that unnecessary nightmare." He grinned. "If I found out how to do that I might even leave a gateway open for others to escape, like one of you, maybe."

Bob then gazed ironically yet hopefully at each of us in turn, long and closely. I endeavored to emanate no defensiveness, only willingness, alertness, and preparedness for adventure. Princess emanated steadiness and depth. Pauline radiated readiness, a developed taste for adventure. "Our project," he continued, "will be the living out tonight, in an artist's mode, with a scientist's precision, an explorer's ship-shapeness, with a sense of risk as well as of possibility, of the sexual history of humanity. . . but to live that history as if there had never been the eruptions of repression, suppression, shame, humiliation, torture, condemnation, religious fakery, moral hypocrisy, neglect of hygiene, the snigger, the prurient, the madness, the demonic, the cruelty, and self-abasement, the fetish, the self-despising, murderous jealousy, futile possessiveness, an end to happiness, dissolution of romance, ambiguous ambiguities, false smiles, sinister gestures, morass of terrors, illimitable ignorance, lies without end, shrieking, hysteria, furtive mumbling, sweat-drenched sheets, tear-dank pillows, leers, sodden heartaches, sudden assaults, silences in which time erodes . . . Loneliness in which space contracts. . . .

"As you know," he continued softly after a silence, "I in no way consider myself a teacher of anything, but rather an explorer of ideas and practices relating to attention upon attention, especially the quick experimental shifting of the basic attention to specific forms, perceptions, images and combinatorial patterns thereof combined with successively recollecting the body, the species, the biosphere, and the cosmos in order to determine the macro-effects, if any, of different kinds of micro-behaviors and vice-versa.

"Nonetheless, in this one-night pact that I am risking to propose to you, I wish you to understand that this expedition must have a leader, much like the Captain on a ship, who has command, has the charts, and the course to be navigated. Each of you will be like an able-bodied seaman, particularly in that so far as doing any specific task, tying a bowline knot, handling the pumps in an emergency, reefing the sail, you may well be better than myself, therefore don't wait for me to tell you anything other than the timing, the course, and the ship itself. Tie and untie the knots yourselves!

"The timing has been correlated by me with the new moon, and consists of a four hour session. The ship will be this room. When the ship vanishes magically, and the library returns, each of us will be free at that time not by my permission," he said sarcastically, "but by the facts to incorporate anything of what we have learned into our future functioning if we should so wish and see the possibility." He grinned again, this time wolf-like, "Of course, by then you might already have incorporated several elements you can't dump so easily even if you wanted to."

A long silence ensued. The tenseness of our sitting relaxed. The mood became comradely and expectant. It brought me back to sitting around a long brown table in Chicago, preparing for a demonstration for Willie McGee, about to be legally lynched in Mississippi, knowing that my life would be irrevocably changed, if only by an FBI record, in those fully racist days but some of us would rather be nowhere else. We wanted to change the history of power.

I watched Bob closely. He had hit my mark, my efforts to be an able-bodied seaman, ready to traverse and study the seven seas, carrying my notepads and handful of books in my seabag, never contradicting any Captain, but always ready to jump ship if he went mad or mean, or if a more romantic voyage offered itself. At other times I thought of myself as a working passenger who wanted to sign on as many expeditions and trading ships as possible to explore parts opening into the panoplied empire of multiversity.

Princess adored Bob. She had said to me that she found working with him in their dance-dramas exciting and an end-in-itself, her definition of objective art. Glancing at her, it was clear she found obvious happiness in the fact that I, an uncommitted individual, but in actual authentic touch, however marginal, with some of the Tangier and New York mystics of the day, should also find Bob's ventures rewarding. "It's got to be real as well as far-out," she said to us. "And it can't be real if there's not someone around who doesn't give a fuck about whether or not predetermined results actually occur or not."

Pauline had told me she "wanted it all before getting married and rearing children so I'll never have regrets about what I didn't do with my youth like everybody else I've heard bitch and whine." She possessed a simple, cheerful philosophy of life as a series of separate stages, childhood, youth, marriage, old age, and a peaceful death at the center of the loving attention of an extended family of children and grandchildren, her several generated bodies, bidding respectful good-bye to the originating body. She'd like to marry Bob, eventually, when he arrived at the same earthy wisdom, if he could do it in time, but, with a proud consciousness of her beauty and practical intelligence, she knew she would "make out alright no matter-what" if she could work out the hang-ups "from a few things like being nearly strangled in my crib by my father."

Bob, I couldn't figure, but that was the essence of his actions. Never to be figured out. He changed directions like a man being hunted by a team of snipers. He said that was in his heredity, not individual merit, from three centuries of frontier survival plus at least one of English outlawry. A revolutionist without a party, a poet-playwright without a publisher, a leader without knowing where he was going or if anyone were following, a madman with no diagnosable insanity, an athlete without a game, a rancher with no ranch, even his yoga, such as it was, had no yoga, a laughter without any other joke but life itself to amuse himself, a connoisseur for whom fluffy scrambled eggs topped his own cooking skills, a lover of existence who thought that death canceled all purpose and meaning for the individual, but who would have done anything to gain immortality if he had thought there was a real chance, not Pascal's billion to one gambling mathematics, a mystic with no powers such as telepathy, clairvoyance, mind-reading, or tradition. . . . "I love Haight Ashbury," he said to us. "Here I can be perfectly anonymous and do whatever I wish, know, and am. Joe, get all out of it you can, because this area in 1967 is the scene for the most important event in human history. It's a freak wave, the one we never had before in America, maybe anywhere, a cultural frontier where the taste of freedom has a chance to become an indestructible transmittable addiction for humanity, so that it will never die until our genus disappears, if then. It depends on enough of us getting enough of that taste that we'll never do without it again, and our passion, our addiction, will transmit from a thousand lively centers until the planet's vibes shake down all the walls of all the uptight oligarchic Jerichos. Shatter all the stone tablets, too."

Bob then passed gracefully but without ritual to each of us half a tab of what I knew must be LSD. He put his in his mouth, and we followed, silently. He began to remove his clothing, stacking it neatly behind his pillow, and, again, we joined in his action.

First, we did a few yoga positions, mostly animal ones, the lion, the snake, the camel, the eagle, and the archer, ending with a long stretched out salute to a visualized sun rising in a blaze across the Ganges. Bob motioned us to resume our cross-legged sitting position, but the one small candle in the corner now lit up every detail of the book and rug packed room in its aromatic light.

"I want you to do some exercises with me based on the most ancient text I know, and the best, so that our inner attention will be at the level to use our rocket launcher, not be used by it, and both experience vividly and impartially observe the events we will make together."

He indicated clearly by gesture and glance that we were to stay in touch with our body and its smallest movements at all times. We laughed watching him comically act out someone forgetting his body in ever-increasing panting of sexual excitement.

His precise, gestural setting out of steps to follow, treating the enhancement of attention as if it were homologous to a chemical procedure requiring a cascade of operational facts, his calm, distinct demeanor, left my rising passions free from excitement's take over. Our individual efforts to synch with Bob's postures and state created an atmosphere of impersonal intensity that now illuminated eyes and forms far more, as if the candle had become a small sun.

"Before the Repression, in the tribes of old and even in some tribes today, even in ancient Rome, every year the social masks of class, of power, of sex, of education were dropped, and everyone acted in darkness or in masks from essence desire." Bob blew out that now-blazing candle. "Close your eyes. Follow any movements your body wishes to make." I was amazed at Bob's need, at how completely he opened himself to us. "Bob must be so desperate to gain experience that he is forced to trust us," flashed across my mind.

An amazing world of neither personal nor impersonal touch, kiss, skin and moisture, of breath, of hair, of tremulous pleasure, anonymous, without names, memories, or expectations, intensely individual and yet so empathetic, engrossing, ever-changing, so rich in phenomena to explore that little temptation remained for the voyeur to arrive, to open eyes to sate an unfulfilled hunger. Sinuosity, suppleness, and relaxed spontaneity I had never hoped for.

"Sitting," Bob's voice arrived in my head. Tuned, understanding exactly what he meant, all four of us almost instantaneously again sitting cross-legged in our silent square. A deeper noiseless breathing subtly moved Princess's torso. The coalescence of our attention poised the cubic space's time into an invisible cat licking up thick vibrations.

"Growing up," Bob's voice resounded inside my head, his tones an objective blending of historian's objective description, a tantric's dry precision, and a poet's glamour, "the girls wanted to explore the boys' power and understand it intimately after the annual ceremony where they first had learned exactly where nature's power most intensely incarnated." He and I by imitation so quick I could have thought it magical except for my now minute discrimination of muscular movement, sat backward on our haunches, I gazing upward into a leafy forest that came without effort at visualization, while the girls alternated with first one and then the other testing and experimenting with our power. The girls, not coldly or factually, but totally investigating the properties of the power and its underlying secretories, and this with such grace, delicacy, and even second-by-second developing art, that defenses, rigidities, apprehensions, disappeared from my body and consciousness and I surrendered all would-be control for the first time in my life. The alternation, every minute, on Bob's signal, of the two investigators, thrilled me with the observation of two different approaches and tempos, each intelligent, ascending at almost the same rapid rate the learning curve, and as they learned, I learned, and I saw how all my life would have been so betterly different if this essence knowledge had been mine earlier, and how betterly different it already had become.

The sitting indication again and the reversal of roles. At last, the leisure, the pleasure of learning all I had ever wanted to know, the alternation to keep the learning at maximum interest, the learning advancing to discovery of two subtle teachers. The range of sensitivities covered in one stroke of the tongue, one touch of the moving finger, the different jewels of touch in the cave of Ali Baba and the magic lantern of Aladdin going on and off until Sheherazade herself appeared with those thousand and one stories, that legendary mirror of myself.

Bob indicated a stop again. I sat more alert than ever before, these alternating stops turning on and off of the sexual current producing intervals of desireless almost samadhic lucidity. I felt deep chested, almost literally breathless from the long attentive bodily absorption of other bodies.

"Thousands of years ago, perhaps tens of thousands, special shamanic groups in the tribes noticed an even higher energy, later to be called Eros by the Greeks. Eros holds everything, no matter how different, together, even the strife of opposites provoked by sexual energy, that terrifying dance alternating creation and destruction of androgynic unity, the terror that gives a psychological basis to the Repression, still ruling the world, that first deviated and then almost destroyed the development of a magnificent sexual history for humanity, reducing it to a grim and limited history of reproduction, prostitution, variant dogmatic family, state, and religious forms, in short an encyclopedia of mental and physical diseases, capable of keeping the population going, even increasing, but no longer capable of producing delightenment.

"Namely, this higher or erotic energy evoked by the combination of sex and visualizations, directed the free flow of energies throughout key centers of the body toward concentrations in the magic wand and the magic cave and then spread the concentrated energies back throughout the entire body. The magic substance not to be ejected, but drawn back into the organism." He indicated gesturally how the women and I would pull our full sensations back into ourselves, the women while not blocking the muscular outflowing orgasmic reactions, and for myself not to orgasm. Otherwise, and here he made us laugh by his mumbo-jumbo imitations, I would fall into floppy oblivion, a happy dog.

Bob indicated for the women to lie down between us. I was to transmit directly from my eyes to his the energy arriving up my spine into the center of my head, and he to descend that energy directly to his touch, and the women to complete the circuit.

The room lit up as if in daylight, but a daylight without a source, each object distinct without a shadow. An ever whiter light satisfying, impartial, warming (I began to sweat). While as aware of sensation as in the sequence modeled on "nature," I became aware in addition of the new quality of the energy circulating around us, and that this energy was indeed finer than the purely sexual energy. I could sense not only motility of individual muscles, but the entire muscular sheath itself easing into positions without strain that allowed a whole new happiness of organic motility, of heart beat, breath, and neural network, a fantastic unitary synchrony of those four beings as if one. The lack of this energy was what always before had caused my disappearance into the river of orgasmic forgetting. And it had always been a happy disappearance because I had thought it was the highest energy that could be attained. But now I saw much better not to disappear.

The astounding series of historical stages to be explored that followed, each separated by a stopping, a sitting period, a silent glow, a new set of gestural indications, took me into regions of understanding I had not even dreamed possible. I also saw, no, felt as if it were deeper in me than my own feelings, the extraordinary sadness in Bob about the mangled happiness of humanity, its ruthless sexual-emotional torture and imprisoning, and his even more extraordinary passion for the marvelous, for the frontiers of possibility. How did he hold those two forces together? Then I knew he couldn't do this exploration without my help. What I'd learned in Tangier, in India, in Vietnam was helping out. I didn't know what he knew, but he knew that he could count on my not flaking out or going weird. I didn't want to see these two great horses, high joy and deep sorrow, pull him apart. He was right, I could not let him down, his daring swept me beyond myself. I would go with him till the end wherever that might be in this already fabled night.

The most profound of these stages to me was a reprise of the boys and girls alternations but with the addition of being done in turn with each the four qualities requisite for shamans and priestesses, and then with the four qualities together of each of four distinguishable stages of initiation, the alert hunter (for power), the impeccable warrior (the finder), the tantric network (the unifier), and the alchemical quantum (the creator) where we endeavored to do the operation of detecting quantum changes in the hormonal molecules. I could not do the latter but even its visualization produced a complete standing beside myself state where I could observe not only minute sensations, but minute ecstasies and see that the general state called ecstasy was as gross in comparison to this as, say, sight without being aware of line, color, hue, tone, size, shape, and form. I saw how ecstasy can be composed, like poetry, or a painting, or music, and that this art, produced for oneself, unreproduceable for others to see, was the supreme art from whose bounty all other arts gained their courage and force to manifest. This supreme art served as the irrefutable assessment of the achievement of all other arts.

The four of us once again sat, synchronously, lightly, as silent and "there" as cats at a mousehole, or as roses on a windless dewy morning.

Bob spoke as if drawing words up bucket by bucket from a deep well, "One last energy remains to isolate and become familiar with. Although sexual energy contains the power to create the new and destroy the old, and erotic energy to hold all the parts together, I believe that there is a transcendent energy that imparts direction to each part, and," Bob smiled the smile of Kouros, "the direction of the cosmos is the sum vector of all these directions. Without transcendent energy we can at best balance the flow but remain helpless to influence the direction.

"This energy was contacted and concentrated in high civilizations such as Greece, India, Maya, Yoruba, and Egypt through visualization and ratcheting up, through several stages, till finally a god or goddess form actually entered the body."

I could now see everyone and everything in the room quite clearly.

Bob somehow let four forms successively take over his body while we watched: Apollo, Dionysus, Artemis, and Aphrodite. Sweat poured from him. Then he and I alternated between Apollo and Dionysus, the radiant form and the emanating formless, and the women between Artemis, the huntress-investigator and Aphrodite, erotic attracter. I saw secrets of tragedy and truths of comedy, fission of forms and fusion of formless shadows while below this vision the now established sexual rites of unconquered tribes produced bodily flows, and ecstatic experiments of initiate and priestess societies continued holding steady-state mind organizations together. Then new internal chemical changes adjusted the capabilities of the nervous and muscular systems to perform supple feats. Happy immortals feasting on ambrosia of senses and nectar of ecstasies while making archetypal loves with easy direction of intricate implicate wave forms of the human body-minds at instant disposal of their incarnation's wishes.

Then, following Bob's inspired full-body gestures, we entered the sublime intellectual vistas of the Bodhi of Time pulsing images of realizations into the forever receptive Dakini of Space, the Bodhi of Reflection forever flowing onward and never introspective with the Dakini of Water, the Bodhi of Analysis gazing at each material particle with the Dakini of Earth, the Bodhi of Compassion seeing the neediest body cell receiving energy from lightning quick Dakini of Fire, and the

Bodhi of Freedom enjoying chosen forms of chosen biospheres with the fearless Dakini of Air. Below, drunken tribals danced, and ecstatic mystics lost themselves in learned caves with exhaustless manuscripts of enlightenment being found at rhythmic intervals, like Tibetans applauding readings of newly recovered manuscripts by Padma Sambhava.

Another stop, and for the first time, I and It seemed the others, even Bob, needed not only to glow but to rest, but rest without descending from this point and state. This rest took place in me with a few delicious breaths within, breaths rippling along sides of the lungs. A few muscles deep within the abdomen flexed subtly into a more integrated tensile network that showed me the directions for future postures. The room's light deepened into golden refulgence.

We then entered the realm of those who deal directly with sex, death, and esoteric madness as a splendid diet to maintain a soma for their unconquerable and undismayable delight. Maha Shiva and Kali with eight arms and eight legs and four incarnate metabolic centers, each now magically moving by synchrony, initiation, and intuition toward an exact vibrational note which, when struck, shattered the costly crystal from which before I had drunk my taste of time. Each Maha Shiva head transformed in turn to, and then transfigured Brahma, Vishnu, and Shiva with each new vision of reality's story. Each glorious head rolled to the floor, beheaded by Kali the insatiate who drank the blood from each world with the sword of sharpest discrimination and the bowl of total catchment. Nothing, no matter how wild, inchoate, or ordinary that Brahma began, that Krishna-Vishnu could not bring to the tumescent fullness of a three hundred muscle dance, that Shiva lord of animals and the twenty-one known yogas plus the fool's yoga of improvisation could not bring to a satisfying climactic end with elephantic and benign breath. Kali killed used-up form quickly and painlessly while dancing on Shiva's samadhic ecstatic trance form of death. Civilizations, Egyptian, Babylonian, Western, arrived, gloried, traced-out architectural samadhis to die consciously delivered deaths. Empires, Roman, Aztec, Han. Planets. Biospheres. Stars. Universes.

A stop. We had lived and learned with the gods. Bob handed each of us an apple. The light had become an even monochrome, a subtle gray diffusion in which we bit, chewed, tasted, and swallowed bite after crunchy sweet bite, content in our presence.

Bob dropped his physical acting out and spoke simply, humbly, almost begging us to stay with him for something that he himself really wished for. "The last part of the session takes us to the point of profiting from chemistry. We have now altered our chemistry, by a process in older days called alchemistry, which means *the* chemistry. For our work with magic wand and magic crucible, magic cave and magic mirror, there now remains to reap the full rewards. Each sex misses a vital essence-substance that can only be produced by the other with most careful and prolonged attention such as we have done. But something more remains."

We men first assumed a position in its fourth recurrence, from the tribal boy through initiate, through Maha-Shiva, to alchemist. With emphasis upon the last, he and I were first to be natural, then use the qualities and states of the initiate, then incarnate the god of choice but through all changes concentrate on the alchemical procedure, which was to retain all substances as long as possible by rolling our eyes and alternating our structural breaths, and then to draw back one unit into the body for every unit leaving. The women using all their knowledge as tribal girls, initiates, priestesses, Kalis, were to make it as difficult as possible for us to retain any substance, and to take all of it if possible. This relentless charm would make alchemists work self-control to the utmost or else lose substance in a bitter sweet oblivion. The attention needed was all-consuming to carry out the cool precise final chemistry while gods played, initiates labored, and boys went bonkers with sensation.

Bob indicated stop again, the Kali-alchemists replete, breathing deeply. "The Shivas, initiates, and boys will now feast themselves, while the Kalis, priestesses, and girls will now let their energy pulsate outward as it desires, while at the same time drawing their sensation back into themselves, stripping the orgasmic energy of a percentage of the substances for their own self-creating."

For the first time I felt resistance, but this transformed into strange and wonderful interplay until finally tipping to exquisite tiny splayed detail gave micro tastes of finest spray.

Bob called a stop. We ate another apple. Everyone looked relaxed, wide awake, in repose, refined. We put on our clothes, except for Bob, who embraced us quickly and lightly before we left, each alone to their bed. I took a hot bath and drifted to sleep.

The next morning I said to Bob, "I am so lucky to be here in Haight Ashbury, to have met you and Princess, Pauline and this Theater of all Possible Time Lines."

"Yes, " he said, "I feel exactly the same way. We are both old enough to have been prepared for it and young enough to live it. There can be no greater happiness than to live at the height of one's life at the height of one's times."

"It does beat," I smiled, "living at the height of one's life in the depths of one's time, or at the height of one's time in the depths of one's life, my only previous alternatives."

Suddenly I saw the cause of Bob's world sadness which put such a nostalgic perfume into all his life-loving, creative oriented actions. "But you really want to be immortal, don't you," I surprised myself by probing with the knife, "real immortality in the flesh?"

"Yes," he said, acquiescent to my strike.

"You don't believe it's possible?"

"No."

"And yet the ideas and exercises you use were found by those searching for immortality! So that's why sadness interweaves your golden moments. They end but only your acting in the illusion they won't makes you go on."

"Yes," he said, "profounder the joy, deeper the sorrow. Left foot, right foot. I don't discuss immortality; I thought about it until each culture's notion became a refuted hypothesis to me. What was I to do? Commit suicide and hasten my exit to meaninglessness, or act as if immortal, drain each drop of life given to me? I try to act that magic if, but can't always do it. I think each man determines his exact place by how he deals with this inmost longing of the I, and it is for no other man to tell him how because finding his own way creates secret personal power to deal with his death, and therefore his life. Nor does he have to tell anyone else why he does it."

Taking Sides in Oakland

"Superspade was killed yesterday."

Princess and I had just made our way up a sun-splattered white painted back stairway to visit a "drug-dealer", a hippy who distributed a fair amount of grass and hashish. I had never met a dealer, since these substances had always seemed just to appear before me in Tangier in 1963 and Kathmandu in 1964, the only times I had actively experimented with their spectrum of effects. Princess knew a representative type, or even a genuine individual, of every aspect of the Haight Ashbury, indeed, of the whole living cultural scene in the Bay area. "The last four years, since I was fourteen, I grew up with the scene," she said. "Ken Kesey, Stewart Brand, Dick Alpert, Chloe Scott, Anne Zalbin . . . and, of course, many of the essential supporting casts."

"So, come on," she said, "You're curious, I'll take you to visit one." Jason ("because I search for gold") Talisman ("because if you touch me, you can turn on"), lay back on his bed, bare-chested, blonde-bearded, long haired, bare-footed, blue-jeaned, white-teethed, and smiling happily. Doris sat by him on the bed, silent, but vibing in, also blue-eyes and long haired, but clothed to the ankle in a thin light brown dress that managed to drape itself from every curve and every angle, an everchanging still life.

But when I asked Jason, after Princess made the proper soft-voiced introductions, what was new, and he had answered with report of Superspade's murder, the light and smiles seemed to fade out of the room and I caught a flash of an old grey Chicago room in a Southside slum back of the yards with left Communists and right FBI closing in on courageous union men that had organized the area, except this time it was Mafia and narcs closing in on liberated space.

I hadn't known Superspade but his name had been infamous on the street as the introducer of heroin to the scene.

"Yeah," Jason continued, "this means the mob is moving in on the new people coming here. Superspade had gotten himself into dealing the heavy shit with lots of money. This also means cops will be around investigating. Small guys like myself doing sacred stuff as part of the magic scene are gonna be wiped out in the crossfire."

"Don't get uptight," he said to Doris whose face began crumpling, "No way I'm going to stay around til that happens."

Long silence as we contemplated the first reported killing associated with the community.

"Well," he continued, "the police were getting tighter anyway, and the laws meaner, and so you couldn't any longer dare to openly tell people what's what, and so the acid-grass sacred scene was already being split with speed, with STP at too big a dose, with some H, and new people pouring in for the action not as well prepared as the first wave, needing lots of straight talk they couldn't get anymore, and being handed free samples of shit."

The talk became friendlier, we let the topic of Superspade alone, but its sliver stuck in my heart as we walked back down the stairway darkened by the arrival of fog.

"Princess," I said, "I can see the petals falling from the rose of revealed mystery; it's happened before. The masons built Chartres and Amiens with theater, dance, and high mathematics but soon there was only the walled-up back of a dark cathedral with a few stained glass frames left to glance at while the priests of lawful lawlessness and ordered disorder preached at their controlled populations, making an example of anyone who dared speak truth or act publicly about enhanced states of consciousness."

At dinner that night, Bob became openly excited addressing the ten of us that constituted the house.

"What's happening, in this time-place, with these extraordinary energies creating real magical properties to balance fantastic mystical influxes, is an event without precedent in the West since the death of Pan, and only seldom experienced in tribal and pre-scientific Asian societies.

"However, to gain access to all the energies available, and not to miss the ephemeral contemporary scene, we can't neglect what's occurring across the Bay in Oakland which is polarity to our event. If we do, we shall become unreal, although remaining in bliss so far as that exists on planet Earth so long as freedom continues to be tolerated in this ever more isolated enclave."

"In short, tomorrow there's going to be a major attempt to stop several busloads of draftees for the Army from entering the Oakland induction center. The Oakland police will be out in force, in black-helmets, shields, with gas and clubs, ready to use them on hundreds or thousands of protesters. We will go there to act the role of protesters, but in no way as leaders. There will be risk, so each of you feel free to stay here. Those of us who go will be cautious, study lines of retreat as we go forward, and use the occasion as a chance to observe the behavior of our organisms and emotions in a conflict zone as well as the behavior of our society and crowd passions at one of its historic impasses."

Princess managed to produce a veteran infantry man's look; Pauline betrayed excitement; Sally, the painter from New York looked serious but committed; Mike, the tall broad shouldered merchant marine sailor who read his Jack London as well as Beckett and Ionesco, leaned back in his chair and stared at the ceiling; Kama, the ripely beautiful black-haired Hindu girl said, "I will have to think about going, I came to San Francisco for love, not war." Ed, the elder of the house, a philosopher unable to hold a teaching job partially because of occasional homosexual flings, but mainly because unable to make up his mind between Pierce's radical reconstruction of metaphysics to fit science and Hegel's radical reconstruction of metaphysics to accelerate history he had become in his own words, "an observer of movements in American life during my time." A minimum position that could combine detailed observation with dialectical sweep. Ed shrugged his saturnine shoulders. He said, "this is a correct decision, otherwise, as our existentialist friends would say, our communal existence at the house would become inauthentic.This act is one of the options involved in our choosing an alternative cultural route to the nation's police and war machine;" Len, the young Jewish introvert, engaged in writing disconnected passages he hoped would become a book, "Notes From Under the Underground", a total discombobulation without a trace of throughline to organize the emotions, one of his most hilarious/depressing pieces being ten detailed pages on his unwrapping some French blue cheese and slicing a piece of it in front of his girl friend, grimly nodded his head with its blue whisker stubble, clearly resolved that this crazy episode would provide him with "material." I didn't take in the other three because I fell back on studying Bob and myself.

Bob suddenly and quickly pushed back his chair with his feet and a right-handed spin from the table, rose with his special puppet exercise ascension (visualizing a rope attached to the top of his head pulled by a Bunruku Master), magically turned (following his nose exercise), quickly left, and then I heard the door of his bedroom deftly close, almost silently (result of a decision exercise). When Bob ran three quick intentionals in a row that I could see, I knew that a very high state had entered my organism. Generally he looked like, and often he was, simply letting a very well-trained and nutritioned body respond to circumstances, and the actual moments of intentionality were invisible to me.

I found myself walking rapidly, automatically, for quite a distance, past the Panhandle, and then turning down the Fillmore. A number of people, including Pauline had reported losing their wallets or purses to a snatcher walking down Fillmore, though no physical violence had as yet occurred. A relatively poor black district, the Fillmore had only James' House about ten blocks further down to represent the Haight's influence. I decided to walk by to say hello to James, but tactically made my way down the middle of the street, keeping a slight swing of my head going to increase the peripheral vision arc, the better to pick up on motion. My body slid into the making-it-down-the-street glide.

Suddenly, I heard the choppers again, felt hot bright sunshine, engaged again the no-bullshit camaraderie of the Special Forces with Sergeant Jackson, saw terror on the faces of the Montagnards whose Chief had just been executed by Victor Charley (the ominous mantram given them by the field sergeants).

One subject I could not speak about in the liberated territory of that fabled part of San Francisco, was Vietnam. Some who where there, like Bob, never lost sight of that true revolution, the revolution in dealing with states of consciousness, with sex as love and love as flowers, colors, cool textures of silence and tea, conversation, perfumes, contemplation, making the scene, and making the scene and economics into art. But Marxist ideologists had moved in with their ever-ready radar for anything that could possibly become a nucleus for a mass movement to avalanche themselves to power, to bring an end to a history which had trapped humans into acting as profit and loss commodities. They saw history as a malicious succession of now unnecessary superstructures. They thought material progress would take care of itself by itself when run by the workers with the superstructures of theft overthrown. This doctrine of 1848-1859, when the practical world was visible (before electrons, the periodic table, quanta, relativity, and, most of all, ecology and the biosphere were discovered), dubious then for its anti-intelligentsia prejudice, had become a farce, a planetary murderous farce, in a world of continual invention, world market. Garbage in, garbage out. In this new world of bytes, micrograms, alloys, space and the subliminal, in which innovative intelligentsia had become the key to productivity, I could see their ideological power grab's inevitable demise, though perhaps only after decades more of propaganda, tortures, jails, wars, and bleak mindscapes. However, their indictment of a world run of, by, and for profit would remain, a detailed warning that outdid Jeremiah's.

I had been catapulted into this state of ultra-awareness of hell-beings in the political realm by contradictions that wiped out thought by Rob's pragmatically Dadaist call to experience a struggle in the streets. However, my considered opinion about Vietnam was, from an originally neutral position changed only by my months there of close observation and experience traveling through twenty-three provinces, that Victor Charley for all its romantic national elements ultimately served strictly as an arm for ideologues of Hanoi. Victor Charley was one of the chief hydras of that absurd doctrine whose self-righteous oppression exceeded fundamentalist Christians and Mullahs, if only because they had mastered the intricacies of bringing organized state power and modern technology to bear without check upon whomever they decided to target as the opposition.

At the same time, when I had gone to Washington, by invitation to accompany a friend, to share my experiences with high officials, it had become only too clear that the brief re-appearance of political intelligence in the Kennedy era had been destroyed in America. Even while I had been in Vietnam, Johnson had followed exactly the Goldwater-avowed program rejected overwhelmingly by the American people which he had hypocritically opposed in the election. Namely, he underwrote the doctrine of airpower and ruthless bombing on a mass scale, abandoning Kennedy's emphasis upon agricultural aid and special forces living with the people program. American troops, now isolated from the population, in concentration camps for soldiers, waited helplessly for the enemy to strike, while hoping terror bombing would weaken the will of fanatics like Giap who proclaimed that 20,000,000 lives would be a small price to pay for his triumph. Even at a kill ratio of 20 to 1, it was clear the United States could not, would not, and should not pay one percent of that price to win, not even a fraction of that.

These draftees would not be the special forces I had met, volunteers, specially trained, devoted to the local area to which they were sent. They would be useless cannon fodder, twenty-five per cent written off in advance as dead or permanently diseased and wounded.

They were just to be killed holding the strategists' fort while the bombers killed masses on the other side. And even if, against all probability, the policy should "win", they would put into power slimy bureaucrats and sleazy profiteers in Saigon, as unreliable a bunch of puppets as could be imagined.

However, I knew the protests would do no good, and would even be used as an excuse to move against my beloved Haight Street in a general reactionary offensive against freedom, especially a living freedom that drastically cut down on material wants and demands, threatening to cut down profits. A Hashbury House of ten adult member's sharing its infrastructure represented a five hundred percent drop in refrigerators and other equipment, just for starters.

Nonetheless, sidling thoughtfully down the Fillmore, toward James' commune, I had decided to go to Oakland with Bob. Perhaps I could help, in a drastic situation, to save one of my friends. Perhaps, but I admitted the truth. Like Bob, I wanted to see the conflict. I wanted to be part of it. I didn't want to be blissed out on cloud nine, oblivious of the metal fire on cloud one. And if I was going to be part of it, I didn't want to be cheering on the police and the busloads of victims. I didn't want to build up the power of the demagogues, the rhetorical slave drivers by engaging in rash and fruitless action, but I did want, in the final count, to have put my body on the side that would show some people had dared to witness against this stupid escalation of Apocalypse. Bob's approach finally melted my cautious antagonism to street action because it seemed to have as much merit as any act could have in the maelstrom: basically to appear, and then to disappear, to have made an act, without being caught up in the activity, providing, of course, that we could really carry out this challenging operation. It would certainly test my belief that my capacities for subtle action had improved.

I slouched in my best confused humility style up the steps to James' porch on his frame three story house and knocked. People sat and sprawled around the living room in chairs and on the floor.

"Hi James."

"Sit down, Joe. You know Peter Zurg?"

The other white guy and I shook hands.

"We're talking about liberating territory. You know how we took over that store and started selling second hand stuff so the ladies could get off the street?"

I glanced at three or four of the handsome women. "Yeah."

"Well, Peter thinks we've got to really get into this liberation of space. If we don't have the space, and we don't, then we can't act, we can only dream, and even our dreams are gonna become distorted caricatures of our true desires."

"Yeah, man," came the antistrophes around the space. I'd heard of Zurg, but only that he was connected with getting the fresh strawberries and produce the Diggers put out for the hungry in the Panhandle, along with their delicious thick soup. Donations from well-to-do merchants who dug whiffing molecules of the action. All of San Francisco vibrated to the Haight and even some of the straight bent, hoping to get a little.

"Guerrilla theater," said Peter. "A guerrilla theater that takes space, does its thing there in one minute to several hours, and then moves on."

"Create and run," I said.

Several of us slapped palms with a licking final finger withdrawal.

"Hey," Peter said, "Next week we're going to liberate City Hall for lunch hour on Wednesday. We start coming up there with our music and dance from the Panhandle at eleven."

"Be there," I said.

Would be the perfect counterpoint to the Oakland stand.

All of us got into the bus that began our journey to the Oakland induction center (two transfers away), except Kama who said she was going to meet a guy at Golden Gate Park and listen to the bongos. "I'll be hoping it all happens right," she waved good-bye. Indeed, I thought, why should a Hindu, even an American-born Hindu, become involved with these madnesses of the West, though Asia had also become infected with its raging viruses? I gave her a specially warm good-bye embrace. She glanced at me before she turned to go, sending vibes of impersonal compassion.

A hundred or so people had already gathered at the street corner from where we were to walk up to the buses hauling in the draftees, three blocks away, and then attempt to persuade them not to go through with the induction process into the military.

In the distance, some black uniforms with shields and helmets stood around in informal clumps. Excited exaltation coupled with alert wariness became the predominant mood of the crowd, now beginning to increase by several new persons a minute.

Bob knew how to start things. He waved his right hand in a circle and strode forward. We followed him a block toward the black uniforms strolling as innocuously as we could. "I want to check the next street corner," he said. "If they charge, we need to split quickly to make it past the first corner because they could easily send a flanking detachment down that street to cut off the retreat. At the same time we want to get out of the line of fire as rapidly as possible. That makes this street our desired turn-off, the second street back from the front line. We want to turn down the rightside here because, see, it's got the most probable open doors to avoid the gas. But, if it's really bad, we'll duck down that first corner to the right. Stick together unless it's real bad, then let's use the buddy system, each buddy is responsible for the other. If an hour after anything starts, any buddies don't show up at the bus stop we got off at, we'll come get you out of jail. Or you get me and Joe out." Bob and I were the only ones that had been in the army and been through tear gas training.

I looked up at high face-crowded office windows. Everyone, it seemed, had quit work to peer entranced through those high safe windows down at the street. Several hundred people had arrived by now, and we jostled in the crowd. I had no idea who our leaders were by name, but I could see them getting it up for the action, checking their watches.

"Let's go," they waved. We started walking behind them, Bob motioning us to be in about the fourth rank, although the ranks formed unevenly and changed slightly as we walked closer. The police quickly assumed a solid line, three deep, when we crossed the corner two blocks from them. Bigger and stouter than nine out of ten of the walkers, with uniforms, helmets, shields, gloves, clubs, guns, handcuffs, and boots, all black except for face shield and white flesh behind, all masked in impassive stares, Oakland police's finest clubbers looked capable of doing basically the KGB bit, but with no concentration camps in Alaska to back them up and with an occasional judge occasionally to overrule excesses.

"Don't see any media," said Bob. "Good-bye to one restraint." I pointed up to the office windows on both sides of the street where impassive observers packed for the view, "Lots of witnesses, though."

Pauline almost pranced, nervous as a high-strung race horse. Princess gave me a cool glance. Bob got into it. Mike strode beside Sally obviously determined no harm should come to her. I tried to see the event through Sally's abstract expressionist eyes and saw blonde blue red and yellow arcs, waves of kaleidoscopic ocean about to crash against a black granite pier protecting and hiding a hideous and exotic slave traffic. I imagined philosopher Ed taking a Bakuninist stance against the Prussian State in its turned into-the-opposite dialectic filled with Sartrean nausea at the useless commitment required but with an up-beat Jamesian awareness. Empirically, I could see him calculating his chances. Len had his notebook in his jeans, left hip pocket. Ready to write up post-absurdist jail notes, a wry amusement snidely whispered to me. Mike had anarchist thoughts of martyrdom. The other three had waved good-bye and left soon after the walk started. Bob waved them jovially off. "Less responsibility, good," he had muttered to me, and indeed, the burden lay on him, since none of the rest of us would have initiated this action, though now, obviously, we were caught up in it. In search of necessary experience or shoved in the ass by accident, karma, type, and abstractions? Both, I answered my question. And for the first time, I realized I had come there not because of Bob, nor Princess, nor my own hip alchemical investigations of some scene I deemed historic, but because I had finally decided about the Vietnam war.

"You know I'm only here because of you and the war," I said to him.

"And I'm only here because of you - and them," he replied, pointing to the other citizens of the house. I could not abandon history with a meaning and he could not abandon life being beyond history, an end in itself. We smiled at each other, at last friends enough to reveal our opposition.

Silence fell, palpable as touch, when black archetypal roles of terror and prohibition stiffened their human bodies to readiness. The front rank of the walkers, colorful California replays of European archetypes of roles of vanguard and revolution, slowed to a cautious approach, endeavoring to make eye contact with individuals inside the masks. Black uniformed superiors stood behind and to the sides, with half-raised bullhorns. Some sweatshirted and sleeveless flower-bloused leaders narrowed their eyes, then deliberately opened them wide and innocent. Some girls walked slowly along the front of the police laying flowers at their feet.

The hundreds of walkers loosely filling more than half of the last block all stopped. The watchers at the windows stood in tableau after tableau, the salary-slaves and whip-worded overseers of business watching their society's skin stretched to the thinnest, where thoughts and speech, exhausted, had given themselves up to gesture, and gesture trembled in the urge to advance to rhetoric or blows depending on which side won.

The buses began to appear down the street behind and to the left of the police. Boyish, taut faces turned to the left to look at us looking at them past the police. The walkers shuddered forward, a foot from the police, shouting,

"Hell, no, we won't go!"

"Make love, not war!"

The bus windows stayed rolled-up. Fierce gestures demanded they be lowered. A second bus, a third, I heard the choppers again, saw the terrified village elders, suddenly, the black powers moved, and yells, screams, some falling figures, rising clubs, the first two ranks charged through before we could react to turn and run.

We raced down the right side, Bob kept in the middle, urging on Princess, Pauline, Ed, Mike, and Sally, who, ever the artist, wanted to look back "to get visual material". I had to look back myself, and saw incandescent motion except for a few bodies rolling like dancers between giant robots reaching and striking. "Gas" somebody yelled. At the second corner we cut sharp right as planned, in between dull square cost-conscious concrete columns, and into a lobby built to squelch emotion. We watched the chase continue outside down the street, til the uproar disappeared out of sight except for a couple of people being hauled away, arms bent hard behind their backs.

An Initiate in Sonoma

Pauline bubbled in a couple of afternoons after the Oakland charge to discover some of us plopped on oak stools spaced around the thick pine kitchen table where vegetables were knife-chopped into tiny pieces. Bob insisted this was the easiest way to pick up more energy, surface energy. "The secret of all great chefs" he pronounced in his best gnomic straight face routine which meant he considered the statement to possess "a deal of truth." At various times Lapsang Souchong, or chamomile tea was steeped and served to those who vibed in.

"I just got back from Sonoma where I met Count von Landers", she announced. The name meant nothing to me so the significant pause had been wasted, but not on Bob and Princess. "William G. Landers?" asked Bob who never asked questions. "The way to learn is to observe, visualize, and do, not questions," which he pronounced as Quest-shuns.

"Yes, and he will meet you and up to five others on Saturday morning at ten o'clock!"

Bob, Pauline, and Sally took the front seat of Sally's old white Datsun pickup, while Princess, Mike, and I piled into the back.

Apparently Mike had first showed up at the ramshackle adobe compound Bob shared with Sally on the La Cienega outskirts of Santa Fe for one of Bob's Thursday night "Theater" talks. Had a major heroin and minor alcohol problem. Had hung around doing work on re-plastering adobe, making wooden tables for a living. Taking long hikes back into the Jemez mountains every month, re-appearing after three days, reminiscing mystically about secret hot springs. True, Bob had slipped the four of us a tab for our one special history session, but basically he was a sleep, yoga, and nutrition hound and would not tolerate drugs in the house. "I'm not against anyone taking them for a purpose, even if that purpose is . . . only . . . ecstasy (he grinned), but you must know that I think that ecstasy is man's natural state, so you should use a crutch only when you can't walk naturally. And never use H or speed is my advice."

In any event, Mike stopped his habit, though he took up a regular Saturday night whiskey, to became a key crewman of what Bob called his "ongoing ever-lovin' expedition." According to Mike, Bob had at first derided the hippies filtering through La Cienega, calling them "heapies" because, he said, "they have no more social structure than a pile of sand. Grains of sand just pile up where they fall till the wind blows them away again."

However, always one to check out his denials, and confessedly "as curious as a young hound dog," Bob finally made his trip to San Francisco in mid-1967. Blown away like myself upon being handed a candy and a flower by two beautiful, and beautifully costumed ladies, who boarded a bus he had gotten on, performed their rite with each passenger, and then laughed their way out past a suddenly jocular bus driver at the next stop.

But Haight Street itself really grabbed Bob. Clear sound of hammers, nailing wood, storefronts going up, carnival business, seeking, and tripping all going on together. The same magical autopoesis as a forest, a human body, an athletic contest. "There's a new principle of human organization behind this manifestation," Bob had called Sally in La Cienega excitedly, according to Mike. "Drop New Mexico. Come here. This is the top break through of the last two millennia in experimenting how to make a truly human culture!" Mike told me, "Bob really wants to be Crazy Horse and Sitting Bull combined. That is his real ambition. Chief and Medicine Man at the same time. But he has to find his Dakotas and his wide open range. He thinks we're his Dakotas and Haight Ashbury is the Bad Hills before the white man come."

Bob had known Pauline from one of those hot springs rendezvous deep in the Jemez and, before Sally arrived, had moved in with her. Sally and Mike took the other room in the pad, then Bob had made a decisive move after meeting Princess at a Zalbin happening. "Is there anything beyond the avant-garde?" she said, the same type of stroke that had gotten me. "Yes," he said, "The Theater of all Possible Time Lines."

Three days later Bob soft-talked the five of them, including himself, plus his old chronically broke philosopher friend, Ed, to put up their total cash, $250, and rent one half a Victorian house for a month, plus the month in advance. "Now," he proclaimed, "we have a territory, we will maintain this territory for the duration, and we join this life and this battle. We are here!"

I had met Princess only a month after their start-up. Bob's first lecture on prophets of the West, starting with William Blake had brought ten people. These ten, later fifteen, at three dollars a person per week, by lecture, paid a quarter of the monthly rent, after Bob took his fifty percent. "Everybody will put in a dollar and a half a day for the food."

"Where will we get that?"

"Make jewelry if you have to. Pauline will take it to the counter in the store she works at and they give you fifty percent if it sells."

"William Landers," Princess informed me when we were turning up the hilly road from the bar where Jack London had hung out on occasion, on the last few miles to the Count, "has the reputation of being real. You may remember his book, 'Drugs and Psychology.' Supposedly he is also master of yoga, Gurdjieff, the Tibetan tradition, Sufi music, and surf fishing. He is considered a teacher but hardly ever takes a student and belongs to no special tradition."

I did remember looking at his book in Manhattan, at Weiser's on South Broadway. Had read half of it trying to avoid shelling out my vanishing dough. A civilized book written wryly, and a little dryly, I smiled to myself, that weaved its way in a curious channel between the factual and allusive, as if the writer was not in the least eager to reveal all he knew, certainly not more than a fraction of what he felt and a very small part of his experience. One phrase stayed with me because of its suggestiveness about the inner life of the author, "the playful spirit of hashish." He must be at heart an artist.

Our pickup stopped in a narrow graveled rectangle between the road and a small white house. A damp hill rose up behind it, and redwoods clumped in the ragged dark green draw of the creek just ahead that ran down the hill, under the road, and then steeply past a small plant-filled garden on the other side of the road.

Pauline and Bob strode through the gate, looked around, then waved us to follow them around the cottage to the door. A few seconds after knocking, a ruddy-faced stocky man of medium height in rubber boots, straw hat, and working clothes emerged, deftly opening first a solid wooden door, and then a screen door showing its age with a few bulges from the odd nudge.

"I brought them," Pauline said, "This is Bob, Sally, . .."

"Allright. I'm Count von Crap if you use titles or William if you don't. Why are you here?"

"To learn," said Bob.

William laughed sardonically. "Learn what? Ten years it took me full time to learn chemistry at Cambridge, where they know how to teach it. And you want to learn metachemistry right away. You look like a weekend warrior at best."

I could see Bob almost boil over before his decision intervened to shut his organism down to half-speed. "To learn from you what you choose to give out and what we're able to absorb from that."

"We?" William cocked his head. "Look," he said "I'm fifty-four, I don't need anything but to write my books, take care of my garden, go fishing in my kayak, where, at the right time, about eighty, since yoga will keep my body in good shape till then, I wish to die in the breakers. So let's get it straight, there is no we in what you're looking for. There is only I. Each I must find its own way over a difficult path. I cannot accept you. Good-bye, I must work in my garden.

William Landers, Count von Crap, strode quickly off, through his gate, across the road through another gate, and down a small path through his garden to pick his hoe up from where it leaned, carefully placed, against the wall of a covered tool stand. I was amazed that Bob had simply quit his effort to make contact upon receiving this rebuke, harsh by American standards, but familiar to anyone who had read accounts of certain Sufi masters, which I knew Bob had poured over. Almost as if Bob agreed with his critique, and that's what astonished me, that a man like Bob could still have a place which, when touched, would make him quit on the spot. No matter that the touch might have been truth. As Bob himself had said, and which we both knew, a change in attitude, or state, or knowledge, could change a truth to an irrelevancy.

Bob leaned on the gate post, all of us standing beside him, looking intently at Landers chopping the weeds out of his strawberry patch. "Well," he said "Let's go back. That was an interesting meeting."

Pauline dashed him a look, withering, desperate, inspired. She knew if Bob walked away he would have lost, given away his momentum. She had bet on Bob. She didn't want him to lose. She had been brought up to help men when they turned into boys. She clicked the latch with her long finger, opened the gate and ran down to Landers who refused to answer whatever she said to him, continuing to chop his way expertly down the row. Without glancing back at us, Pauline then walked behind him, matching him step for step, her elegant knees flashing high in the air as she leaned forward pulling each of her sandalled feet in turn out of the moist cloddy earth that William sturdily and easily, with a practiced sureness, set his boots down in and out of.

Row after row William hoed his way down, turned at the end, and started back in the opposite direction, Pauline matching step for step behind him until they hit the synchrony of dance that gradually became one motionless image, growing intenser and more detailed in my vision, both William and Pauline motionless to my vision, deepening into an unpaintable painting beyond Titian's most metaphysical color, just as, doubtless, they were doing innerly and deliberately at this point, though their bodies continued their successional traverse. This image, I knew, although phenomenon, was no hallucination, but real because of its point and relevance. William could not deny that he taught because she learned, and he could not deny she learned because she had attuned herself to his exact pitch.

He stopped, having finished his rows to hoe. William looked at Pauline, he looked at us. He smiled, waved us down. Though I felt eager to go, I was again surprised by Bob, who had dropped all resistance, and walked directly and freely straight toward William without stepping on a plant. One of the unusual things about Bob was that he could physically mass his resistance, but when he dropped it, he dropped it completely. That quick change ability undoubtedly was how he had become, in the main, exact and precise. I loved flow for flow's sake, but I often missed the fine points of when to stop it to build the power for better flow. He called it "waiting for something new to enter the war of opposites."

"Let's go in the ashram and sit down," William said. We trailed behind William, Pauline, and Bob, past a small path at the side of a bamboo roofed, Japanese rice-paper walled building. A small rockbuilt pond where a fat golden carp lay motionless mirrored the small wooden bridge that led into the ashram. "Lao Tse," gestured William at the great carp. He slid the panel back. We removed our shoes as he had his boots. We sat cross-legged on straw mats in a semi-circle in front of him.

"We start with some yoga," he said. "You can take off some or all of your clothes." Quickly, he sat before us bare chested, wearing only his pants. The three women removed their scarves and hats, and the three of us also took off our shirts.

The provocative Count von Crap, the sturdy, expert peasant farmer, became a precise yoga master who quickly located the exact point of no further of each of us. "Do not mind if at first you can't do it. Do the approach as correctly as you can until you reach your limit on the position. Observe. Visualize. Do." He would do, while we observed, and he mentioned fine points we might miss, such as the exact placement of the hands. Then we sat and visualized. "See exactly in your mind the successive steps of getting into the position, then holding the position, then returning from the position."

"Then, do."

After about twenty minutes I was sweating, and breathing deeply, having failed to achieve about half of the positions beyond half-way. I noted that Bob had not noticeably recoiled at being placed in an exceptional position for him, namely a relative novice needing correction. Then I remembered he must have done that a lot to have learned so much. "Now we go to music and dance," said William.

He showed us definite positions, calling one FORCE, another BEING, and another EFFORT. Another WILL, another FORM, and the last one DANCE. Each position called for special attention to the feet, the knees, the hips, the shoulders, elbows, hands, and neck.

He sat down cross-legged in the half-lotus, after satisfying himself that we could go into the gesture called for immediately upon hearing the word, and picking up his masterfully made and decorated guitar, began to sing a sustained and almost seamless melody-rhythm that immediately put me into the Middle East of legendary power and mystery -- far away from time-short America. "Force!" "Being!" "Effort!" "Will!" "Form!" "Dance!" The words vibrated in three dimensions as word, vision, and sound.

At first, the exercise seemed arbitrary and pointless, something like a German movement class on effort patterns. I became a bit self-conscious and missed putting a hand or foot right. Gradually the feeling changed to being an automaton, moving quickly, puppet-like and easily to a series of repetitious images that became sharper and more colorful. Resistance left my body. William's voice and guitar became quicker. Intonations entered each word and the rhythms of their enunciation became exceedingly complex. A visualization of gestures transforming one into the other, synchronously operating my body in this ever-changing ever-same drama. Soon I could observe visualization as well as gestures themselves. At the final climactic series of changes I saw my observer observing images and images responding by observing movements and subtly correcting them if they began to deviate. The most excited calmness filled my experience.

William called, "Stop!" I froze in almost exact position of his call, in transition between Dance and Force. Then, at an easily recognizable gesture, we all sat down. A companionable quiet filled the room. A quiet light gray light filtered through the paneled paper walls.

"You can come once a week. Same time," William said to Bob. "But someone who works with me must do something besides yoga and sauna. Make an object."

"We're thinking of starting a restaurant," said Bob. "We need to make some money, but of course we also want to provide a definite atmosphere, a place for conversation in the front half, to be painted red and yellow, and a place to be silent in the back half, basically bluish light and rugs and cushions."

I was surprised since I had heard nothing of this before, and, glancing around, thought no one else had either. Bob was obviously riffing with William giving his subconscious full rein to respond to the challenge. He had just thought of it himself. Once again, I would be forced to decide.

"Then you must have the right name," said William. "The name resonates within itself the power that holds the manifest possibilities of an event. Our karma composes the event because we are too ignorant to do so, and we can even become conscious of our karma, but until we name the event karma cannot move forward to the point of recognition. Do you have the courage to put a real name on this restaurant?"

"Of course," Bob said. "Life's too short not to be real as I can get."

"To work with me," William said, "and to understand something in yourself, it must be called the Sign of the Tarot and the third thing that you will do on your visit here is to paint each of the twenty-two cards of the Tarot, carefully choosing which version of the forms you will use, the colors, the aimed-for quality, and to understand meaning in the same way you were beginning to catch and see meaning in that simple dance you started with."

Bob started to say something after William's pause had allowed him to glance around at us. William raised his hand to stop him, "I will see your answer by whether you show up next Saturday or not, with your preliminary work. I will have some of my students here also."

A ruddy-faced peasant farmer with straw hat and boots waved once at us as we drove off, walking then around his house where I knew a scholar-scientist-mystic would emerge, go to his study and commence his writing. I could visualize him doing that after entering into communion with other initiate authors seeking to formulate his ideas and experience in the light of classical standards of irony and clarity.

Jazz at the Filmore

Princess held one major difference with the dominant cultural forces emerging in the Haight. I was following her on a bizarre route over the tops of buildings, one guarded by a snarling Doberman, but the only way to get in free at the Filmore. You finally dropped down on a back fire escape and went in through a door on a iron balcony used for a breathing space by some of the customers.

"Tonight Charles Lloyd, Keith Jarrett, Jack de Johnette and Cecil McBee are playing great jazz. It's jazz that should be the musical center, not rock. But only Charles has been able to get a gig in the Filmore. I want you to hear real jazz make it on a big crowd scene where it's got lights, slides, and action going for it. Jazz cools the action, throws it back on the individual and team effort which is what it's all about. Rock's playing emotional mass politics with these high energies in Haight. It's what's winning and it's better than what is, but not at all what could be and is for some."

Princess turned out to be on. The endlessly looping run of a far-out kiss film, the streaky, wiggle lines of color, packed standing crowd, changing lights, all a lot different than the sit-down smokey whiskey jazz bars I had known and cherished. Lloyd leaned up into his height and let go with the sax, Jack deJohnnette scored with the drums, Jarrett melded with the keys, and McBee on the bass beamed in with the beat.

"Rock's gonna make the big money," she said, "that's why Graham went that way, but it won't have the subtleties of jazz, won't have the combo, won't have something we need to be creative for the long haul, open up the rarer emotional chords. It will have Stars and it will move the masses up a notch, but the edge will dull. It's like Kerouac and Ginsberg instead of Burroughs and Gysin. Anyway, tonight you'll see the alternate universe of possibility manifesting."

I didn't take acid that night, but half the audience had, so I made my contact high, and just that difference from whiskey and coffee transfigured the jazz, plus the audience standing like the front rows of a rock crowd, moving to the riffs, the complex forwardness of this quartet I had never heard or even heard about made me catch a new vision of sound. "Music is the image of the will" I had read years before in my fervently underlined *Birth of Tragedy Out of the Spirit of Music.* This jazz, individual, combo'd, structured and improvised, witty and uncompromising, beautiful and jagged, always strange but never alien created a sound-image of the kind of will I wished to attain.

Afterwards we paced excitedly back down magic San Francisco streets, divided into that realtors' gridiron of American boosterism, but with houses and trees so distinctive, so right for the climate, so imbued with living, that these simple earthquake tested streets seemed more romantic, more promising than the narrow and artistically changing streets of the finest old towns of Europe.

Who Has This Unlimited Love?

My grandmother died that early December of 1967 leaving me memories, a flow of love, and fifteen hundred dollars.

I had visited her just before leaving for Tangier in 1963. Her face that had borne the dull pockmarks of smallpox turned translucent and faired out the old scars. Her white hair hung down turning into small wisps of curls at the ends. We held hands and looked far into each other's eyes. She was ninety and had made a boy out of me. A boy can make a man out of himself with energy given by the blows of life and fate, but a child needs a lot of discipline, space, and love to make a boy out of himself and without that boy only a grown-up can emerge, not a man. I stayed with her several summers on her farm just past the edge of a little town of less than a thousand people, with its few windproof red brick buildings on that three block long desultory mainstreet, its white painted houses shaded against the sun by elm trees lined up against the wind, with sloping roofs for the times a cloudbuster crashed down its thunderous deluge. Only main street and the national highway where everyone had to come to a stop at mainstreet were paved. Not that many people drove in the depression and the depression lasted there till after World War II. Each house had a cellar for home-canned produce and tornadoes and rods on the roof to divert the fiercest lightning.

My grandfather, killed in a fight with a government agent in 1937 when I was eight, and he a blackhaired sixty-eight, had left the farm's core, the garden, the house, the barn, and milk cow, the pig shed, its yard and wallows, the cellar and smokehouse, in such top shape that grandmother could take care of the place by herself till in her eighties with only a little help from her eldest son, Uncle Frank, who now ran his own farm down the road.

"Bob," I said, "This fifteen hundred dollars from my grandmother needs something special to be done with it. She had eight children, and my mother died, so that's one-half my mother's share or just over six percent of the material surplus she left behind from a life's hard good work. She always wanted me to have space and freedom so I'm going to leave, go to Australia and Indonesia, especially Bali, for a couple of months. I'll come back to the house then if that's OK with you."

"Go," he said. "don't look back till you start back. Aim high. If you've made something for yourself, you'll being moving forward no matter which direction you take."

"I've got three days till I leave." Couldn't he see I wanted to make a deeper contact with him?

"Come with me this afternoon, then, I'm meeting Lord Zealand of the Institute. Landers wants to see if we can ally forces."

The Institute had hundreds, no one outside its leaders knew how many hundreds of members. The Institute had no external aims. It claimed as its main asset a teaching that could be carried out in the middle of the marketplace, invisible to the crowd and the players. There had to be much truth to the claim because I never heard of its members doing any projects as members. The proper carrying out of this system of exercises was supposed both to make one better at whatever one did by balancing the different human faculties, and more importantly to produce an inner seed capable of flowering into an immortal soul. The latter claim of course, was unproveable, but at least the Institute stated that only a handful could hope to reach this goal, and that no one might be able to do it, other than, of course, its Founder. The Institute avoided publicity by not seeking it and by assiduous prevention of scandal. At the cost, Landers maintained, of not doing anything interesting enough to provoke the energies one needed to make a body ready, willing, and able to deal with moment-by-moment demands of life's ever-changing reality, not to speak of the impact of death.

Landers drove Bob and me into a villa section of San Francisco, up a drive with tall eucalyptus. Suddenly a spacious lawn, landscaped with ponds and redwoods, set off a white mansion with substantial outbuildings.

"He wants me to direct their dance movements," Landers gruffed. "They're useful and beautiful, but I have my own work. I told him about your group, Bob, and that he should talk to you. . . . After all, one of your influences is the writings of the Institute's founder."

"Yes, but like Marx on Society, I like his diagnosis much better than the prescription."

"There is no prescription," said Landers, "for death, disease, and old age. You have to deal with them."

A high, stately carved door opened, and a grave man in coat and tie politely ushered us down a long corridor, where a somewhat smaller door opened into a roomy office with refined plaster decorations adorning the ceiling. A picture window opened on to the central grounds where a couple of white gowned no longer young ladies strolled in alert ease.

"Well, Zealand," said Landers, "I brought you Bob and his friend Joe because his approach seemed somewhat akin to Lurdyeff's."

"That will take some time to ascertain." Zealand replied affably but with no nonsense in his tone. "Just what approach do you use?"

A black and white photo of Lurdyeff hung over Zealand's desk, for all the world like a guru's photo in the office at the Pondicherry Ashram or in numerous other places on the subcontinent. That impression came not from the photo itself, but from its being the only photo in the spacious area of the desk, and of its being hung at eye level.

After some silence, Bob began. "Basically, I do theater that aims at the physiological understanding of all the emotions, including the negative ones, a special series of exercises that aims at the individual accessing finer energies than the reflex or automatic to attune his muscles, and a series of ideas and experiences presented as opposites that the individual must find some way to reconcile, or else leave our theater to escape the tension he can't handle."

"This is not our method," said Zealand turning abruptly in an unconstrained manner to Landers. "I don't see how this can fit in at all."

The energy rose sharply in the room. For the first time, I saw Landers slightly lose his cool and a faint red appeared on his forehead. Bob sat forward, ready to move in any direction.

"I think Bob should talk some more," said Landers.

"I'm willing to listen," said Zealand.

Landers had told us Lurdyeff liked to work with a certain type of aristocrat, and I noted the interesting synthesis that this Lord and this Count had made of their aristocratic manners combined with their decades long discipline that endeavored to distinguish insight from impulsions, compulsions, and reactions, and to drive these two horses, manner and discipline, from a single chariot. I suddenly realized I learned by imitation and empathy and not by observation and doing. Joe Madison was the ultimate chameleon I had spent years trying to make into a unity, something that could be seen like a star, or a river, or a human. I was a quick change artist, not in the body like Bob, but in the will, happy as long as I got a piece of the action.

"The time has come," Bob said to the polished sixty-five year old leader from his thirty-eight year old passion, "that real ideas and methods, from those who know and can do, should make their appearance in life, on the street. Haight Ashbury contains the greatest concentration of seekers and freethinkers on the planet." These guys, Bob, Landers, Zealand, all fascinated me because they weren't chameleons, they had a point of view, they had a destination in mind for themselves, they were unstoppable until they died, and then their momentum would carry on.

"I work with ten to twenty people," he continued. "Others do the same, maybe up to a hundred or two hundred people. But you and the Institute have many skilled people, instruments, costumes, ideas. We need your help. This opening occurring in tens of thousands of individuals cannot continue much longer without new inputs. Come out into the public area. Lurdyeff talked about action yoga, action in inaction, inaction in action, the unmoved mover. Give of your stored-up power, of your dances, music, yes, of the legend of Lurdyeff. Only legends transform creative imagination."

At last Bob had revealed himself to me because he had to reveal himself to these men to make his pitch for allies. His glamour as a leader of the new disappeared from me forever, but I loved him for the first time as a profound throwback, an adventurer into archetypes, revealing to me not any new future but the past, the great past of adventures with the archetypes. You've put your foot in it, I thought, you've mixed up what's new in the Haight with the Esoteric Past, just like the Diggers are mixing it with the Revolution, and Rock is mixing it with Star power and the People's Rally. You'll be made to pay for your rashness by the gurus dependent on "their people" and what was handed down to them. You're exposing yourself to them as a threat and competition. But I loved it, I loved his going down the line on legend. That's what Bob was bucking for, I saw it now. He also wanted to become a legend. To have travelled to strange frontiers of the psyche, survived, and returned to attract the mythopoeic powers of artists to create his legend. That's why he wanted me, a writer, and Princess, avid for theater, so closely in his circle. He was a Gilgamesh who wanted his desperate search for the ultimate in the relative to become immortal through the agency of artists. What if artists should ever write about artists, I thought, and remembered Gertrude Stein's saying

Hemingway never wrote his real book, about his own real life, and Hemingway saying how his secret depended on what he left out of the writing.

After a silence, Bob continued again, but dryly as if exhausted into brevity. "You will gain back as much or more than you give from the fresh creative energy of this extraordinary concatenation of desire and aspiration."

Zealand reposed lankily back into his chair. He had absorbed the full attack of his opponent endeavoring to induce him to change his position vis-a-vis current events.

"What you are proposing is impossible. To manifest in public and not to lose everything one has gained, not to cause even more overall confusion, is impossible unless one can maintain a balance of force and form. And to maintain the balance of force and form under conditions of that intensity requires unlimited love. And who has this unlimited love? No one. And so what you ask is impossible."

Bob began to argue heatedly, dropping his mask of ultimate enlightenment's uncommitted interest which even I had thought might be real. He used rhetoric in a last-ditch effort to win. I was appalled, fascinated, certain that he would fail to take Zealand's entrenched position, wondering how Bob would take the first defeat I'd seen him suffer.

"You," he directly challenged Zealand, "cannot turn aside from this situation. You hold the greatest uncommitted psychological force existing in San Francisco. History will judge. . . ."

"You are hypostatizing an idea into a false being when you use history with a capital." Zealand replied.

Landers had gotten red in the face in the argument and appeared about to burst into an explosion. He glanced agitatedly about the room, and then split, noiselessly opening and closing the door. "I will wait till you finish" he said to Bob.

After a couple more minutes Zealand and Bob both fell silent and gazed at each other. I knew they were each trying to digest the happening, so as not to lose the energy that had built up inside them, and also to transmute their incipient gut rage to a hormonal harmony in their blood, that "juice of rare quality." I had jumped too soon to the conclusion that "they had lost it." But still I felt a deep sadness. At least Lloyd had played once at the Avalon. He had laid out a choice though few had taken his path. Zealand wouldn't make a move. Landers was shook. Bob would go on alone. He would continue to play in his small theater. But he would play. No way to become a legend except by playing it out for all to watch, even if only a few actually saw. At least he would become a legend to himself.

Bob and I left with a courteous handshake from Zealand. "You just saw incredible timidity that will cost us all dearly," Bob said. "To be a general, and not use your crack battalions at the decisive moment! They will become a historical museum."

"Or perhaps prudential wisdom that will save something if the worst happens."

"Prudence without boldness makes it more likely the worst will happen. Come with me to see Raimondo tomorrow. He has boldness but little prudence."

In the car, driving back to the Sign of the Tarot, Bob said to Landers, "He's an advanced bhakti yogi, but he understands little of his action yoga."

"Are you indifferent to the fruits of the action?" asked Landers. "Or are you just a mesomorph showing off?"

We finished the drive in silence, in companionable loneliness.

Hello, Stranger. Long Time No See.

The next day we drove to Marin County to see Raimondo, a half-Armenian, half Peruvian crazy guru. "This guy's the dark half of Zealand," Bob said, "the polarity to the white robes and white mansion. What all his types do with Raimondo is pretty simple: surrender to the teacher and see the trips you get out of it, only these trips aren't just chemical or ascetic highs, they come from one who," he capitalized the next three words, "Incarnates The Teaching. The is an operative word that puts muscle into incarnates and teaching. Anyhow, I got to explore my dark side in a six week relationship I had with this guy, Raimondo, in Los Angeles."

"I needed it." Bob making a confession to me? This must have been building. "I had screwed my life up by some force grabbing me at decisive moments and turning me into a rabbit, whether man or woman facing me, it didn't make any difference. Raimondo mercilessly kept pushing me to manifest, manifest, manifest."

"Once, during an acting-out scene with one of his women students, I was hurled against a wall by literal white light bursting out of me, at least a two hundred twenty volt charge. I collided with the wall."

"Curiously, at that precise moment none of the twenty students there were paying attention to the stage, they each claimed not to have seen any of it. But the girl and Raimondo both confirmed what I had seen."

"Another time, doing one of his exercises, I was hurled against the wall of my own room, and this white light stayed for many seconds crackling soundless energy into the air."

"But he came to San Francisco where I gave him Pauline's address with whom I had enjoyed the briefest fling one night amongst the head high May flowers on the ridge above the beach in Malibu. Pauline introduced him to her group of friends, on the basis of my note to her that this guy had powers. . . ."

"He turned them loose to act out their repressions and desires, instructing them to fuck, fight, make money, spend, give a percent to him to make sure they had a higher purpose. . . ."

"He called himself the next-to-highest man, five levels above the lowest man, well on his way to becoming the highest man, he wouldn't claim that yet, and so was credited with a becoming humility. . . ."

"Then I arrived and visited Pauline where we hit it off immediately -- after Raimondo's course, I admit -- in a sort of Shiva-Shakti way. I went to one of his meetings with her, and he decided to make an example of me. He told me to go on my knees to each of Pauline's friends, and then to Pauline, begging forgiveness for presuming in my heart to be superior to them, when I was actually a pretentious fake. . . ."

We had crossed the Golden Gate and I turned back for the last glance at the Wonder of the Bay. After a minute, Bob continued.

"Astounded, I watched myself doing exactly what he told me to do. I had no power to critique the instruction, to pause for even a second, to stop never occurred to me although, of course, my entire being suffused with outrage. My body went through chemical changes I had never dreamt of, adrenaline fight and flights, serotonin, dopamines, testosterone, I believe even squirts of estrogen! My only mantram became 'ride the chemistry'. . . ."

"I actually felt death, then realized being forced into this grotesque humiliation occurred because I had literally become a slave of another man. Then understood I had always been a slave of another man one way or the other. An interactive wrath clarified all my chemistry. From the weakness that seemed endless suddenly strength began flowing into my arms, my fingers, my feet, my legs, my back, my eyes, my lips. . . ."

"It all reversed. I began to willingly beg forgiveness because actually I had nursed a pretentious fake inside, not all the time, not all the way, but even a little pretension is far too much, and because I could detect feelings of superiority to the others. Yet, I asked myself, would a single one of them have been so craven before Raimondo? Certainly no one could have behaved more cowardly. . . ."

"I finished. An immense strength now filled my body, an immense clarity my mind. I will never bow again to another man, I said to myself. I sat down easily in a chair and turned my head effortlessly to confront Raimondo directly face-to-face. At that moment I could have annihilated him spiritually, exposed all his falsity, but . . . he grabbed his only certain friend, an assistant, and split like a squid squirting gobs of inky blots of unconscious terror. . . ."

"I looked at the assembled group. They all sat silent. Not a word of communication. They had all gone along with Raimondo's humiliation scene. Their allegiance was total to Raimondo. I had been exposed as a . . . stray dog. They had become faithful dogs, seeing my abject behavior as the result of a supreme power possessed by Raimondo. They had seen the facts, but not my transformation. Only Pauline and Mike, who had also somehow gotten there, looked human. I waved to them and we left. . . ."

"Right after that we formed the House. My true life began in that moment. I owe it to Raimondo to have created a situation from which I precipitated something beyond any mental-emotional realization, however cosmic, namely an organized tempo inside my body that renders me invulnerable to the rabbit, the main state descriptor of my essence life till then. At the same time I see that he truly does not give a damn how any of his power plays turns out as long as he makes money, power, and highs for himself, nor does he have any real knowledge, so his disaster rate with the people he plays with is very high. Yet in one way or another, to his credit, we all asked for it. Two or three of us learned what perhaps we could not have learned in any other manner. Us truly stubborn jackasses!" He laughed, a long rolling laugh that wound up in a loud hee-hawing parody of itself.

We drove down a long curved entrance road to a rich man's stone house with a large pond behind it with swans. A loose-armed blackbearded man strode to the terrace.

"Hello, stranger," he said to Bob, "Long time no see."

"Hello, Raimondo."

"Have some tea."

We silently sat down around a glass-topped table on the terrace. Raimondo went inside and brought out saucers and cups. "Come in. While the tea's steeping, take a look."

The living room stretched about fifty feet by twenty five. Two large blue Chinese rugs lay across most of its parqueted splendor. "See you still have the Ming vases," Bob commented in front of the glass-doored case that rose to the twelve foot ceiling.

Raimondo carefully poured the tea. Two big cats sizing each other up. Raimondo had obviously already made up his mind that I was a non-combatant. They both seemed eager to get started, waiting only for the right moment.

"Well," Bob said, and the very fact that he started off with that probe word showed he was up for Raimondo even more than with Zealand. "The scene is becoming ever more intense, cops moving in more, heavy drugs arriving, sacred drugs being cut, younger kids arriving out of desperation and hope, living on rumors that have even reached Dubuque, but there's still a lot can be done."

"And just what do you propose? Are you never going to give up on negatively steered automatons that like to call themselves people?"

"Why not lighten up, Raimondo, save your full trip for your all-out few, and get some basic ideas out there. It's not likely to come again, this experiential opening. Even the Renaissance kept tighter limits on behavior."

"Maybe that's why it created so much. No thanks, Bob, I've got my way and my people out here in Sonoma and that's how I'm going to handle it. I don't get swept up by frothy moments."

"You've skimmed enough people off of that froth."

"They come to me, just like you did today. You can't stay away. Hungry for another taste? Truth, now."

"Create spaces in the full action, Raimondo, like our Sign of the Tarot. People love it. The place itself transmits ideas."

"I disagree with you and your approach."

I saw Bob flare, and then decide to go with it. Could he have actually stopped himself? "I disagree with you and what you're doing to people," he replied to Raimondo.

I had heard Bob say, disagreement is a sign of not-understanding. Not-understanding signified bad in his logopoeia, namely a state of lacking skills, consciousness, or both. He distinctly realized that his saying to Raimondo I disagree with you meant a self-critique by his own terms. He flushed slightly, an organic apology.

Bob stood straight up. He strode to the car with index fingers curled to touch his thumbs without checking whether I was following or not. I rotated my head to the right as we drove away. Raimondo still sat at the table, sipping his tea, Lord of the Manor by right and profit of psychic conquests.

Sober Ecstasy

"Look," Bob said to me the next morning. We had, at his gesture, poured a second cup of coffee after breakfast and walked through the edge of Princess' room, the old closed-in back porch, down the painted wooden steps, still in good shape after all those years. We sat down facing each other across the two inch thick, three foot wide, eight foot long pine table that Mike had carpentered when they set up house.

"Why don't I go to Australia and Bali instead of you?" he continued. "I need to get away from here. Too many projections building up on me. And since there has to be at least a tiny hook for any projection, they're gonna fall on me anytime now unless they get a break. Besides, you've just finished a big two year trip around the world in sixty-five."

"Why don't you go to Australia and I'll go to Bali, and I'll meet you in Bali in three weeks," I said.

"You're on."

Bob and Princess had rented an abandoned small grocery store just across the street from the Sign of the Tarot for their acting classes and rehearsals. "Hey," he added, "Come on over to the acting class this morning. If this is our last day together in the States for a couple of months, let's make zocco-rocco!"

I had never intended to get involved with Bob's acting work. Joe Madison was an observer, a traveler, and a writer from time to time when I had distilled some quintessence from the multidimensional experience emerging from inexhaustible phenomena. I loved to watch great actors on stage, including Bob and Princess, even right in daily life in their case. But maybe acting skills would open up new ways of traveling, new data to observe, increase Joe's resilience. Joe was, after all, my only true pal and instrument from which to make observations. "Okay."

Everyone (fourteen now) wore blue jeans and shirt or sweat shirt. Sally and Pauline each had a colorful silk scarf tied around their neck. Everyone barefoot. Bob did not allow flesh other than feet, hands, and head to be visible in his acting classes. "I work too much with sex energy to play around with flesh," he laughed.

Everyone commenced running around the wooden floored space. "Break him in, Princess," Bob waved to her and me.

She ran easily by my side. "The actor starts off becoming aware of breathing and environment. Run lightly as possible, watch your breathing until it operates on its own. Notice when breath becomes an independent force. At the same time, observe the environment, its space compared to your kinesphere, your need and ability to move, any chairs, platforms, equipment you can run into, or jump on, or pick-up. Notice when your organism feels at home in this space, ready to go all out without hesitation because it knows obstacles and possibilities."

A new side of Princess had appeared to me, one that would brook no repartee, that spoke with authority and to the point. I ran and found that paying attention to lightness, to breath, to the environment, made the others disappear as solid entities to become dynamic parts of the environment. A subliminal connection kept us from any collisions as we weaved in and out of ever-changing patterns.

We all stopped within seconds of each other. As the others commenced their series of individual exercises, Princess stood in front of me. She gave a new exercise, directly from the student of Stanislavsky's, Chekhov, who had managed to flee to New York to escape being killed like Meyerhold.

"Modern life conditions us to straight lines." Princess looked straight ahead. Stood straight up. Did a right face, an about face. Walked a straight line. "To be straight is an epithet on the street where life throws us curves." "All bad, bad, bad," she smiled. "Our muscular and sensory systems lose ability to mold a variety of shapes, appropriate to a given moment. Muscles and joints become machine-like, restricted to back and forths." I remembered Tommy Faraway with his studies of back and forth with ladies across the table.

"And up and down," I said.

She demonstrated rotating her hips, then the head, shoulders, wrists. I observed, tried to visualize, and then to carry out the movements by sensing correspondence or discord with the image. "Now put a snake in the spine . . . let the small muscles of the face move how they will . . . give up all efforts to keep a straight face." She undulated like a vision from the Arabian Nights.

I began to feel aches and a great resistance to continue. Not quite daring to stop, I watched my hips, head, and shoulders slow down, the snake disappear, my face resume its grave position.

Princess picked up on the slackening immediately. "Crucial moment, Joe! Visualize your body as a donkey. Win now, it will obey you in the future, lose now, you continue as it's slave. Separate rider from donkey. Do not let the donkey win." She continued her undulation and rotations in front of me, an exemplar of an astounding fluidity that seemed dreamlike, a living nostalgia for something beyond the ordinary that was manifesting directly into my astonishment.

The exercise became interesting, and gradually all-absorbing. Could I continue to ride the donkey?

Because definitely the donkey resisted. I had played hard sports, been through the army's basic training, and knew how to push myself. But however the donkey had subtly or openly tried to provide rationalizations and feelings to stop, to slow down, to fake it, there had never been open resistance to its training, only a testing of what minimum it could get by with by enlisting my thought and sympathies. But here, molding enraged the donkey, an only partially tamed higher animal, that saw itself being lassoed, put through paces to reveal itself, with no sexual rah-rah, no patriotic shilly-shally, no social threats to lure and drive it on. Princess confronted the donkey forcefully, suddenly, precisely with an entire new area of experience and effort, in which it found itself a novice at the age of thirty-eight, in which I was at last paying critical detailed attention to limitations the donkey put on my muscular meta-system.

Princess came in to support my attention whenever it white-flagged. "Left shoulder rotating. Opposite directions now . . . twice as fast . . . half as fast . . . like a macho . . . silkily feminine. . . ."

I couldn't take it any longer. The exercise had become ordeal. Sweat poured out of pain and stiffness. I could feel the donkey about to sit down abruptly, to quit. This was one stupid pile of shit. Who was I, Joe Madison, to have to take this from this unmentionable broad?

Princess caught the exact second. "Two minutes. Two minutes. One hundred twenty, one hundred nineteen . . . make the donkey know you won . . . one hundred seventeen. . . ."

Bob caught me on a point on each shoulder with his big thumbs pressing down, down, down. All the pain went into two points, my head flashed, and suddenly my shoulders swung loose. Then he grabbed each shoulder in turn, rotating it like a well-oiled shaft aligned with a smooth-toothed gear.

"Small muscles alive! Hips rotating! Eighty-seven . . ."

Just after Pauline reached "one . . .", Bob called "Stop!" and, in relief, I almost slumped down to the floor, but my nerves and attention had reached a state of such transparent density, that I caught all the others stopping exactly in the posture of that exact moment. I snapped into an arrest, the esthetic arrest? But, of course, this arrest or stop of mine actually took several small movements which slightly modified the last molding position. The sudden muscular stop sped-up the flow of loosened lymph and energy around my system.

"Okay!" Bob sat down and as quickly as he performed the motion, all of us were halfway or more down as his tail caught the floor. Princess seemed to be there at the exact same moment. My face felt open as sunrise.

Bob began to demonstrate muscle sets that organized striking, moving and alerting sensibilities of animals which we enacted. He became a bear, and we imitated. My hands became paws. They tightened the elbows and shoulders to swing great crushing strokes. He became a lion. My ears quieted my haunches to immobility, ready to spring, while the head rotated to the right and left picking up on every sound, distinguishing its sub component parts. He became a horse. My nose leaned forward until the spine began to pull from the pelvis and the scalp tingled over the skull, sniffing the molecules. From a place in the small of the back the arms and legs coordinated a four limb gallop that zoomed around the space, eyes flaring into small muscles of the temple. He became a monkey. My fingers wild and loosely defted into peoples' pockets, dappled strands of their hair, plucked folds of cushions and rugs, their touch outsaw sight, their dexterity transforming wrists, lips, eyebrows into quicksilver changes. He became a mouse. Skittering on toes and fingers, hurtling a rubbery back into the air, my shoulders filled with a dancing evasiveness.

Who would've thought, I said to myself, that this guy actually knew anything unique. Of course, the House did run well, but with Pauline managing the kitchen, Sally a weekly clean-up blitz, Princess the interface with artists, and Mike construction and maintenance, why wouldn't it? Preparing dinners rotated around the entire household. Bob had been a rancher, then a jack-of-all-trades, a plaid-shirted, blue jeaned, corduroy coated guy, for years, picking up an overall organizational sense from all the jobs he had done.

His talks had a zing to them intellectually, but considering his six years at universities studying every recondite subject under outstanding and individualistic professors from cultural relativity to the metaphysics of the pre-Socratic philosophers to tensor calculus, his talks were not unpredictable phenomena. If I had been ambitious probably I could have done about ninety percent as well. Even his great evening on the sexual history of mankind, while the éclat and skill he carried it off with was a tour de force, none-the-less the factual outline was not unknown to me from my own studies of the literature.

But to experience these animal souls or sensibilities as he called them, by his simply touching a set of muscles, setting them into action by the transmission of our enabling energy plus concentrated attention plus the mantram and visualization of, say, "bear", this could only be from a direct perception and translation by advanced homology of the essences of the animal kingdom. I looked at Bob with a newer scrutiny. Obviously his somewhat extroverted Western rancher physique striding-around persona was an act that covered a being much more at home in other worlds than modern America, or even, as he would probably say, post-Socratic Europe. In other worlds, other than even my fascinating Asia. These other worlds went down to archetypes working their will at levels deeper than any civilization or tribe, back to magical clans and their multitudinous patterns of manifestations out on the original Savannah mosaic of econiches.

Suddenly I switched to that world so different from thought-blanched behavioral civilization, where it was all in the body. Joe Madison had at last disappeared. Sitting in a semi-cross legged way, leaning forward, taking in the sex energy from Pauline, Princess, Sally and Diana, my body responded to every signal from Bob.

Really alert as to what Bob would say or do next, ready to imitate. I had reached the state of sober ecstasy. Standing outside myself, but not carried away by intoxication into weird mind trips. That voyage into acting lion, bear, wolf, horse, mouse, and monkey, somehow opened the door to a world I had never dreamed possible. Genuine, heart-warming, laughing, fearless attention. Fructifying worlds where I understood that the living body is not just the most complex physical unit we know in the cosmos, not only an apparatus for the interplay of the energy flows, electrical displays, and chemical compounding, not simply a relativistic link with quantum worlds of action and multi-dimension worlds of probability, but also a being with access beyond frontier battles of space and time, to an experiential coalescence with a fundamentally different mode of reality. A being that could transfigure to a mode of fulfillment, even past fulfillment to overflowing. At last I had momentarily escaped the metaphysical boundaries of pure thought, escaped its most spacious and well-equipped prison, even its last and most comfortable position, that of the trusty who is allowed to move freely around its time-space grounds.

From now on I would not take my living body, or its perceptions as given. It was a cosmic being with its own agenda. I became interested in everything about it. This being with its at least three point eight billion year old DNA was the philosopher's stone, the door, Aladdin's lamp, the winged horse, the face of Medusa, the flying carpet, the bottomless flagon, the Holy Grail, the Great Pyramid, the magic wand, and the three superimposed cathedrals of Chartres. It was the autonomous, resilient, synchronous, vital, intentional, contact point for joie de vivre, savoir faire, and instinctive well-being. An epochs and even stars old product of evolution, magic, mystery, hallucinations, morphing, resonance, chaos, and possibility. My body's mask was called Joe Madison. I would dance behind that mask from now on using all its permutating powers. That mask, Joe Madison, which I had thought of as myself was only a totem of that world of worlds to which I had just been granted entry. But that mask had been a totem that contained an animal taboo that had nearly killed my connection with living beings. I turned around inside to slam shut this door leading back to dissatisfaction, satisfied that I had had all I wanted, plus some, of that miserable domain of masturbating mind-body separation, artful enough in its fantasies, but forever incapable of the pure act of unifying perceiver, perception, and perceived, of full alliance with my living body and all its . . . incluctability of animal modalities of perception.

Trance Liberated From Constraint

Bob uncoiled to stand loosely on the balls of his feet. "Stop being ahead of the game, heady with delight, headed in the right direction; going to the head, even heading onward and upward or straight to hell, heading off, heading out, heads up, heads down, heading back." His head jerked around to all these positions, his eyes glistening with obedient rapture. "Let's get out of the head and into an entire body that knows this world intimately, from its toes to its balls, to its heels." Laughter.

"Namely, our feet. The feats that poets sing about, the feat of arms, the feats of derring-do, the feet to which we never listen, but instead let our head shod them in shoes, generally the wrong size, pound them on concrete, keep these born dancers and mimics and explorers motionless under desks, on floorboards of cars, told to step on it, step out, step up, walk right, always told by the headbrain what to do as if they had no intelligence or experience or dreams or wishes of their own, as if they didn't know the ways of Earth much better from direct experience than the head can ever do with its abstractions." Nervous laughter.

Bob demonstrated standing still until his feet betrayed an impulse to move, and then let his feet take over his entire body without putting up any resistance to that impulse. He lurched drunkenly, punched savagely, danced flirtatiously, tiptoed in panic, strode determinedly, all on immediate changes in impulses originating in his feet. He became a multitude.

Watching Bob move like a punch drunk prize fighter, shuffling, throwing punches, ducking, then like an old, infinitely weary gentleman pacing some endless city street gave me energy to let my feet take my body into a gliding dance that changed into a swaggering tough in eighteen nineties New York that became a young man prancing a private scene of narcissist glory. I saw trance liberated from constraint of stasis, kinetic trance foot dance of all unlived characters inside, mimic of colorful characters my feet had envied for some special expedition to Everests of the muscles.

Pauline's weary insolent sex-satiated slave girl mumbled a glance at Bob's blasé boulevardier who slouched into a world-sorrowful German romantic halfway through the glance. Princess's guerrilla alert hit girl slid by my impatient stockbroker hurrying to make a deal who segued into a jazz trombonist sashaying the stage. The feet stayed only a few seconds, hardly ever more than thirty with each new life they eagerly explored. Sally's debutante waltzed champagnely around the room before changing into a worldly wise peasant woman harvesting rice. Mike's violent drunk flinging wild hay makers changing into a maudlin pleading drunk changing to a suicidal drunk waving a pistol at his head to a jovially ironic poet surveying the human race.

"See how many people really live in a room of feet!" Bob called. "Keep a corner of the eye open and dig the crowd. Feet are never lonely. The billion-footed crowd is in your feet."

Again we all dropped cross-legged in a rough circle at the hint of a gesture from Bob.

"Now we ride on the magic if," said Bob, "to choose a judgment whose force will generate a plot, our characters, thoughtforms, poetry, a myth, a spectacle. Here are the choicest judgments! Condemned to die like a dog; Condemned to make an ass out of ourselves; to lose everything we cling to; to circle around a fixed point until we collapse; to starve in the midst of plenty; to seek and never find; to destroy ourselves by opposing villainy; which shall it be today, ladies and gentlemen, tragedy, comedy, social, absurd, mystery, epic, or heroic, the stage is on the stage, in life, and in your mind. Which judgment strikes us today with such force that we must say fuck you, and fight until we rescue our life from or lose it to that particular judgment of doom?"

Now I wished to become an actor. I had never wanted to be anything in particular because each particular thing came to a no good end. Now I saw that a real actor could live an entire microcosmos, an incredible world of which a whole civilization would use only a fraction. An actor could no more come to an end than a cosmic observer could, whether any particular play closed, or even if a whole theater shut down. Actors and observers could live as long as human life itself. They had started even before in animals and possibly would continue after us in yet new evolving genera.

Existential I and Thou

"Let's forget Australia and Bali for now," Bob said. "The action is here and it's getting hotter. All the judgments are coming down on this street. How we handle ourselves here, whether to go all out to win, or get out while the getting's good with some big winnings and leave the street to them, or whether we are smashed down and have to flee, this unique concentration of energies will leave a fall-out of seeds, of insights, of legends, of poignancy, that will set the stage for the entire Aquarian epoch." Ah, so that's Bob's specific aim, to be a seed-legend for the next two thousand years, thus even play a role in Plato's Great Year of twenty five thousand years. Now I understood what a dreamer I was dealing with, why he relentlessly hastened onward. I felt a bit bloodless in comparison, a bit thin, watery, but I wanted to become thinner yet. I wanted to become a thin transparent film, an almost invisible substance adhering to reality only by surface tension like water moving upwards in the xylem of a tree. Except at those moments when I also wished to be an actor.

Bob and I stood on Haight in front of the I and Thou coffee shop. Laura, the plumpish good-natured proprietor, waved at us through the window. Laura still went in for talk and waving and handshakes, the tested emblems of the existential social contract. She served great coffee, and, as in Europe, your seat remained yours, unhasseled even by a glance, till you left.

Bob said, "Laura's place fills a necessary function on the street. A nostalgia for the vanishing past, a belief in narrative literature and portrait painting, intellectual conversation arising out of a slack musculature and a restricted sensorium with aim-displaced emotions, stimulated by coffee and alcohol, turned-on by tobacco or cannabis, resolutely non-acid, non-opium derivative, non-speed-blurred quickness, non-rock or raga, a neo-Hegelian dialectic of symphony and jazz, Mozart and Miles. Let's go in and have a coffee."

Her competitor down the street, the India House, started off with hashish smells, glances, a salute from an unpraised palm, a study of rich colors, textures, shapes, incenses, perfumes, and iconic yantras of blue-bodied gods and manuals to attain various siddis, such as lasting youth, geometries of love, mental powers over infinity, and the conquest of death by shifting electronic bodies through the top of the head at the precise moment. Existentialists were located by India House devotees on the Bodhisattvic maps of the cosmos above hell-beings but below passionate animals, among hungry ghosts, talking endlessly about everything, but starved for experience. Essentialists occasionally found in the I and Thou seemed to the coffee-drinkers one step this side of an insane asylum, barely able to carry a dialogue exchange beyond a sentence every few minutes.

Enjoying the contrast of our rambunctious vigor among sallow voiced table talk of the I and Thou, sipping our cappuccinos, Bob and I commenced to talk for the first time in order to discover and uncover what we each thought. Each level on that cosmic map on Haight Street had its uses and knowledge that played a role in the action. Before, Bob had transmitted techniques to me partly as a wary teacher to an intelligent, eager, but dubious learner and partly in friendly confidentiality to a fellow frontiersman accidentally run across in the Big City. We exchanged vibrations, and co-operated in energy transformations and the Oakland action: but we had not talked. We had felt each other out by the non-verbal organic surprises inherent in such mutual probing of being.

"Two Russian boys who get together talk about God," I said, "or so writes Dostoyevsky. What do two American guys talk about? About Life. What they think, where they've been, and what they're going to do next."

"Well, on your theory of this being the seed place for the epoch, and that's why I'm here, to seed my legend, yes to a degree, but no," said Bob, "I don't think that Haight Ashbury alone is going to set the stage for the epoch. While probably there is one quite concentrated point for the impact, there must be others around the planet. An epoch can't start without a planetary action; that is, if there is anything to this notion of the Platonic Great Year of twenty-five thousand earth revolutions, corresponding to the wobble of the Earth's poles. If each Great Year marks a stage in the evolution of our species, each epoch, so to speak, must light up another aspect of Earth's entire stage in order that mankind create a conscious record, an accessible memory, of its entire existence. Anything on that vast a scale must be a planetary, not a local action."

"For its sages, scholars, and fools to study," I said.

"And for its cultural unconscious to be influenced by symbols, monuments, traditions, rituals, myths, technics, and costumes made of such power that they survive the wreckage of greedy and envious centuries."

They sipped Laura's perfectly dripped coffee. She bought special filters. Today the bean came from Blue Mountain, Jamaica.

"So," I said, "you don't think we should call off our trip after all."

"I think we should expand it. One of us, maybe me, goes to New York, London, and Prague, it's supposed to be the hot place in Eastern Europe, they use acid for psycho-analysis there, and Dubcek's calling for a communism without tyranny, and you go to Australia and Bali."

"And then we rendezvous back here and see how it all fits together."

"If it does. This will be critical info if it doesn't."

"You're running a big risk leaving the House for six weeks. You've got no idea what would happen."

"No idea what would happen if I stayed. One day of revolution equals twenty years, Marx said, and this is revolution. Not Marcuse and Maoists with their dried-out ideology, blind to the stifling boring dictatorships of the left, but the real revolution calling into question the state itself, as well as established church, oligarchic forms of private property, thinking itself out of that primal source of mind splitting complexes, the nuclear-exploding money-centered caricature of family which is upheld by and upholds planetary structures of violence and conditioning, hundreds of millions of micro concentration camps of physical abuse, idea dictatorship, sex repression, and economic and cultural struggles against poverty . . . poverty no matter how much money because this limited form cuts off sharing mutual effort. Even an American billionaire leads a life, apart from his million things, of a poverty of experience no struggling artist could feel anything but pity and terror for."

"Bob, I see twenty to thirty years of incredible hardship for you, trying to attain ever more enlightened states, legendary experiential explorations in acting and at the same time struggling openly against ancient injustices, now ingrained into human behavior. You will wind up wishing you had stuck to and won at one or the other of the three instead of failing, heroically of course, at all three." I kept up a light, ironical tone, but I wanted to touch him, to plead.

"Joe," he savored his reply, "I see a lifetime of emotional torment for you endeavoring to obtain an ever deeper insight into truths, independent as possible from social struggle, when your own isolated death will disappear whatever insights you reach, as if it never existed. What is the use of all this effort for a finite individual is your secret aching question. At the end you will get your answer: no use at all except to me, and my life was so brief."

"And 'why do they betray me who worked so hard for them?' is going to be yours," I flashed out of a previously unknown place of prophesy, wrath at his wasting his potentiality, his restrained personality that kept us all, even me, at a distance. We looked at each other, reverted to glance and vibe and lightened up.

"So, I'm headed for Europe," said Bob.

"So, I 'm headed for Aborigines and Asia, " I said. "See you February one."

A Magical Operation

After a long step-by-careful-step hike over tangled barnacle-sharp mangrove roots buttressing down into the salty water, led by a small boy, I climbed inland over a low rise that opened on a small secluded beach where an old Fijian sat cross-legged on a mat by his one-man thatched hut. He slowly carefully put a root into a cloth bag, after smiling hello to me, as if my arrival were no surprise, although there seemed no way he could have gotten advance word.

Then he beat the bag against the side of a boulder until the bag swung limply with crushed root, before placing it into a kettle of simmering water perched on the banked red coals. Of course, I flashed, he does this as a daily routine and the boy knows that he welcomes a certain kind of visitor.

The kettle water turned brownish. After a peaceful while, we sipped the liquid which the old man had poured into cheap glasses with the same languid grace as tea served in a Sussex country house. The afternoon glowed through the blue sky punctuated by a few floating clouds. Glad I stopped at Fiji. Decompression. Some simplicity left, to pass an afternoon in cheerful silence. Living bodies here receptive to new patterns of behavior that would open inner spaces and increase cosmic connections.

Then hitchhiking from Sidney to Perth, across the continent. Blue Ridge haze, reminiscent of Appalachians slowing up the American advance westward. Wheatlands. Sheep lands, kangaroo-filled stream valleys, tall and ghostly trees allowing sunfall straight past leathery leaves, pastel palette, moonlight carrying forty thousand years ceremonial initiations into the bone-breaking stick guarded secrets of wildness and wilderness, into songmarked trails across the desert, and fleet chases after morning rain clouds, standing on great thick boughs above billabong watering holes. Long and empty flat lands full of meteorites, the Nullarbor Plains, the place of no trees, half a continent long, huge mountains of sand thrown up against stark cliffs by Antarctic breakers and winds, the guy with his fishing dory whose catch-filled bow had been crunched off by a white shark, sheet iron remnants of gold rushes, abandoned holes in the ground, brownish-yellow gangue heaps, camels a continent away from home, the Swan River gliding to the Indian Ocean, dollar a night rooms in old frame houses on the other side of the railroad track. The land had not yet found its new voice to match the old chants now protected less and less by taboo-enforcing bone breakers from all profanations by profit, or by insolence of uninitiated youths. The immense vacuum of future pulled power into me, vague dreams of achieved romance glittered out of the night sky. When, lying on my swag on the beach that first night, I looked straight up into that great river of stars, the Happy Hunting Grounds my Indian teachers had called them, but, South of the Equator, brighter, clearer, by far.

In Perth, rested up on my dollar cot for a couple of nights, I decided to see what would happen if Joe Madison took to the street here in this most remote city on the planet. How had my being changed from the Haight Ashbury event? Let my being find its own new level. Here I knew no one, I would not contact the House, would get my visa for Indonesia, and for two weeks would live off my wits in Perth. If people were generating Haight Ashbury energies here, I would make a permanent contact with Western Australia to be invoked at some future time. A magical operation of solitude in public aimed at contacting the time line of history on these eastern shores of the Indian Ocean, where the East was West and North, and the Present held a tiny beachhead into the longest continuous Past on the Planet but where the English language Computer-Space connection formed an entree into the furthest Futures being contacted.

The first night sacked out in a tree-filled park silvery with the waxing moon. Abos seemed to flit by on emotional radar, tall, quick, and powerful by night. Not even the glance needed at Haight to make contact, but direct body emanations. Contact, make the read-out, integrate, move on. Faces chiseled out of a genetic time when genuine masks grew right out of bone and flesh, caved, cubismed, prognathous with unconcealed will-to-live. The great purges of the genetically revealed that had taken place for thousands of years on the other continents with tribes, nations, states, and empires, here had begun to select out smoothed-down faces of camouflage only one century before by the use of guns, medicine, and jobs that demanded the appearance of conformity.

The second night picked up on a bearded guy sitting on a bench behind a picket fenced wooden house that faced the Governor's mansion across the boulevard. The guy definitely wigging from behind his impassive face and motionless body.

I leaned on the picket fence, "Hi, just arrived in Perth. Where's a good place to hang?"

"Yank, aren't you? Come on in. "

Commune of seven. Neat well put together house from old craftsmen. We grooved together till midnight. The Australians wanted to know all about Haight Ashbury. "We know it's happening there. We set this up to be part of the action."

At midnight I followed, hand-in-hand with one of the girls, about four months pregnant, blonde and frank, without display, back to her small room, formerly used for tool storage, facing on their rows of radishes, carrots, and cabbages. The energy like a knife of sensation opening a brilliantly edged surprise of perfect dance.

The Dreamtime Theater, Ronald Match, handsome gay director. "Why don't you teach some acting classes while you're here. Some of those techniques sound interesting." The red-haired beauty, ballet dancer Glenda, back to the home country after three years in swinging London, "Yes, I'll come." I sacked out at the Dreamtime, on my swag in the lobby. "Just get out before the people arrive at ten," said Ronald.

The next morning she came quietly at nine o'clock through the unlocked door and stood over my head. "I came," she said. After I'd kissed my way up towers of ivory into the palace of the Sleeping Beauty, and discovered that, indeed, she could dance, I jumped up and we ran into the theater, nude.

Bob's exercises had become my own. Glenda and I did animals, and moved on through unleashing the movements of the tiniest muscles that could suddenly from apparent twitchings set the whole body into a series of extreme and marvelous elicited postures. Her green eyes set off jade resonances of Chinese sages. Precision clicked in tiny cranes and levers that not even Bob's work outs had discovered.

"See you tomorrow, same time," I said.

"Okay." she slipped out, tennis shoed, blue jeaned, white cotton bloused, leaving a faint perfume of ripely flowering summer.

Two days later, swimming in the ocean on the late morning almost deserted beach north of Perth, our swimming suits held in our hand, we joined together where the water, four feet deep, rose and fell with gentle waves.

A chopper rattled over, low. I found myself somersaulting back and away from her, though I had been totally into the moment, enjoying communion flying on sensation. Vietnam, hot, green, hills, gunfire, choppers, alerts, voices, "we just caught you, we're going to get you, you are worse than the Viet Cong, we'll throw you in jail for being naked with that girl on a public beach, watch out, we're watching you, we aim to get you."

Terrified, I pulled my trunks back on and ran blindly to the beach, throwing myself down on the sand behind a boulder. She knelt by me. "Joe, what's wrong, what happened?"

"That chopper, that chopper, I couldn't keep going with that chopper flying over us. It was them, they were all there!"

"Who, Joe, who was all there?"

"The police, the army, my father, my mother, the fanatics, the powerful, the no-sayers, the jailers, the torturers, everybody who hates what we were doing, what something in me also obviously really feels and thinks. Glenda, I'm a coward, they scared me, I thought I had transformed myself, escaped this fear, but it's all still there. Just a chopping chopper, and suddenly it's all back and I'm running for my life, I'm hiding, I'm abandoning you. . . ."

She stroked my head. "You're not abandoning me, you're letting me see what's inside. . . ."

"I don't want you to see what's inside. What's inside, still inside, are those dark, hateful forces and beings, but furthermore they're not just inside, they're not just an illusion, I would be thrown in jail by these people if they knew what I did, they do look, oh maybe not for me specifically, but for all of us, and even any of themselves who break out from time to time. They make great random searches and then find a person they can mobilize their forces against and destroy him to make an example. We have at best fear and camouflage with a few guerrilla theater strikes, a small tribal enclave surviving by magic here and there for occasional happinesses whose memories save us until the next time . . ."

Indeed, Glenda's husband caught us the next afternoon coming out of the movie, "The Pawnbroker." We held hands tightly, I reliving the emotional accuracy of the portrayal of the old Jew's life, his wife turned into an army comfort girl by the Nazis, his children killed, he barely surviving concentration camp, and then his pawnshop staked by American gangsters, his protégé killed, his own life to be ended at that moment when his killer decided it would pain him the most, his life force propelling him, innocent and persecuted, through the carnage of the century.

We had turned to each, the same emotion flashed our eyes together in a union of courageous apprehension; I swung her in the air, exaltation, then a car stopped. Two men inside, one, broad shouldered, jumped out. "Glenda!"

Suddenly he was standing three feet from us, a man looking at Glenda, ignoring me. Glenda, after one side glance, looked only at the man. "Get in," he said brusquely. She slipped in the backseat, the man clomped down in the front passenger seat, and they drove away without looking back.

That last night in Perth, Ronald took me to the Richard the Third performance at the University although I had low hopes. "You can always leave after Act One," Ronald said, "but you won't."

Richard carried off deadly strokes as a wickedly brilliant motorcycle gang leader, surrounded by lieutenants in black leather jackets. He and his gang created terror and then Richard exploited the fear to ruin a kingdom.

Yes, it was all America needed, a Richard to run rampant with fear to become an overt tyranny, it was all Germany, Russia, and China had needed. And America had a Richard.

With foreboding I hiked with Ronald into the night. "Oh, by the way," said Ronald, "I'll have to ask you not to stay at the Dreamtime tonight. Two friends of mine, guys, need a place to do their thing, and they said it would be a big hang-up for you to be there."

"Yeah," I said.

"Sorry," Ronald said, "but you know how it is. These guys are part of my scene."

"Sure. I'll stay down the street at the dollar hotel."

Walking with my swag on my shouder, I saw the pregnant girl. "Hi," she said, "where you been?"

"In the theater. Leaving for Bali tomorrow."

"Got a place to sleep?"

"Going down to that little hotel."

"You can come back with me."

She was a no bullshit person. I walked on with her.

She showed me into her small room, and touched the palm of my hand. "I've got to talk some with the others. I'll be back when we finish." I lay there for an hour. Suddenly I struggled for meaning in any of my time at Perth. No one here really as intense as Haight Ashbury. But I liked them. Relatively unspoiled. They got what they could out of life flowing through and around them. They strove for something more.

Better than the Americans in their frenzy of things, worship of images, and victorious armies, their lack of time to smell roses and lies.

At the end of an hour she had not yet returned. I fell out of the impersonal, vivifying erotic tempo with its casual arousal. To regain tempo, giving her silent blessings, I slipped out, and headed for the friendly airport benches, to sleep there till boarding time. The airport had a hot shower. Western Australia lived, but without knowledge, alive as a boy and a girl in their first kiss. I had made a permanent connection with their sheer livingness. Bali! In its dance, architecture, and cosmology I hoped to find real knowledge of what lay behind life and to compare that with what I had experienced in San Francisco. Then Bob and I would meet with Princess and the House to see what together we make of the planetary fire. I fell into a deep delicious sleep on my swag stretched out on a bench in Perth's non-paranoic airport.

Valor and Villainy

The dancing master at the Denpasar School of Balinese dance had given me detailed instructions on how to get to a village where the Rangda-Barong struggle would be enacted that night - the entire ten hour play-ritual for the village. No one else would be there except for the village and the actors.

I asked the dance master, "The dances at the court in Jogjakarta were more precise in their beauty than yours in Bali, but somehow the visual pleasure, the beauty, of yours seems still greater."

"Ah, this is because," his whole lithe body suddenly in action, energy flowing from the fingers of his two hands, both upraised, "in Jogjakarta they allow the dancer only this much variation in a movement." His fingers demonstrated a sixteenth of an inch variation. "Whereas, to attain the maximum spontaneity the form can carry, we allow this much." His fingers demonstrated an eighth of an inch variation in the same movement as before.

"This makes the difference, other factors being present, of the continuous creativity of Balinese drama-dance as against the highly conscious but tradition dependent Jogjakarta drama-dance. Remember to go over this map carefully with the truck you hitch a ride with, because," he laughed, "a variation of one small road will make it impossible for you to find the village."

The two ton truck halted in moonless glitter by the side of a tree-filled darkness. I slid off the high-stacked bales of cloth in the back, dropping lightly down in the dark. "Thanks," I smiled. The driver smiled back, then smoothly accelerated the truck down the narrow paved road.

I slipped into my cosy long-distance gait to climb the small lane's incline. I turned on the first lane leading off to the right. As my eyes fully adjusted, stars filled the night. Forest fell behind and star-splashed lower rice paddies commenced. The warm night, silent steps on the unpaved road, my inner preparations reviewing the scripts of the forever battle between evil witch, Rangda, of not-to-be-destroyed power, and good Barong of not-to-be-destroyed delight, coupled with my attention to particles of breath and minute movements in my toes conspired to gift me with that state "where everything is perceived as perfect."

After the next three turns, though, and another mile of walking, eighteen hundred steps, without seeing a person, I began to fear being lost.

One more turn, however, and a vast panorama of star-glinted water motionless in cascading paddies insouciantly challenged the star-glittered spherical crystal of sense-imagination in the center of which the earth revolved our points-of-view. As I stopped to savor the four to five degree change of Orion's position since starting, signifying among many things the passage of about twenty minutes, a figure walked off the paddy ridge onto the lane, a hoe over his shoulder.

"Rangda-Barong?" I executed a body pantomime of the witch, but with a low smiling laugh. The man also laughed lowly, and waved to follow him.

Two more turns, and five minutes later, we entered a village through a carved wooden entrance, past a temple, to an open place on the other side of which a temporary bleachers had been erected. The open place lay adjacent to the temple. On the side opposite the temple a few booths stood, with small articles of food, carved figurines, and colorful paintings of Rangda, Barong, and Hanuman.

My friend took me past the booths and into the bare planked stands. Soon everyone in the village was sitting there. Packed. Some shadowy figures could be seen entering the temple. The dance master had told me the actors must enter that sacred space to obtain a blessing and to attain a definite state of consciousness before entering the theater space. "You see, the theater space is two levels higher than the actor who enters the village although this actor is already higher than the daily life level. So in the temple, the actor contacts the gods, then in the theater, the gods contact and enter him. Therefore, the beginning of the theater depends on the actor's prepared skill accepting the decision on when from the gods. We know only that they will depart at early dawn."

The gamelans crashed my spacious sensual night, a three-level construct of Ptolemy, Copernicus, and Einstein, Earth, sun, and stars, on into the fourth level of cosmic light in which the triply scientific night space became only a temporary stage set for a cosmos of universes, each universe a theater for immortal forces to fight to control emotional constructs of authors, actors, and gods: the Earths, suns, and stars of the worlds beyond my world.

Role-scripted by an author who had seen, listened, lived and created with the roars, conversations, threats, and speeches from that realm of organized qualities, hero and heroine, god and goddess, loyal friends, best friend transfigured to monkey-god, villains of demiurgic magic, kidnappings, mind-rapes, the emergence of witch Rangda in kinetic trance, all rocked and rolled the stage. I saw that all the unceasing evil that befell the hero, heroine, friends, and even the villains had not been an end in itself but a calculated and performed means for Rangda to increase her power, to attain sole rule of the world. Evil, then, controlled both hero and villain. Evil needed energy and this hideous show of valor and villainy in mutual slaughter was Rangda's face happily feasting on the finest food.

The Oakland black-shouldered and visored, club and gas armed powers, the float of costumes, music, and love in the park, outstretched arms from the traffic jam buying Oracles, and the cool hash-enhanced interiors of India House and warm coffee clattering chatter of I and Thou, the dance-dramas of the House and Raimondo's psychic rapes, all part of the witchcraft configured by Rangda to prepare her tasty cuisine. No wonder I had to split that scene, yet in Australia it had been the same, but on such a smaller scale, that, starved, I had fled precipitately to the airport. I myself was Rangda! The thirty-nine blows of my escape, my fleeing from America to make a journey around an extraordinary planet dancing in a mad alternation of Jogjakarta precision and Balinese ecstasy, all of the struggles in that Manifest Destiny of the Progress of Profit clashing with the Historic Necessity of Revolution, all were but one smile on the face of Rangda feasting on the casualties of life cooked up by her remorseless needs. My entire existence, punctuated by enlightenments and hardships, all was Rangda! But, contradiction! Rangda’s world would come to an end if she were allowed to eat it all. All would die by losing hope, by seeing their puppet master, the wicked witch trance continually dancing the energy of all creation into inescapable destruction. When all canceled, even Rangda herself would starve to death, the bewitching cosmos fall down to a factual universe of energy-decaying abysmally separated solids, time's inevitable victims, bowing to the implacable trinity of Ptolemy, Copernicus, and Einstein, all magic reduced to a sleight of hand joke.

Rangda morphed from the savage intelligence of ugliness, as her dance moved incredible ligaments of lightness, into a full moon of baleful attraction flooding the night skies. I nearly fell off my bench seat realizing I had fallen in love with her. No woman could move with such articulated exhaustless passion, no man dare advance toward her without dying, yet Rangda was calling for an eternal lover, a lover beyond sexuality, a lover who would fight her for the soul of the world hanging half-devoured from her slavering mouth. When would he, it, come. Surely she would have to quit, the exhausted goad and killer of the world. Who could challenge her?

The gamelan split into architectonics of struggling passions throughout many ages, many long lost passions but now remembered. A gorgeously intelligent white animal, Barong, charged-undulated out of the temple onto the plain of a meta-kurukshetra. Around me and in me, the leaning forward. The village and I made our investigation of next year's destiny. The drama occurring on the stage, in them, and throughout the local night concentrated the temple, the village, the space, the time, into two costumed energies fighting in trance realms, through muscles, breaths, and sensations trained from infancy for thirty years, in competition with the best, to refine destiny itself.

I vibed now without thought, emotion, or sensation, to each movement of the struggle. Coming down to the waking-up state I saw Rangda disappearing into the dark, Barong dancing, hero, heroine, and friends reviving, bleachers stirring, stalls opening, the night almost gone, my eyes irrepressibly closing. I made a gesture, could I sleep behind the bleachers? Yes. I fell asleep on my swag, into a deep sleep far beyond dreams, beyond delicious, profound fatigue, into unmodified deep sleep.

Ashes In My Brain

Returning to Haight in early February, Sixty-Eight, my eye staked out the battle ground where I resolved to stay until just before the enraged establishment, suffering a near-mortal wound with their bloody engagement of full-scale ground forces on the Asian continent, devoid of strategic objective, wrecking the economy and thereby stifling the one real war, the one against poverty of body, of mind, of spirit, would turn on its own people, makes both dissent and difference a crime, and sends in battalions of police and squads of narcs to imprison or at least terrify into silence both the intelligentsia celebrating and the black youth revolting in the hearts of American cities. Yes, truth, experience, and freedom seekers would be harassed and jailed in the general repression which would be called morality, the American code word for fascism, the rule of the state in the interests of the rich. The inane and profane would strike soon and hard to destroy sacred dances being enacted at last on a global stage before cool electronic eyes. Though the vast majority of humans remained safely herded, divided up into national state paddies, a Rangda's dance had evidently begun in full force upon the planet. Could she build up the energy needed to attract the Barong? The ultimate world war of values would be decided on battlefields of archetypes. World War I had been won by bodies, World War II by minds, but the last one would be won or lost by sacred theater. I swung down the street toward the House, my seat at a table of the world casino, determined to focus my energy into the final escalations of piles of chips on Haight Ashbury.

The decisive battleground included the Panhandle, the liberated area of the Park, Haight Street to Ashbury, some blocks of Victorian houses on both sides of the street, some outlier houses on Pine Street, James' on Fillmore, some studios on Division Street, the House and its Theater of Seven Judgments next to the Sign of the Tarot, some allies on North Beach, in the Mission, in the City University, in Berkeley, in Big Sur and Sonoma, and a handful of sympathetic professionals in the arts, in law, in religion. In New York, London, and Prague, hot spots of action flamed, rock and rumor swept the planet's youth, Bali, Perth,

Kyoto, Saigon, Tangier, Kathmandu, Oaxaca, Ibiza, Goa, King's Cross, the Beat Hotel, East Village, and a thousand other places synchronized the action in separate engagements.

All this complexity panicked the thought of powers in Washington, seeing the coming first defeat in war threatening the history of America. These graduates of Harvard and Texas A & M decided to treat this archetypal war in higher levels with the lowest level of brute force, the charge of treason. I remembered my talk with Johnson's budget Director, Bell, upon returning from Vietnam and how, Bell, confronted with ground truth by men of experience, confirmed by his own top assistants, had swung in his chair, placing his back to them until they left, grimly signifying that nothing could be said in the White House that cast any shadow on its insistence that victory lay just around the corner. Now the President, besieged by popular uproar, hardly dared leave his imperial palace. By a predictable stupidity of ruling classes losing a war who had run out of ideas, and therefore relying only on force to maintain their privilege, the American power holders would now commence to escalate the use of propaganda and force, primarily against their own people, satisfactorily helpless compared to the disciplined legions reporting to Hanoi. Americans would be reduced to initiative-obliterated fellaheen unless their billionaires and politicos could be overthrown by a split amongst themselves with one side calling in the intelligentsia. But Republican and Democrat alike, both paid for in advance at the elections by the oilgarchy, called for war and repression, uniting behind an ex-President of an auto company in charge of winning Vietnam. The majority of the people ceased useless voting in the apathy of empire. Academia, fat with imperial contracts, postured as intelligentsia, strutting on its reductionist leash, and with a Darwinism manqué talked of the accidental arising of humanity, and its not far-off extinction, a "meaningless twig on the bush of life." "Why bother with anything except a career?" they asked the blacks, women, and longhaired students, engaged in all night arguments and demonstrations.

Bob had arrived back the day before me. "Come on," he said, "The battle of Prague was lost, but the Runaway Children's Conference is being held at Glide Church. All the media will be there. Communication Company's decided to confront charges of bad things happening to teenagers."

Glide Church, interface between the street and the power, furnished the one space left in the battlefield where all parties could meet on the level of discourse.

Cameras banked around the front of the church. God the media was now for sure, photographing inscrutably until His judgment caught guilty postures and attitudes somewhere in the congregation, picking up their slightest sounds, and tiniest squirms and eye white rolls. The congregation sat alertly holding their inner positions secret in the best way they knew how. Examination by the media, a linguisitorial, jealous, revengeful, relentlessly scrutinizing, and puritanical god who outdid any priestly tribunal in arousing mass lynching of heretical and deviant behavior. This deviant devil's litany of true names had been discovered by the media: non-married sex, consciousness-expanding drugs, opposition to expansionist wars, and satire against pompous ideotheologs. The media sold this war with mantrams: Sex, Drugs, Treason, and Cults. This fairheaded devil would be burned in blazing images. Bodies would follow. Prisons would flourish. Morality, prescribed drugs, loyalty, and a literalist Christian Church would be the two parties' line. No one would be allowed to deviate from the two parties' line. It would become tighter and taughter than the Russian one party line.

Nonetheless, Ralph at Communications Company, a red-haired ex-Madison Avenue advertising vice-president, who had helped decide to call a car a horse, "Mustang", a great success story in the market place before his tuning-up, dropping in, and turning neuron, entertained the hope of desperation in launching this media party, risking flagellation and burnings by sound-bite caricature. "You're playing with fire, literally, calling in these priests," Bob said to him.

"Yeah, but I know these guys and all their tricks from the old days. I'm not the typical provincial who dared to think for himself that they laugh at while annihilating. Besides we've got no choice. Did you see the headline last week? Twenty thousand children descending on San Francisco in June! They've already doubled the cops on patrol in Haight. Anyone they find under eighteen they're throwing in the tank and calling their parents. They're starting to write up sex charges on principle against House leaders who've let one of the kids stay."

"There's not room for twenty-thousand more people on Haight anyhow," said Bob.

"Right. There's only two thousand communes and most of those are inexperienced with their own problems learning how to live together. . . . So we need to get that story out, to keep some of them from coming. But no matter what propaganda's been put out against the Haight it can't sound worse than their present situation that's made them desperate. In fact Haight at minimum's going to sound hopeful as all get-out to anyone who's bright. We need to make sure the city helps or at least doesn't attack us for their flight to here."

"Lot's of misery and boredom out there. I'd come no matter what if I were sixteen or seventeen," said Bob. "I wish to hell there had been a place like this for me to come to."

"Yes, you can't stop them from coming now. But when they get here, how can anyone take care of them while they get their bearings?"

"I don't know. How many people can a dream take care of? Hell, we are free as you can get on this planet of disease and conditioning, and unjust allocation of scarce resources, but we only got forty to fifty blocks plus one newspaper, one clinic, one switchboard, one free lunch, and maybe a thousand experienced places for one or two to crash left if we push it. It'll take another year for us to get it down."

The media guys imperiously summoned Ralph to the bright lights.

"You're pulling a hundred thousand kids from ten to seventeen here next summer promising them drugs and free sex, freedom, but what about disease, crime, the pain of the mothers and fathers? Whose gonna be responsible?"

"Sure, we estimate twenty thousand sixteen or seventeen year olds, mostly the really bright ones who graduate from high school early, will make the scene to take a look. Most will go back very quickly. We are not responsible for the fact that many of the smartest youths want out of armored, hopeless lives, surrounded by a thousand meaningless gadgets, growing up to be job fodder to be thrown on the scrap heap at every recession, and cannon fodder to be thrown to the jungle. Why do you try to make us a scapegoat for the national failure?"

"Here," Ralph said. "talk to one of these runaways. . . ."

A hooded boy shyly makes his way on stage to face the mikes.

"What's your name?"

"Can't tell you."

"Can't tell me your name?"

"I'm scared."

"Of who?"

"My family."

"Scared of your family? How can that be?"

"They'd beat me and yell at me for coming here."

"Then why'd you come here if you knew they disapproved?"

"I couldn't stand it there. I came here and found friends."

"You'll never be able to go to college."

"Don't know that I want to go to college."

"You run away from your family who's going crazy because they don't know where you are, you don't want to go to college to educate yourself, you probably will take drugs. Would you fight for your country?"

"If it was attacked."

"What about if it was going to be attacked like Pearl Harbor and you and we had to attack first to stop that?"

"I don't know."

"How many drugs you been offered?"

"A few."

"How many drugs have you done?"

"Only some grass, hey, man, this is enough!"

Millions of Americans watched a selected montage beamed their way by studios of technicians directed by a producer calculating the dollar value of excitement and 'cutting to the action,' determined as a Soviet agitpropist to carry out the policy to obliterate dissidence.

I felt immense pain. This would be the end. Children and drugs, sex, and anti-war. Headlines. Ralph had been a fool. "Children" was the ultimate rhetorical club to fire up panic. To my surprise I heard Bob bellow out, "tell it like it is!" to another hooded figure, this time a literate sixteen year old girl. Bob glanced at me, "Only chance is to increase the energy!"

I rose and left. The cops and narcs would be fully unleashed now that they could claim to be saving children from pot and sex. How could someone sixteen be called a child anyhow? I had left home and gone to work at fifteen, on my own. The actual facts of misery, alcohol and rising illegitimacy due to sex ignorance would be silenced. Would the moral police ever be called off until America became one total prohibition? Then, of course, hundreds of thousands more uniforms would be needed to enforce the prohibition. The crushing rationale of American political tyranny: Morality, More-ality. By more-ality meaning the behavioral standards of a mythical American Literalist Christian family, mother, father, sister, brother in a three bedroom suburban frame house, of a middle income, middle meaning at least three times above the poverty level, and with no divorces, only quiet desperation, drunkenness, delinquency, alienation, and credit card rat race. The complaining middle, scared to death ever to do something other than they should, should, that is, according to commercials (advertising for things), sermons (advertising for god), speeches (advertising for state), lectures (advertising for schools), and flattery (advertising for sex). Scared, because if they got fired, they would be poor and they knew what poor meant in America: you're no longer human. More-ality meaning cowardice in the face of herd pressure, cowardice instead of thought and bravery.

I remembered going to work on Saturdays when I was fourteen, leaving home that summer and working as and being treated as a man in wartime California. I had never been a "teenage-kid". I had made my living, read, thought, danced, dreamed, and grown patient in front of mysteries, had seen the necessity in thinking for myself. Ralph had been betrayed and exposed by his indoctrinated unconscious to accept the description of the sixteen and seventeen year olds as children. They could fuck, fight, think, express, survive, act just as he had, or even better than him, because more knowledge now existed and was available, because they hadn't been conditioned for so long.

Bob, a fighter, was going to get involved. I had seen Bob become identified with the hooded figures who had run away to search. I would not get involved. I had escaped, I had no hope to improve anything by external action. Anyone else who escaped could do as I did, keep investigating this life and following deepest desires and insights until it clicked. Nothing would really change until enough people thought and acted from their own experience. But I saw now that escaping itself was not so difficult as not being caught again. The figures of Bob and Ralph strangely strained in a combat with the odds totally against them and against their actually helping anyone left ashes in my brain.

Even the Ghosts Depart

Bob raged in that temper that arises from being ground between unbearable contradictions, contradictions that are forbidden to be lived out, but must be reduced to one side or the other by the demands of the local society. The temper that rises unbidden in a man when he knows himself compelled by force to truncate his life.

"So these people, sixteen or seventeen years old are coming to Haight, twenty thousand, we estimate, as soon as school's out," he said at the breakfast meeting, "and they need a place to stay, a chance to ground themselves. The city is going to throw all of them that they catch in the tank till they tell who their parents are or show their I.D., and then call their parents to come get them. If any House is caught taking them in, it's going to be busted for suspicion of underage sex."

"We've known that for a long time," said Pauline. "Our rule has always been you had to be eighteen to be here." A faint puritanical tone flavored her statement.

"That was our rule not an imposed rule," said Bob, faintly defensive.

"Sure it was our rule," Sally said, "we picked eighteen because of the objective fact on that very day humans like tadpoles becoming frogs, just suddenly change into a different being." Everybody laughed, even Bob, reluctantly.

"And, Sally added on the wave of her success," it had nothing to do with California's statutory rape law, the fear of families hunting us down, a story in the paper, potential jealousies, oh no, we as free intelligent enlightened spirits chose eighteen from purely scientific considerations." Nobody laughed, but they had to smile.

"Oh, you're right," Bob slowly admitted. "After all, we didn't start the House till Princess' eighteenth birthday even though it meant a two week delay. All the same," he yelled, "I hate it! I hate it!"

"The comic judgment. You're condemned to make an ass out of yourself!" Sally and Pauline laughingly chanted to Bob.

So it came as no surprise when Bob called me to his library room for a talk after breakfast.

"Joe, you, me, Pauline, Princess have reached a point we must go onward or lose it. Standing still doesn't work in a dynamic universe. So we'll have another meeting tomorrow night. We've got to go past sex,"

"Past sex?"

"Alright, have to expand our structure so that sex and erotic energies are part of the pyramid, not the apex."

"This age bit on the House and the crackdown by the city aren't just making you uptight?"

"Of course they are. Obviously when the nose of the state enters your tent and starts sniffing around, its long arm is right behind with its brass knuckled fist, and then the legs with their jackboots kicking people into jail."

Once again Princess, Pauline and I met in front of Bob's door at ten o'clock to file into his library-scene-bedroom.

This time we immediately sat straight, backbones gathering their presence. Clearly, Bob was up for something. He had not flicked a perceptible muscle upon our entrance, already cross-legged on a three inch high black velvet cushion.

"Tonight," he said after minutes of quietness, "any of you can leave at any time. I only ask you go straight to your room until everything wears off. Don't wander around or out. Agreed?"

"Yes," we replied as his gaze fixed on each of us in turn.

About five minutes of silence. The room densened with vibrations, which almost physically resisted the smallest movements. Bob distributed a palm full of dried mushrooms to us, one after the other, then a bar of chocolate. "Eat the chocolate first, then the mushrooms which have a bit of honey on them. Dish of Aztec emperors and probably the Toltec priests.

"Last time," he said, "we explored the ideal history of sexuality and erotic energies. This time we study the ideal history of transcendent energy."

"Are you really sure anything transcends erotic energy?" said Pauline with a slightly joking tone, gazing straight at him. Bob could not avoid the faintest movement of irritation. Pauline smiled ever so lightly.

Bob looked back at her, choosing to bounce off the front of her eyeballs. "Transcendent energy, silence, shadows, twilight, sleep, death, ghosts, nothingness. The energy that gives the direction anything takes when it changes form. That energy which determines the direction taken by all the energies required to hold the attention together, the energy that gives direction to Eros itself. Otherwise, Eros would only create those vast non-historical cycles of cosmos hypothesized by the great Asian sages."

We ate our substances slowly, thoroughly, running the saliva rich rubble beneath our tongues.

"The history of contact with transcendent energy began with the silence of sunset. The wind often stops. Animal movement stops. One can look straight into a fat red sun momentarily sitting on the horizon. The moment heightens, the apparent motion of the sun apparently stops. The direction of life prepares to make its daily change. Sunset may be the first word invented, a sign of astonishment, of warning, of celebration, of check-out, of coming together, of changing from hunter to hunted psychology and behavior, of the time to start the fire, using precious wood, of beginning to fix up dinner, of securing a place to sleep, of stopping the babble of day, of silence, that silence that will prepare for storytelling after dinner, that storytelling that digests and renders nourishing the day's events, that in turn sets the stage for the engrossing theater of dreams."

Bob returned into silence. I saw sunset after sunset, especially a long chill one in the high Uncompahgre and a warm red one through persimmon trees and scrub oak. I began to hear silence in the room broken by an occasional catch of breath. My sight grew vivid, subtly changing shapes and colors of faces and things from accustomed and undusted images into living ever-changing mirror-clean intricacies. The room relaxed into alert friendliness and readiness.

"Of course, well before sunset, the shadows had begun to lengthen and had become longer than any shadow-maker, man, woman, rock, or tree. Already intimations of the day's end had begun to produce a cautious eye, a musculature readier for unexpected action, to hasten steps toward the sunset rendezvous, to bring up images of being lost, alone, unprotected, beset, stepping off ledges, into holes, of encountering some indecipherable mask concealing both insights, looking-ins, and ambushes, looking-outs."

I felt a certain objective fear creep into my mental set. Now past eleven, on the way to midnight. The two candles in the room guttered in the immense shadows from which I could see six eyes peering, grouped into three sets of two. What did I really know of these people anyway? The shadows of their lives had not been open to my inspection. The sunset of Haight Ashbury could not be far off. When the shadows became longer and darker what poisonous naga of unredeemed antiquity might strike from Bob's unchecked experimental attitude? From Princess' hip avant-garde cool? From Pauline's aroused instincts of female mystery and sex-sharp iridescently lacquered nails?

I tried to mask my searching gaze in casual nonchalance. I felt the failure of my camouflage as each set of eyes gazed steadily back at mine in turn, weighing me as I weighed them.

Would they indeed all prove good comrades when the sun set and the shadows drifted into a dark chill, only the tops of trees and heads lit faintly by the twilight high above? If we became an isolated clan, would we survive, or betray each other?

"In the twilight," Bob spoke again. Joe could hear the drumbeats of his heart. Was this drumming the first music as sunset the first word, and shadows the first alarm system? "In the twilight," Bob repeated lingering on the word, "all became ambiguous outside the circle of the fire, the magic ground of the hearth, where the taken animal became transformed to delicious meat, and sacred herbs to states of laughing consciousness. Outside the fire, shadows of the watchers stretched away to rejoin the now universal glow beneath the twilight in the high branches, high over the feathery grasses, beyond the hilltops."

"The drums stone-adzed from burned out tree trunks, covered tautly with totem-skin, began talking to drumming hearts throughout the wilderness. People eyed their partners for love and sleep, complimented the cooks and every cook earned a lover to ensure new feasts. Hunters told stories designed to engrave in magic outline procedures proved to succeed, followed by enchanted stories told by herbalists of elfin help to ensure confidence in finding specimens of these plant masters that raised the consciousness to detect any flaws in magic procedures, those formulas of ancient science that could coalesce a group of wills to succeed in tasks they undertook."

"Have some more chocolate." I chewed my chocolate, gazing into the eyes of Princess and Pauline in turn. Who would be my partner in love and sleep? Pauline returned my gaze with a franker interest than ever before. I could see them both stare deeply at Bob. Princess looked at Bob with an appraisal that seemed for the first time to be rooted in critique, though still with high regard. I could feel the fire dying down, the chill advancing, the twilight gone completely, all the stars emerged to emphasize the night around us. Invisible predators roamed to whom my entire life with all its mystery would mean only one day's eating, little different in value to them from catching a wild pig.

"Through all the forms of the history of sexuality that we explored plus torments and sighs of associations, dreams, and visions, Eros comes and goes, and sleep arrives. Sleep in which I disappear, go somewhere I can not remember, perhaps die, in which perhaps I am not at all, anywhere, in which I am helpless should whom I lie beside turn traitor to enslave, to steal, to kill, to plot in whispers on the other side, to study my features to know me better when all the guards are down, sleep so close to death that death comes most easily, without perceptible difference."

"Close your eyes."

I closed my eyes and seemed to fall down an almost endless ladder my hold slipping from rung after rung, until my grip slackened and I fell abruptly into weightless fear. I issued myself commands that Bob had taught. Quiet! relax! rest! (where I watched, unable to move my attention from muscles and sensation, the slow increase of energy). Dream! (of eros and violence, fear and incredible courage). Deep sleep! (where I enjoyed total surrender to the will of a hypnotic sage, "ah, at last, this is where I go to, to wisdom's refreshing catalepsy", and, indeed I experienced no actualizations except, amazingly, seeing the word 'potential' hieroglyphed darkly in stygian morpheus, waiting until some random ending, when, camouflaged again, transcendence faded away and chaophany manifested its needy call to cosmos once more).

"All things must come to an end, all energies transform into another, all intentions turn into their opposite, each idea call forth its antithesis, each sensation give way to its successor, each emotion use up its chemistry, each mask be changed, and each life use up its time; each of these is a death, when whatever exists changes into something else, dissolves, no longer to be found by the most passionate, the cleverest, the most desperate, the greatest suffering seeker-lover."

"Enter the world of your deaths."

Suddenly my spine tingled as the room fell past silent to deathly silent. I saw the death of the House, departure of its occupants to different directions. The death of my belief in Bob's sanguine and sustained energy carrying himself and his friends past the common fate. How could I have believed so strongly that Bob could help me create a soul that could resist the shocks of death? Shocking that I had grown this unconcious belief. Now in general slaughter I beheld separate deaths scattered, in twisting pain, over a battle ground where the enemy struck invisibly, irresistibly, as and when the enemy wished, with or without warning, and no possibility existed to strike back, to kill or wound this enemy, death itself, who made his will effective with invincible strikes. Death always one stage longer lived than life, the old stagehand striking life's sets, the one certain arrow of direction in a quiver of directions.

I examined Bob's unmoving face, death mask of a courageous man who had fought with heart, skill, and learning, struck dead in the midst of an objectively insane effort that would require at least a thousand tireless years of a thousand tireless heroes and heroines to achieve its purpose to understand reality well enough to change its shape. Pauline's death mask, ancient, lined, weary, while beside her body leered old calculating children, and rangy grandchildren gleefully prepared to enjoy property she had labored to accumulate and who had harassed her out of mind. Princess's deep shadowed irony mocked the conqueror and revealed the melancholy wisdom that had foreseen ultimate futility, refusing ever to have believed victory possible, having extracted many precious moments from the flux with which she had concocted mysterious perfume, luring subtle actors to her subtle theater.

At last I dared sense my own death mask and saw a grim hatred frozen into defiance that died without surrender. No fact, no wisdom, nothing and no one could make me believe that I would ever die. I refused to die. Death might make me die. Well and good if death did it, death once dead, no more dying then, but I refused old consolations of poetry much less religion or alchemy such as Bob pursued. I wished to live and not to die, ever, with such intensity that I realized I had lived a lie and would if escaping from this supertrip of Bob's alive, continue to live a lie, if a lie was required not to look at death. I would lie that I would never die. I knew seeing my dead heart spread out for the first time that I would never accept death as my sovereign, or even as my all-powerful enemy. I preferred my poetic lie to the prosaic truth of death's invincibility. Somewhere, somehow, somewhen, I would master the secrets of cellular reconstitution, DNA re-programming, organ replacement, the making of a new world without disease and catastrophe, even colliding meteors could be steered away or exploded before they destroyed whatever biosphere base I happened to inhabit at the moment.

I had not realized before that I incarnated defiance. I did not rebel, I did not hate, I did defy the facts. I defied the facts. I would lie defying them. I would die defying the facts. No, I could feel each movement within the pulse of my heart, each space between my vertebrae. I would defy death and I would get by with it. Even if I were wrong my death mask would be the greatest death mask ever seen, total and absolute defiance, so great that even if I did die my death mask would be the most alive event present so long as it endured, and it would endure, because generations would preserve it for the high it gave. All the knowledge available would be used then by all those present to reconnect me just so the secret of that defiance could be possessed by all humanity. Never say die.

For the first time I heard my own voice speaking automatically on its own with a peculiar authority in this circle where I had previously chosen to play the part of silence. "After death, the ghosts of the passionate ones fallen from the demiurgic world and the ghosts of humans whose will to live refuses to accept the rules handed down by prophets, these ghosts from above and below held by resonant knots in molecular ropes to the decaying ship of their last abode, decide to continue living by eating and digesting the most refined food, namely intense alchemical quantums, obtaining those by shocking hormonal catalysts into emitting finer energies. Thus ghouls ever burst in on scenes of fear, murder, lust, despair, and loneliness that beset humans. Battered exposed synapses hunt murky lairs of haunts of hungry ghosts."

Each of the others huddled into a heap upon the floor of a desolate castle. I looked at the others quickly, disdainfully. Fellow ghosts, they had no more to offer each other. I felt ravenous to haunt living neurons pouring events into rushing torrents of blood, sugar particles, dopamines, adrenalines, and serotonin. Living neurons in which I could strike a frayed resonance causing it to explode the fine energy I needed to absorb to keep my defiant wrath together.

The others each seemed to have disappeared under a collapsed heap of clothes. Then, a spectral bat, I flew out of my pile of clothes around and around the vast space radaring and spectroscoping for the blood of blood.

Then far away from myself my voice croaked out phonemes, each a slowly flapping crow, that formed themselves very slowly into words and those words receded over vast horizon stretches of time formed words.

"At last even the ghosts depart so that nothing remains, nothing to catch a photon, nothing to note a picosecond, nothing to absorb a quantum, nothing at all remains. All and everything disappear."

I would have screamed or gone mad but nothing remained to scream or go mad with. Then I wanted to laugh and laugh but nothing remained to laugh with. Then I wanted to orgy without restraint but nothing remained to orgy with. Then I wanted to call on God, or Devil or Nature, or Holy Man, but nothing remained to call upon. Then I accepted nothing, but nothing remained to accept nothing. I saw all I wanted of everything: worlds, biospheres, civilizations, species, myself, Bob, Princess, Pauline all falling into nothing, a constant flow of bright-eyed phenomena disappearing without a trace except to leave the vacuum of their path behind so that anything new would be sucked in and ongoingness maintained. I had successfully defied death, roamed as a ghost, but nothing contained everything although nothing disappeared everything, but if everything disappeared without coming to be then nothing would starve and disappearance disappear. I saw that nothing reigned almighty because a mighty swarm of everything issued from the nothing that matched everything disappearing into nothing and that nothing continually made slight alterations in the everything entering into it, a connoisseur continually evolving its tastes, fragrances, and quintessences in a feast of feasts.

A voice called out in my brain, in music, chant, and mantram, "truth sets you free." Tears rolled out of my eyes by their own volition, no recognizable emotion. I now knew for certain, but what it was I knew, I knew I could never tell, but I did know that this certainty had now worked its way into every molecule of my totality, and would work wonders of perception, invisibly, undiminishing, advancing the frontier of my being beyond the furthest reach of tyrannies of the day.

I fell into a deep sleep that a remote region of attention patrolled, a night watchman in a remote village at four o'clock in the morning, breathing in silence, peaceful, quiet, aware of stars overhead, the fact of the unobtrusive patrol allowing the village to drift securely into sleep that merged into night beyond the night.

Hospital Meant Hospitality

Bob sat erect at the pine table around which they had all been summoned. No pot of tea. He breathed silently with a forced control until they all sat and fell silent.

"Alright," he said. "It happened." Obviously he hated what he had to say because silence again took over. Pauline sat wrapped in impenetrability. Princess watched Bob ironically.

"I got gonorrhea," he said, "Pauline went out with this guy a couple of weeks ago."

"You went out last month yourself."

He glared at her. Bob detested speaking about his personal life. But consequences of personal life had obviously become a social issue. Obligation had taken over from his desires and he didn't like it.

"Whatever. So anyone who has had a contact with Pauline, me, Princess, and," he nearly choked the words out, "with Joe, must come with me to the Free Clinic this afternoon."

Sally spoke up with her artist's worldly viewpoint spiced with New England ruling class practicality. "Bob, I don't think you need to make such heavy weather out of it and revert to a Christian-Maoist confessional. I suggest we all go as a body to the Free Clinic, get tested and anyone who needs it take a treatment."

Pauline giggled. Bob's face turned red, the first time I had seen him blush. Princess smiled gravely. Mike grinned. The others relaxed.

"Okay," said Bob, "Let's make an expedition out of it. Let's check ourselves out, get the cures we need if needed, and dig the anthropology of The Free Clinic!"

"How about digging its archeology?" said Princess.

In the afternoon they joined a line of twenty healthy-looking, smiling, determinedly up, well-costumed residents of the district on the balcony porch of the clean but bare offices of the Free Clinic. To my surprise, surprise because I harbored a visualization of slouching, run-down, shabbily-clothed nondescript no-goods among whom I had unluckily fallen, the good-looking, intelligent people in line stood straight, carrying on conversations, grokking the scene. I saw many guilt trips still ruled vast regions of my inner being. I watched it all unreel, these guilt trips I had believed totally destroyed. "So, caught while fucking around, well, inevitable wasn't it. You thought you could get by with anything, well, there's a rightful inescapable price to pay for flouting. . . ." I turned off the recording with great effort. Evidently I could overcome guilt conditionings by reasoning and conscious effort, but they survived like ancient snakes in ancient tombs, ever ready to strike again if some impact opened again a door to their chambers of engraved tablets of sins and wages of sin. Life, sex, sin, disease, disgrace, death, and hell, the word associations again throbbed. Rulers hated life for so long because it represented their powers'greatest threat. Since sex could carry life to its height of freedom, naturally it must be restricted to reproduction, its minimal social function, life at its minimum. In monasteries and nunneries life restricted to masturbation and same sex.

Chopping at the roots as fast as they sprouted, I cut the associations out. I found a place inside from where to look at the calm sky, above the balcony, by some chance clear with a wash of blue, then at the people, then especially at Bob who had taken the hard, necessary first steps, thanks to sensible and diplomatic Sally, of the volunteer nurse, then thought of the doctor inside who had made such brave commitment to a new community with such new ways and networks of living, then of scientists who had developed antibiotics, reformers who had made the information public, of the great enemies of social life: the emotional plague, cholera, gonorrhea, syphilis, guilt cults, hepatitis, suppressed information, disinformation, dysentery, poverty, and indoctrination of hideous ideologies and fanatic theologies.

Somehow I felt uplifted at being part of the group of people in the line bravely and cheerfully going to take their medicine. The Free Clinic suddenly seemed to me a holy place, with flying banners, and the nurse, a trim blonde mesomorph, a disciple of Aesculapius. I now knew why the Greeks had worshipped Aesculapius as one of the greatest of gods, with his daughters Hygiene and Panacea, his knowledge of rest, of dreams, of climate, of environment, of herbs and potions, his acceptance of the ill as fellow humans deserving the best vibration and environment that he could give, when a hospital meant hospitality and not a house halfway between prison and a pulpit. Of all the changes I saw in this stateless, churchless liberated space, the Free

Clinic alone, if its example spread, would justify the entire experiment of history being re-made as an open process.

Green On Green

A week later I didn't see Pauline at breakfast. Generally first there, full of laughter and bounce, she would be flipping golden brown pancakes for Bob and a couple of others, or scrambling eggs to the fluffy perfection Bob liked, with rye toast and fig jam. Princess specialized in a coffee dripped through a certain paper that, with the proper amount of hot milk, "set the day off right" as Bob would say with his love of setting old sayings in quotation marks to make sure everyone knew he was consciously using a bromide.

Mike and Sally alternated frying up some meat to go with their eggs, generally ham, but sometimes a lean bacon. The philosopher ate his oatmeal and shared in either the pancakes or the fried eggs. Bob hated the word commune, and insisted on co-op. "It's 'co-operations'," he would say. "Communes imply a false idea of equality as sameness. Real equality is to be able to exercise differences as a set of co-operations. Behavioral diversity."

The vibrations quite heavy that morning. Princess scrambling eggs with meticulous attention. "Pauline left last night," Bob said. No one said anything although clearly everyone registered the remark. After a while, Sally asked, "for good?"

"Whether it was for good or for ill," Bob answered, forcing a wry smile, "I doubt that she's returning."

Later that morning I strolled toward the Panhandle with Bob. "It was so strange," Bob said, "the night before, we were making love. When I first met her, I said to myself, at last I've met Shakti, and, indeed, some new flow loosened my body past some armor embedded deep inside. She had joined in on a long mountain hike, about twenty miles over rugged country, with inadequate boots, her feet had been battered, but she finished. Two weeks later we sat in a mountain hot springs, no one else around for miles, gliding on a joint, looking at the stars, played a little, and a month later made out together, and the word Shakti came to my mind in sincere gratitude."

A long silence till we arrived at the Panhandle and made our hit with the scene. I waited for Bob to continue knowing that he detested anything that smacked of confession. “Internalized terror of spiritual tyranny causes it,” he had one time whipped out. None-the-less, Bob wanted, even needed, to talk about this drastic change in his life, and this blow to his hopes, since Pauline had been an ever-creative force in the House succeeding. And, Bob regarded the House as the key experiment of his life.

“She turned her back to me while sitting astride, and suddenly … suddenly I saw that the sexual power gripping her buttocks and thighs was all that was there. Whether actually true of her, or mainly my projection, I'm practically certain it's true. At that moment I was totally certain it was true.”

They sat cross-legged on the grass. Cool bongos beat in liquid distance. Graceful ladies tripped by with longhaired escorts hanging loose.

“I pushed her gently off and over to the side. My voice came as it were spontaneously. I spoke, not a personal I, because my whole being backed up the voice, but I did not formulate what the voice said, I recognized its truth, for me, and knew a decision had been made in the deepest part. Pauline, I said, it's finished between us. She looked at me, I believe truly uncomprehendingly for a long time, then I saw, and could not blame her in the least, fury chill those green eyes. She dug her fingernails deep into each of my shoulders. I could feel them going into the flesh and blood starting to ooze.”

I said, “Pauline, this act only confirms that we are finished. How can digging your fingernails into me do anything but underline the fact?' Inside, I wondered how much my conviction that she had contracted the gonorrhea influenced the inside click. That made me angry, irrational, of course, since, 'but for the grace of god' and so on. Nonetheless I was not proud that anger had possibly played a role. After all, for more than a year, we had been close not only sexually but in action.”

“Perhaps I could not have started the House without her, from which I've learned things about psychology and human nature impossible except in such a high pressure laboratory. It's inexplicable to me how such a drastic and precise decision could have 'come down' as it were, and also, even if it did ‘come down’ that I so unquestioningly accepted and accept it.”

“Yes, that last part is what interests me,” I said. “You are in for some exciting times. How do you know where it ‘comes down’ from?” My tone of voice ended something in our relationship. Bob loved irony in literature, but in life, while a master of sustaining ambiguity until the last moment, he was too much into action not to smell satire and even ridicule on the horizon when a trace of irony appeared about his personal life. He could laugh, however, if a specific case of this overreaction were pointed out to him.

Still, Bob invited me to accompany him and Princess that night to a dance performance, one night only, of "green on green," by Alice Langley at her studio on Divisidero. Alice had danced with Alwin Nicolais, but this was to be her first production. About fifty people filed into her long studio, each handed a green gown by Alice, long straight black haired, slim, glowing. The gauziest green curtain hung between the dancing space and the spectators.

The dance went off in silence, the dancers in various shades of green, green slippers, green stockings. I leaned forward, marveling at the balance between formal mise-en-scene holds of the dancers, and dynamic movement moods between. Alice danced with intellectual passion. I felt poignancy in her disciplined beauty and choreography, neither with an ounce of fat. Not in any way art as commodity, nor the precocity of art for art, nor psychological teaching as in Zalbin's dance. Art for artists and friends of artists seeking to participate in the creative taste itself, in creating exquisite vibrations to allow the dancers to experience the height of youth, discipline, expression, and form, and the audience to contemplate that experience. Poignant because I wished not to miss a moment of this transient perfection. No cameras, no photographer. This dance existed as pure offering from Alice.

Bob leaned forward as intently as me, but I could see that his interest focused as much on the dancer as on the dancing and the dance. No doubt smitten. The complete opposite from Pauline, Alice's every move emphasized her aim to soar, to fly, to reduce the gravitational component to the minimum. At moments I could almost "see" her moving ahead of her body. By the end of the dance I could almost hear her through line word, discorporate!

A few moments of silence to absorb the frozen tableau at climax. Stunning applause, and then a slow rhythmic hand clapping for five encores. Bob stayed behind to talk with Alice, the others returned to the House, while I wandered toward Haight, inspired by the dance, resolved to cast once again my own life into the moment.

Pausing at the intersection of Ashbury and Haight, I sensed a lithe form moving up Ashbury behind me. Recognized a fellow spectator. We glanced at each other. "That excited me so much," I said to her, "I had to zoom out in the night, I'm too up not to be restless from Alice's dance."

At a gesture of invitation, she hung a right with me and continued down the street, arm in arm in a wordless communion. "Hey, I remember you," I said. "You danced with Ann Zalbin in the candle dance."

"The candle, nude, and ceremonial dance," she laughed.

"Yes! where you slowly climbed up and down and around boxes that cast immense shadows."

We began to skip in unison down the street. I remembered the dark-haired, intense-eyed girl very well now. Her hips and thighs seemed to move almost by magic. "Conscious thighbones," Bob had said when I'd commented on it. I remembered the contrast with Princess who in that same performance had accomplished in public the same extraordinary feat as when I met her of moving as it were through holes in the gravitational field with her long slim torso and proud eyes, like the sails and lookout of a transdimensional vessel.

Where Zalbin's dancers specialized in easy liberated body expressions charmingly moving in loose ceremonial progressions, rituals of enlightened sexuality diffused through an idealized group of dedicated participants, Alice's dance came straight from the pleroma of forms with dazzlingly mysterious transitions presided over by a disillusioned passion already wishing to reside in the other world. "Alice comes from the other world," I said to the girl, "like a messenger, and I see, I love the art, but I don't want to live there. You have conscious thighs and I wanted to join you in your dance."

"Let's go do a workout, I live right up the street there, a couple of blocks, with my friend, Sam."

We swung briskly ninety degrees like two trained circus horses, and moved in hip-to-hip synchrony beneath great old trees and onward in one surge of feeling arrived at her apartment. She flicked on the hall light and turned a door knob with tips of thumb and two fingers into a small studio room, with bare wooden floor, and white painted walls, and one full length mirror.

"I move. You watch till you feel an impulse to move, then you follow that impulse. I follow both the development of my original impulse and the impulse that develops in response to your movement, and we continue this way till a pattern develops, and then we develop the pattern by allowing the wish of the muscles and impulse to gain full expression. We guide by close attention to removing blocks to wished-for movements. Move in the direction of the resistance."

No doubt about it, I thought, after two minutes of workout, a real dance emerging. Our movements and emotions read each other and composed near instantaneous interlinear texts of movement attenuating between the three points of display, contact and resistances. Separate pools in which our Narcissus gathered new energy from direct self-reflections to re-engage Echo rather than drown.

I soon stripped down to my bluejeans and she to her danceskins. "Name?" I said, "Mine's Joe Madison."

"Martha Landin."

Suddenly I knew I could have been a dancer, even that for this moment, I was a dancer. Bob's acting classes, Princess's hints and demonstrations, Alice's green-on-green explosion of forms and lighting, now Martha's unreacting cool at the center of a body awash with cyclic surges of movement originating at the pelvic connections of her thighs as if those two points were where she "stood", gravitationally speaking, my own natural impulse to spontaneous movements that had led me in the past to dash up and down mountainscapes, leap from rock to rock, prowl through ancient forests in Indian make believe of dangers above and below, all these fused to a point in my lower spine from which I found it possible, from the edges of my perceptual glances, to keep in point-to-point synch with her. I could hear the unplayed music rising and falling moving toward a climax as the alternation of movements became synesthetic.

We reached a place of simultaneous stop, right thigh against right thigh, each bent back and away, hands outreached, right knees bent, left legs out at forty-five degrees, heads back, and in silent laughter.

Then she kissed me and led me back to her bedroom. "Sam has the other bedroom."

We had just begun our expedition exploring embrace when a naked form hurled itself on the bed. I felt a strong arm around me, and myself and Martha being brought into a tighter embrace. I could hear the excited breathing of a man and feel sinewy muscles lacing lean bones.

The moment shattered for me, I sat bolt upright. "Sam lives here with me," said Martha. "If he wants to join us, I can't tell him no." I looked at her. I looked at Sam, Sam looked at me. I felt myself go into brilliantly precise automaton mode. My emotions disappeared. No thoughts appeared. The automaton quickly pulled on his clothes, tied his shoes, embraced Martha, embraced Sam, and split the apartment without a single bumble or slip. The arrival of this automaton of precision and power splitting the scene silenced me even to myself. This must be an effect from the transcendent energy Bob had talked about. I hadn't wanted to split.

Mad Naked Love Dance

Martha reached me by telephone two days later.

"Joe, you said you wanted to become a dancer -- and that you're broke."

"Yeah."

"Well, Sam's not going to be able to make it this Friday night, so if you'd like to pick up forty bucks by doing an all-out twenty minute thing with me, you know, that contact-off-contact stuff we played with, but make it, you know, more sexually graphic. You'll have to wear a G-string and there'll be about three hundred in the audience."

"Never done a dance in public before."

"You'll do great. Meet me here an hour and a half before, I'll get you the G-string, and I'll show you how to make the entrance before we climb in the ring."

"The ring?"

"Yeah, it's a little like a boxing ring. We do our thing inside ropes."

"Ropes?"

"Yeah, so we don't fall off, and someone doesn't rush in. They've all had a couple of drinks, but it's alright, a pretty high-class joint, jackets and ties."

Martha laughingly handed him the spangly G-string when they locked the door behind them in the green-carpeted small dressing room with two small lockers to hang their clothes in.

"It covers just exactly enough," she said.

"Can't fly off?"

"No, the elastic string holds the cup tight."

Someone rapped on the door. "It's time!"

"Follow me," she said, "And follow your impulses. You can do anything you want to as long as you keep moving your feet. Then it's dance and therefore legal."

Suddenly, opening the entrance door, I felt a tiny speck in a vast darkened space with an elevated dazzlingly lit roped stage at the center. The carpeted aisle ran straight through a crowded audience seated at tables. The spotlight swung to us and everything became blackness except for some glimmers of light faintly reflecting from candles at the tables off sequins or jewelry.

Martha caught my hand, and we synched into a toes walk down the velvety carpet. I felt uplifted, free as never before, bareskinned, bare-footed, with a bare breasted graceful girl at my side, free to manifest, without even my name identified, in the midst of hundreds of anonymous Americans eager to see our performance. Eager because I could hear the caught breaths, the silence cascading down the numerous tables eliminating sound. The thought thrilled through me, "I will show them unarmored ecstasy dancing a healthy body in its prime, so that they will never forget this vision of muscular, erotic, and emotional freedom." I knew from our sinuous walk, on toes, from the finger flashed signals from Martha that she felt as up as I did. We crawled through the ropes and stood gorgeously, still and silent in the vivid shifting solid colors alternating with a slashing strobe. The rock beat began a down and dirty blues nostalgia.

She took me by surprise, leaping legs outspread nearly flat from those fantastically lithe thighbones, clasped her legs around my back upon the pelvic contact and threw her head with full abandon toward the floor. My fingers had already caught her just between the thigh bone and pelvis, and, rotating, I swept the small of her back up, so that her hair trailed the floor, her head a safe four inches above, her arms thrown also back, her fingers also trailing the floor. My knees flexed, then straightened, as she swept out circles in ever changing altitudes.

My hands tightened, I pulled her sitting upright, breasts against me, and as her legs straightened from my back, my push elevated her to fall on her feet a yard in front of me. I reached, caught her left hand and right breast, and we ruthlessly gazed into each other's eyes, unrecognizably impersonal and ready, my right leg between her thighs commenced to translate into movement the energy of a full orgasmic encounter, curving low, and straightening high, gazes interlocked. Her free hand cupped my cup and that audacity seemed to loosen a flow of lubricant throughout my knees and ankles. Achievements that had never occurred to my imagination began to act out intimations and erotic kinetics that, meeting no resistance, only flesh that magically stayed a millimeter away from total crushing non-danced rapture, crystallized into pursuit I had never dreamed passion could attain.

Just as we found ourselves at the end point of one of these alchemically quick maneuvers, when she bent back from her knees about six inches from the floor, I six inches above her, at the limit of our spring, ready for the spontaneous recoil that would prevent our fall, I heard a gasp from the audience and then upon my back a full contact that would have splashed us painfully and disgracefully upon the floor except that a strong and skillful arm provided just the fulcrum to the right that enable us to spin out and away to the left.

Sam, his face contorted by lips curling in snakey sinuousities, his eyes wide, glittering, grabbed Martha's left arm, leaving me with her right. Her eyes blazed, dazed with data pouring into her dance, then cleared, I reading hate, love, admiration of Sam's audacious foray, and I felt my own micro-second delayed response flashing her my response, to accept this dance of a three-hearted beast, a three-brained artist, and a three-sexed divinity. From then until the music ended Sam and I danced to the last micron our bodies could distinguish, to pour Eros through our receptive instruments into the sheer sheen of she transfiguring magic transformations with no recognizable transitions from breakdown to breakdown, activating silken muscle after silken muscle. I saw momentarily as in a magnifying glass, every small muscle that could be developed by the greatest belly dancers in a myriad display of receptivity across her belly swing taut against her backbone while two jaunty breasts performed a metronome of configurations below the eyes dark, unfocused, tuning in on the changing forms, Apollo and Dionysus incarnated in her eyes, manifesting in Aphroditean thighs and buttocks, Artemisian feet, fingers, and hair.

The music ended, we each stopped at exactly the same note. Applause. We departed rapidly, I holding Martha's left hand, Sam her right as we swiftly moved away.

In the dressing room, quickly pulled on my clothes. I would never not have done it, but didn't wish to do it again. I never wanted to see Sam again. Martha and I would make love, but never reach the same point. Sam's wordless jealous intervention had shocked the moment into pure duende.

I had to be quick to get out of that dressing room before an argument began when the exaltation died down and the inevitable examination began about the happening. I didn't need an examination. I needed to let the active molecules of this experience circulate until they became integral with my life, an organ of memory and action as reliable as, say, kidney or heart. I had received an extraordinary gift from Martha and thanked my lucky stars, probably Vega and Sirius, I thought gratefully. I finally silently thanked Sam after I had walked and run for half an hour.

It's Getting Heavy

Bob called a special meeting of Sally, Princess, and myself. Eighteen people lived in the House now, every room had two people except Bob's room which doubled as House library and day meeting place, Princess's blanketed off section of the back porch, and my closet space. Mike shared Sally's room.

"Look," Bob said, "things change quickly. The establishment has definitely decided to destroy Haight Ashbury. They're losing the war. They need scapegoats. The Mafia has already moved in with their runners hitting new faces before they catch on with stuff cut with speed and heroin. The cops are busting everyone they can find an excuse to bust except the Mafia, you can see cops lurking in the alleys around Haight every day now, three here, two there, waiting for the call to move in for somebody or some House. They turn their heads when hoods from Fillmore move in to hassle the Haight people. And the Haight people can't handle how to deal with a hassling hustler if he's black because they feel the guy's only doing it because of bad breaks. So they get ripped off, sometimes raped, and it's a major downer."

I knew Bob. This setting the big picture stage would lead into the specific point.

"You know this girl, Linda, we rescued from that phony guru's house last week?"

Princess, Sally, and I smiled at each other. Linda was five feet, ten inches tall, and stacked like a Hollywood star. Long blonde hair, nineteen, and so cool she chilled me. I had never thought such a physically beautiful girl could leave my chemistry purring along without a disturbance. Somehow she'd heard of Bob and called him up. They'd met, and Bob had got Mike to go with him in Sally's pickup to take her and her things out the back entrance of where she lived. Linda had convinced Bob she was being persecuted and could get badly beaten up.

The whole affair completely fell out of Bob's pattern, who insisted that people who wanted to move in meet anyone at the House who wanted to sit in on the check-out conversation and that was usually everybody. Since the Pauline incident, I noticed Bob a little uptight, a fraction too quick in his reaction times to ensure feedback contol. Mike thought he'd moved Linda in for an affair, but Bob avoided her obvious attempts to get next to him. Bob had a very deep thing going with Princess, and besides was now seeing Alice, the dancer. Bob did not get too warm with women who relied on sex. "First, intelligence. Second, beauty," he said. Bob had grown up seeing bulls and stallions going after it, but he wanted a lot more than cows and mares. He also prided, cosseted himself on maintaining a fundamental independence even while he played an easy-going old man of the mountains role in the extended group life he had initiated. He was quite cautious with any new woman in the House. Clearly he had been burned once or twice when younger.

"Well," Bob continued, "I caught Linda with her old boyfriend and another couple from the House she left, in the upper bathroom, with their needles out, and with a real nut giving them the H. From his look I knew it was cut with speed. I kicked them out about thirty minutes ago and told Linda if she wanted to do that she had to leave today. I think the drug laws are an instrument of a police state and on rare occasions I make an intentional use of sacred substances, but there's no doubt in my mind that we must have a drug free house and that anyone on speed and heroin has got real problems with their reality check-out, problems we don't need."

"We know where you stand," said Sally. "So what's the point? You kicked these people out and now Linda's got to make up her mind."

"The point is, that nut is walking up and down outside in the street," Bob said. "I don't like the look of it. He's definitely up on speed. He didn't want to leave the House." I realized with a start that Bob was afraid of what the guy might do, and highly apprehensive, if not afraid, to go out and confront him. I couldn't blame him.

I felt the pressure building inside as the silence grew heavier. Princess looked at me gravely, and at Bob with concern.

I felt the words blurt out, realizing they came from my chemistry responding to perceived social pressure rather than from myself, "If you think you need to talk to the guy, I'll go with you."

Everyone seemed relieved by my offer, but I felt an immense wariness, not exactly of physical danger, although I did sense adrenaline building up both our energies so that the fight-flight hair trigger response mechanism could attain full operating order. Real risk had suddenly confronted our way of life, which always before had seemed to move in a magically charmed circle.

"Okay," said Bob, "let's go talk to the guy."

We walked out in late afternoon light that lay like a poet's glance on the curb, on the street, on the trees unmoving in the windless air. Then my glance focused on the boots, the long, thin legs, the frayed army jacket, matted hair, uncombed beard, green hypnotic eyes, and wide open lips revealing big yellow teeth with four gaps.

"You weren't very polite asking me to leave," the youngish death face walked straight up to Bob, his back bowing his face forward, as if ready to strike directly with the skull.

"We can't have needles and drugs going down in our House," Bob said firmly.

"That girl of yours in there, she asked me in with her friends. Hasn't she got the right to have visitors? What if I want to go see her right now?"

"Well, she's making up her mind to stay or not. If she stays, she can't deal with that stuff."

"You trying to tell me what I can do?"

"You do what you do, but not in that House."

"Since when you can tell people in your House what to do and not to do? You a dictator of their lives?"

I saw Bob go red with rage. I sent all vibrations possible to strengthen Bob and discourage the speed freak, whom I estimated at six feet two inches tall, and about a hundred seventy pounds of muscle, bone, speed, and powder keg anger. I didn't see any weapon, though something might be under the army jacket. Obviously the guy could really use his logger's boots in a crunch. His big-knuckled hands each showed scars.

"We have a rule," Bob said slowly, "no needles or drug parties in the House."

"We have a rule," the man sneered, "you mean, you made a rule, and ain't man enough to say so. Linda told me that you the boss man. Well, just how you going to enforce your rule, boss man? You going to take me on?"

I kept a triangle going, loose and unthreatening but as present as possible, at forty-five degree angles to Bob and to the man, hoping, first, to defuse the situation, and second, ready to move in response to whatever happened. I stood about two and a half feet from each of the others. Bob and the man swayed slightly, directly facing each other, about three and a half feet apart, a distance any shortening of it might well move threat to force.

The man sized Bob up, judging Bob's silence and readiness.

"Well, maybe I'm just going to go back in there and give Linda what she wants. Did you ever think she might need an upper/downer to deal with herself? You haven't given her what she needs, that's clear. Look at me, I walk the streets alone, I don't depend on nobody or nothing. I'm on speed because it gives me an advantage, I can see and move quicker and last longer." His gapped yellow large teeth gleamed surrounded by hair stringing down his face.

Bob's silence continued. I could see Bob's intelligence baffled, uncertain, but holding the fight-flight urges in containment by a huge effort judging from his still red face. I let my mind go blank. At last got my nose out of the situation. Let direct perception have a chance if crisis arrived.

"I think I will go on back in," the man said. "I don't think you can stop me."

I saw Bob's body convulse, his fists clench, then relax. "I'll call the police if you do," Bob said, barely getting the words out.

I felt physical horror. I saw, beyond doubt, clearly, the end of the liberated space, its return to the same oppressive stagnation that I had fled to Tangier over four years ago to escape. Bob had acted out a true freedom action, had helped put together a community that operated without police, without edicts, on the basis of vibrations, ideas, community, mutual support. Now Bob threatened to call on the same police who daily arbitrarily arrested dozens of citizens of Haight Ashbury, who smashed all efforts to stop the hopeless far-away war by making war on their own people who disagreed. This man was dangerous, to be sure, definitely on speed, but a man who wasn't armed. The two of us could take him if we had to, of course only after a nasty altercation.

The thoughts flashed through my mind so quickly as to be almost simultaneous. Why had Bob interfered to take on Linda's karma, anyway? Who knew the truth about her previous House? Why hadn't he called a House meeting and confronted the five people shooting up with the entire House, and brought out all the factors? If someone like Bob, under pressure, intense though it might be, had reached such a point as to go big man, then in big man's inevitable fear threaten to call in the police, that is, the state, with all its exorbitant power against the individual, with judges, prosecutors, jails, and asylums, to deal with this angry gap toothed man on the street, that meant that Bob had no confidence in the House or in the community at this point, and if Bob did not, how many of the other House leaders without his vast life experience and pack of skills did? I felt this horror sucking substance out of my body, felt myself becoming straw skittering on the street, blown any which way.

Immediately reacting to Bob's threat, the man pushed his face within six inches of Bob's. "You call the police, man, and I kill you. Kill you like a dog you understand me? Before they get me, or when I'm out on bail, or if they keep me in, after I get out of jail. I'll cut your throat and you into little strips."

I saw Bob himself horrified that the word police had issued from his mouth, saw that Bob believed the man would slash him to death if he called the police, saw that Bob had not and never did have a real intention to call police. That the man had exposed idle threat as empty bluff. That Bob did not know how to deal with a man who saw himself against the world, ready to die, trying to get all he could get while he remained alive, a man in a fully cornered existential jag. And what would I have done in Bob's place, if it came down to that?

I watched myself split, half "for" the man, whom I saw would "get" Linda for a while, who stood face-to-face ready to sneer, threaten, or fight, risking jail and being beaten, wrecking his teeth and shortening his life with the speed that lent wild brilliance to his forays, and half "for" Bob who tried to articulate a new way of civilized life emerging among tens of thousands of intelligentsia, based on ideas and techniques requiring immense co-operation, tact, and closely monitored daring, carefully watching his diet and doing his beneficial theater exercises, whom I saw would "lose" Linda. I felt an immense revulsion that these two men moved so close to a fight over a very dubious woman. And why was I there?

What did I, Joe Madison, count for when, neither accidentally or intentionally, I stood unconsciously at one apex of a now equilateral triangle of three men, so close to physical violence, engaged already in ruthless emotional violence, egged on by intellectual violence in thinking each alone possessed the right? And the right to what? Stud rights to some provocative mare on heroin and speed? I stood also on the edge of physical violence, for had I not backed my friend Bob with the same unquestioning following as any other two guys who were pals in Montana or Western Oklahoma? Had I not participated in the emotional violence by allowing the scene to build by not declaring my take on the emotional situation? And on intellectual violence had I not by emptying my mind left it open to take efficient part in the violence by eliminating the monitoring of thought?

"Okay, okay," Bob said, shrugging.

"You heard what I said, man, one word to the police, and you die." But the man also drew back his head a bit, synching with Bob's shrug.

I let my shoulders drop as low as they could. The adrenaline peaked and began to signal a switch to the flight mode. I made a step to side-by-side with Bob.

The man gave a lip-curled smile, then turned and loped off in a speed-lit easy stride.

Bob and I cast a look at each other.

"It's getting heavy," Bob said.

"Yeah."

"It's still the best if not the only place to be for now."

"Yeah. You wouldn't really have called the police?"

"No. Fuck no. But that it even popped into my mouth."

"Yeah."

Aphrodite In Search Of Dionysus

I finally decided to do the whole trip at the House. I showed up at all the acting classes on Saturday and Sunday mornings in the rented old grocery store across the street from the Sign of the Tarot restaurant.

A good sweat had broken out when after an hour Bob called a halt. "Okay," Bob said, as they sat down, cross-legged or on their side propped by an arm. About fifteen people attended the class. "Let's take up the nature of drama itself. Seven kinds of drama have been discovered, but let's start off with just two: tragedy and comedy. Each commence with a judgment laid upon the main character or characters. In tragedy, the judgment on Oedipus: you are condemned to die, as an infant, on meeting the sphinx, and upon his father-killing and mother-incest being discovered. What makes the matter dramatic, Oedipus shouts Fuck you! to the judgment, and the struggle continues until the life force decides one way or the other. All of us men, according to Sophocles and Freud and to my own experience are condemned since Laius seized patriarchal control of the woman to die in infancy to our essence by a father, fearful of competition, by our fear to speak up to the father's hypnotic archetype, by hiding our inner desires, but none of us experience full Oedipal tragedy unless we choose to struggle against these condemnations, by attracting help as an infant, by solving riddles when young, by becoming a catharsis of pity and terror as an older being brought down by condemnation for starting to kill father by violating some patriarchal rule.

"In comedy, we are condemned to make an ass out of ourselves: in Modern Times, Chaplin is condemned to be inferior to the assembly line, that set of machines quicker and better designed for production of objects than he is, but physically inferior though he is, as a human jackass he endeavors the impossible, to outwork the assembly line . . . of course, none of this convulsively laughing audience has ever tried to outwork the system. . . ." Bob glanced drolly around the circle.

I finally saw Bob's secret, why people liked him, how he maintained the spirit of the House. People howled with laughter or fell silent with empathy as Bob went on to enact in voice, gesture, and mimicry the outlines of the seven forms of drama. He looked at, lived in, and dealt with the entire Universe by the laws of drama. I saw that Bob's insight could be something like, "nothing is true, everything is undecided until the end of the play, and there's always another play if you've had enough of the one you're in." Bob offered a way to switch dramas, switch plays, switch characters, build an expanding repertoire of possibilities, to raconteur impossibility, which could use everything that happened as grist to its mill, whether love, science, adventure, or politics.

At our actor's lunch after workouts, at the Sign of the Tarot, with hot bean soup that had simmered overnight, chunks of ham well-distributed throughout, thick slices of fresh ground whole-meal home-made bread, choice of grape juice or red wine, provolone cheese, and bananas, I asked, "But, Bob, how can you attain certainty by means of theater? Ultimately, is theater for real? You put all this energy into fifteen people, eventually you make a production, which probably only a few hundred people, if that, see, and that for two hours at the most. And even for those few, they get nothing they can hold onto." I was thinking of how I had attained my portion of certainty that the universe was sustained by and interfused with Lilas, the play of delight, when I had sprawled back bent over the heap of sharp rocks in the hot Indian sun at the Sikh truck drivers' stop in Madhya Pradesh. I had determined to stay in that position until I passed out or until I "saw". Lilas came and Lilas stayed on until Lilas had crystallized throughout my body. Riding that secret delight had carried me into experiences before unimaginable to me.

Bob said, "Well, I hear one of your own hidden personal agendas in your talking about the small number of people. Hidden, because you come on as Mr. Individual, one man at a time, if necessary, but you're implying I need lots of people not "just a few" to achieve any real communication. In the first place, in my case, I long ago decided that art I worked on would be primarily for me. If I got something out of it, I won, and that if anybody else got something out of it, well, great, because maybe they'd flip me a cut of that energy, a hug, a love affair, some do-re-mi, some place to crash, a new idea or perception, something extra.

"Second, Joe, in your wanderings and searchings on your own you follow a throughline, seeking certainty about reality, and your failure to find that is what keeps you hung up in your quest-shunnings. To me, it makes no difference that you exist in some ways on a higher level than I do, immersed as I am, and have to be, by the ineluctable necessities involved in putting on drama, forced to deal with diverse people through diverse emotions and changes, holding spaces, watching social finances, and, in general, facing catastrophe of various kinds at almost every turn. Individual contemplation may be higher but men and women make themselves real in action.

"Third, drama exists not only on the stage but in the situations of daily life and in the seemingly individual events of your mind-experience seeking certainty. Those mind-bodies in that Zen monastery up the street from us are in drama when they try to get the goose out of the bottle without killing the goose or breaking the bottle, or those mind-bodies in that Catholic temple on North Beach where they're trying to go to heaven when they die, or in ordinary life when the lone guy tries to figure whether his set and setting are going to keep that bad trip away, and when he turns on whether he will tune into the infinite or into 'No Exit'."

"But," I said, " "doesn't this life based on drama lead you into an overemphasis on excitement, glamour, and 'pushing it'."

"Okay," Bob said "let me get excited about what you said, to push it, and if I become a bit glamorous to myself in the process of accepting your challenge, I think that's preferable to sinking into life's background, cuddling one's contemplative certainty like a teddy bear. Dangerous yes, that's why drama seems to me to be living real experience, even though amateurs and pure professionals may not, to their future misfortune, take drama as seriously as dynamite. Actually, drama teaches the willing student how to do, how to live deeply, how to see through lies. That's why dictatorships shut it down, democracies buy it out, and actors themselves sensing the dangers turn themselves into entertainers."

"How is it actually dangerous other than costing us lots of time, energy, money, in other words risking our investment?" asked Sally.

"Because if an actor while acting, or an author while writing can incarnate without identification the character being architected, then that actor or author wins. Their existence and even essence enlarges and deepens. But if they become possessed, if that architected character becomes the temple of their existence, then their being shrinks to that one character, and even worse, to that character who then escapes his proper play, presumes to be independent of context, and wrecks the other plays that one engages in. In short," Bob laughed, "you get nuttier than the usual nut."

Princess's neutral look checked me out and sent me reeling. I could not find any refutation of Bob. But I did find a desire to find another way than drama for myself. I could see that Bob's way would take Bob to the heights and depths, make him loved and hated, that Bob loved mystery, excitement and the different, that Bob was a leader of a new kind, an organizer of theater directly in life itself. That Bob had learned to live "off the land" both in the known and unknown. That as long as the House kept this level, I would be there, but I could not believe so much depended on the worldview of drama. On the other hand, I certainly didn't want to introduce Zen, theology, or scientism, or any other system promising method-induced certainties to Haight Street. Bob particularly showed in his acting classes how to get rid of deep hang-ups many people called certainties. I suddenly realized my certainty was strictly limited to my own real existence whatever might befall me. I was not Bob, but I had no opposition to Bob's drama as orientation for life with people.

Suddenly I jumped up. "A toast!" Everyone lifted their glass. "To the story of uncertainty, intention, and danger!" The glasses clinked. The red wine dropped wetly through my mouth.

"The world," I said, enjoying the scene now to the fullest, and gently challenging Bob, "is a collection of stories become immortal by poetry that a good theater can make dramatic. Homer and Apollo arrive before Aeschylus and Dionysus."

"And the discovery of drama began," Bob replied, "when Aphrodite in search of Dionysus and the grape encountered the great old story of the moon and the sun, Artemis the investigator and Apollo the revealer of forms." A second toast was drunk. Bob and I looked at each other for the first time as two guys that could riff back and forth on what they really thought. He's after drama and I'm after narrative, I thought, but aren't they two words pointing to the same region, two paths that come within hailing distance at intervals?.

The Notion Of Being A Secret

In mid-morning the next day I reclined on the pleasant slope of the green hill in the liberated area of the park, gazing into the blue, retracing my personal story. The painstaking dismantling that I had done with my American "eventually he'll run for President" personality, the "great frontiersman-engineer-businesswide ranging interests" figure, my efforts leading to successive "escapes" culminating in arriving in Tangier in time to meet the symbiotic avant-garde/Berber community there, to discover timelessness in my first surprising visit to the "hash cafe" when the afternoon had disappeared into fleecy white clouds crossed by three telephone wires, my "journey onward around the planet," reconstructing myself as an Arab, an African, a Hindu, a Vietnamese, then on my return to Manhattan encountering a mysterious trio in Duke's Cafe in the Village on Thompson Street that put me into "a contact" never since broken with "the eternal youth," and thence to Haight Street, where I had encountered twenty thousand Americans who had one way or the other arrived at the same zest as myself to live out freedom, ecstasy, and intelligence. Live them out right in the middle of a once hopefilled country that had become dominated since 1950 by an ideological warfield of endless busyness, grim labor, hypocrisy, split consciousness, and virtuous indignation, all massaged by television, air conditioners, cars, and fast foods. This story seemed to me to be the same in Vietnam, Haight Ashbury, Prague, and Mississippi. I felt "part of a vast network" of experience of pursuit of real happiness, of seeking truth, of psycho-physiological transformations, of mutual care. I really didn't wish to add another chapter to my personal history. I would be happy to end my personal story on this climactic note, stroll around the planet sometimes as bit player that came in briefly to swell the big scenes in great plays but basically as a skilled spectator who would vibe to the throughline and give the actors, writers and directors confidence that their hippest dada was appreciated. I wanted to view myself as a confidant and at the same time anonymous assistant of unknown producers. I adored the notion of being a secret.

The girl next to me shyly touched my shoulder. Brought back from my reverie story review and preview, I saw two frightened blue eyes peering at me from a young face, devoid of makeup, beneath long tousled blonde hair.

"He took my purse," she said in a low voice pointing to the black guy in blue jeans and sneakers, lounging but sharply alert on her other side. "Make him give me back my money. It's all I've got."

I took a quick look at the guy who stared right back at me. If what the girl said was true, this one was super cool. He seemed totally in command.

"Uh," I said, "are you sure he took it?"

"Yes," she continued in a low voice, clearly having been peacefully stoned, but now with a growing fear, desperately wanting her money back, "See that coin purse on his other side, that's mine."

The guy picked up the purse and played with it, laughing sardonically. I felt adrenaline rolling through my body, just like with the speed freak. "Look," I said, "I know you're just playing around, but the lady's scared you'll really take her purse, can you . . .?"

"Man, the lady's purse is now mine. She gave it to me, and getters keepers, givers weepers," he laughed softly. All around on the hillside I could see a couple of hundred people stretched out, blissed-out, doing their own thing. How had my own thing gotten involved in this scene of conflict?

"I didn't give it to him. It was sticking out of my pocket and he saw it and pulled it out. Please get it for me."

"She's a kid. She doesn't have much money. Give it back to her," I urged, but heard with dismay the faintest note of threat in my voice that came from a twitch of deep conditioning I had not ever seen before. That meant, I knew, a heavy scene.

The guy, very trim and lean, about a hundred and forty pounds, flamboyantly shoved the purse in his hip pocket with his left hand, and flashed a switchblade in his right.

"So I stole it. It's mine. And if you don't split, man, I'll steal your life right now, on this grass."

I stared at the guy, trying to feel, maintain my presence but it had ooshed out. A bad slashing at minimum. I could probably take him in the end. Why was I even considering a fight? Taking a chance on losing my life, and for what? Here I was exactly in the position of Bob about Linda, well, yes, we both had grown up in traces of the Old West, chivalry toward the few ladies menaced by bad and evil men.

"Please," the girl said looking straight at me.

"It's your karma," I heard myself saying to both of them. That's both true and the cleverest cop-out of them all, I thought. The guy and I looked at each other a few seconds longer. I saw myself rising, walking away at an angle, keeping my eye on the hand with the knife. About twenty feet away, I saw the guy switch his blade back in, return the knife to its pocket, stretch and laugh, enjoying his coup. I felt about as secret as the sky caught in a sunset. Or was it a sunrise?

The girl sat there silently, looking straight ahead.

The fog came down also silently, quickly over the hill. Drama and story were certainly not all sunlight. In the fog memories, projections, desires, fear were stronger than sensations and perceptions. I was glad to split that scene. Some dramas were not worth playing out. You still could work with the story.

Someone Must Live To Tell The Tale

Plunging up Haight Street, I ran into Peter Zurg whom I hadn't seen since the meeting at James' on Fillmore. Peter was not only a big name on Haight because of the Free Kitchen for the hungry, but because he radiated happiness and energy. Peter strode with intentionality, dressed in a red plaid shirt that set off blond hair and broad shoulders.

"Hi, Peter."

"Hey, Joe, this is the day we're going to liberate space at City Hall for the lunch hour. Want to come?"

"Yeah." I eagerly fell into step with Peter to avoid the morass of thinking about my fleeing the switch blade. Life never seemed sweeter. I lived, and nothing seemed sweeter than life. I had fled, and did not hold it against myself. Backed in a corner, I knew how to fight. Not backed in a corner, I would escape. Once and for all I decided to be a survivor, and possibly a writer, not a hero, but I would move as much as far as I could at the side of real heroes like Bob and Peter. Someone must always live to tell the tale, the words formed in my head. Peter and Bob would lead me on to help liberate certain spaces, but without the conquest of time, the liberation of a given space would be forgotten, every action would disappear, including the heroes. Only story could conquer time. They arrived at the porch of another gabled green three-story Victorian house with mystic signs and mandalas hanging from the windows. About twenty men had gathered on the porch with drums, flutes, and guitars. The men lounged, mostly bearded and long haired with the keen-eyed craggy faces of the American frontier, blue jeaned, shirts open at the throat.

"I'll call up Bob," I said.

"Sure," Peter replied. "We leave in half an hour, at eleven, and walk to City Hall, the drummers keeping up a rhythmic cheerful beat, occasionally a flute contributing a short melody or a guitar a twang and a series of chords. A lot of laughter. Waving to people on the sidewalks, in the cars. Passing on vibes. Lowering the paranoia level." Everyone grinned.

"Guerrilla Theater," Peter said to Bob who got there in twenty minutes, "arrives unexpectedly, liberates a space for a happening, music, scenes, interactions, departs." I could see Bob's ecstasy. Peter putting theater right into the middle of life, Peter's use of the metaphor guerrilla implying intentionality, conflict, Dionysian revelry of conjuring and disappearing forms, forms of future victories. Guerrilla invoking the myth of people learning their real friends and enemies. "Create and run," said Bob "is the artistic and higher level version of the armed guerrilla's hit and run."

City Hall's marble splendor loomed in view. Peter moved to the front while the men innerly elevated their presence. No one lost their cool, everyone stayed physically relaxed.

Up the steps they glided like frontiersmen and Indians. This was more fun than fighting my cousins with wooden rubber guns and dry canestalks with a hard clod at the root. I couldn't help looking for the cops, but none appeared. Three minutes to noon. Peter waved the men over to one side of the wonderful marble porch, to the left side of the silent doors. Silence.

At noon, suited men and an occasional trimly dressed lady began to emerge from the interior through the tall doors. The musicians struck up their folk sound. Peter stood in front, smoking and waving to the outcoming officials, who nearly all stopped or slowed in some surprise. Many of them smiled and waved back to Peter and the musicians. I breathed in deep relief. Many officials poured out the door, on their way to lunch and conversations.

Some stopped, a couple of them knew Peter, some leaned against the balustrade and took in the scene. Gradually the scene died down, with only a few officials remaining to interact. But as the lunch hour continued, several dozen returned with coffee and sandwiches to eat while they listened. A bright sunshine warmed the street and reflected gleaming gold from the clean buildings of the area.

By one o'clock all the officials had left to return to work. A few had returned with their heads down, deliberately pretending nothing unusual was occurring, but most smiled and waved, clearly enjoying the music, the scene, the artistic and peaceful energy of the guerrilla theater.

As the last official went in, Peter started down the steps and the theater moved on like an extemporaneous procession from an ancient mystery rite through the cars and past the business fronts of San Francisco, headed back to the Haight. Everyone playing music or laughing. "Just like it's real," said Bob, his eyes flashing. "Realer than real," said Peter who had overheard him.

Let come what may, I thought, let the scared bosses send in the cops to harass, to give signals to the criminals that they were free to hassle the community, let the media fulminate, let the rulers mired in Vietnam disasters destroy this manifestation, as they certainly will with their crackdown on sacred substances and the Houses. Let them crackdown on these people working through their regressions, armor, defenses, projections, making, of course, their full share of mistakes. Let these human rats do their worst, as they will endeavor to do, and I will be afraid but I will write it down. I am proud to be even the smallest part of this chapter of the human story. I will make sure that this chapter conquers time just as Peter, Bob, the Free Clinic, the thousands of people in the Park, on the street, in the houses, in the guerrilla theaters, in the music halls have liberated space. This Haight Ashbury event vastly increases the quantity of both time and space forever conjoined with a specific psycho-physical creativity, making permanently available to humanity new paths to explore and develop.

I felt perfectly happy being a poor bloody infantry Joe under the command of generals like Peter, captains like Bob, and statesmen like Count von Landers and, yes, Princess. I would fight until they gave the word to melt away into the bush. I would never forget. I would tell the story as best I could, I would put in all the vibrations I could. I gave up innerly reacting against speed freaks, cops in their van moving up and down the street, criminals hassling innocents, media lying by commission and omission. I signed on as a lifetime member of the Guerrilla Theater. I resolved that wherever I stood would be a piece of liberated territory and whatever I wrote would be my infinitesimal part of the time-conquering story that began with the tale of Promethean fire. This time-space tale would also grow ever stronger and more alluring with episodes, flashbacks, epithets, and metaphors that arise from unconquerable poets watching flickering dances of flame and short brilliant lives of sparks. From pilgrims who would return again and again to this space marked as surely as the pyramids and Himalayas with the baraka of achieved power. From dramas that would bring out every tragic, comic, absurd, and epic aspect of the conflicts that produced the forces that made this form, called by us, "Haight Ashbury, the Liberated Space."

Mysterium Fascinans

Bob burst into Sign of the Tarot restaurant while I was finishing cleaning the counter from the small lunch hour rush for our cheap, good soup, 35¢, and slice of thick brown bread, 15¢, a choice of teas and coffees chosen specially by Bob and Princess from around the world, cheese sandwiches, and the House's homemade key lime pie. I worked twenty hours a week at the Sign of the Tarot. That paid for any rent, utilities, and food at the House, with about 5 dollars a week for spending money. I bought second hand clothes at the Salvation Army. Always walked anywhere in San Francisco, never took a bus, so I still had a few bucks squirreled away for my getaway if it came to that.

"Joe, it's Passover, Seder, in a week."

"Yes?"

"Well, it's the end we've talked about. Keep quiet on this, no one's supposed to show up who hasn't taken a real part in the life of the street."

"Show up at what?"

"It's a party to be called 'Bury Mr. Hippy.' It's a full moon. At the end of the party, in the early morning, an effigy of Mr. Hippy will be carried from the party and buried in the Park. That will be the end. Anybody who calls himself a hippy after that will be known not to have been at or even known about the party. Some will go on to the North, past Sonoma County, even to Oregon, Washington or Vancouver, some will go to New Mexico or further east to the Big City, and some will hang on in the Bay Area, but in a different way."

"Some will join the establishment. Some will go into open opposition. We will meet again, those who survive, in the eighties or nineties after we have digested all that we did, and all that's happened, plus what we do on our own. Then, we will win."

"What about factoring in your dramatic uncertainty and danger?"

"So we come back again after the start of the next millennium. We have till then. Never say die."

I poured Bob a cup of his favorite Blue Mountain coffee, with a hit of half-and-half to lighten it up, then poured myself the same.

"So we're all going?"

"No, only you and me, Princess and Sally. This party's not for everybody."

At that point, Mike sauntered in to relieve me.

"Let's go to the back," said Bob.

We passed through the door made of inch apart hanging cards of blue beads that gave into the dimly lighted room with its second hand Chinese and Persian rugs to sit beneath the blue and gold magnificently detailed Hoopoe bird (celebrated by Attar) carefully painted by Princess on the back wall. Bob pulled up a couple of cushions for us. The old windows had a two foot wide sill in front of them. Princess and Sally had painted the windows to resemble stained glass, then set shutters down in front of the sills so two customers could close themselves off for their private interactions. The food and drink would be handed in through a slot in the shutters whose cover could be latched or raised and lowered. The window seats had become quite popular in the evenings.

"All things come to an end," I said.

"One step at a time. Evolution comes in stages and so does History," said Bob, capitalizing both words with faintest intonation on their first syllable.

"You're excited," I said.

"Excited like an electron impacted with sufficient energy to reach a new energy level capable of initiating photosynthesis. I could have continued here no matter how long it lasted. I believe the Haight has just begun to actualize possibilities undreamed of before of experiences and evolution of basic social forms, maybe the first genuine new inventions of social infrastructure since the array of the forms of the blood family developed tens or even hundreds of thousands of years ago with their various rewards, obligations, and taboos. Which of these new forms will survive depends on their adaptation to evolutionary competition."

"You can say that with increase of cops, media, laws, and crime hitting the Haight?"

"Up to a month ago, within limits, these negative factors simply forced us to evolve new forms more quickly. However, there's no doubt now that a major crackdown on all social and psychological innovation in America has begun, that the ruling groups have irrevocably decided to carry this bust through to the full limit of their power. They are frightened, losing the war and their sons' and daughters' unquestioning belief at the same time. They have got to find scapegoats to blame for this, because they will not change, maybe cannot, and the intelligentsia experimenting with different states of consciousness and social forms and the Blacks in the city slums will be their scapegoats. In the nature of these beasts, crackdowns increase in harshness until an explosion of some kind occurs. The prisons will expand their population by hundred of thousands of intelligentsia, experimental youth, and black ghetto males who have armed themselves until crime and revolution are impossible to be distinguished by the searches. The reaction has found the triple tools of demagogic power and repression that will enable the America rulers to stay hog rich and become richer than any class in history: "The left," sex and drugs. The first allows the military force and foreign adventures to increase to levels undreamed of by humanity, the second mobilizes the fundamentalists, and the third allows armed police and internal prisons and conditioning systems using media techniques to whip up the population into a semi-permanent level of unreasoning panic. The cop vans moving up and down Haight making arrests of youth are but the first experiment that will soon be applied all over the United States. Youth arrests for experiments in self-discovery will be taken for granted in a few years. It will be a constitutional selective fascism without a führer, just figureheads, legalistic fanatics, and devoted gunmen in a dozen different uniforms, but still a fascism, a quasi-omnipotent state with oligarchic owners.

"But new inventions, societal, space, substances, media, will be made, new modes of hipness will develop able to act with dissociated states of consciousness in a montage of functional skills under an I-attention of even to us incredible subtleties of informational and emotional complexity. So with great sadness, I will bury Mr. Hippy and, then, rejoicing, prepare to move out into the great world to see what I and others who escape can do with the magnificent energies, post-Nietszchean insights, and hydraheaded relationships we created here."

I looked at Bob a long time, appreciating anew Bob's sanguine capacity for action. Bob would always move forward, always a little ahead of himself, leaving a scent which, if he survived, others would follow although at a distance. I would always be in the search party, looking ahead to find where the Bobs and Peters had gone to, to serve as a link. But in the vertical world of states of consciousness as distinct from the horizontal world of expanding states of action, I would always be looking down while Bob was always looking up from his expanding horizons of activity.

I saw at least twenty years, a lifetime of victories and defeats ahead for Bob in his war to liberate space, to free a few humans from unnecessary restrictions on what they could do, with Bob perhaps to remain until he died unaware of the personal space at his core, his attention so raptly concentrated on grand problems of social existence. Probably Bob would deny his public suffering in the name of eros and his private suffering in the name of ecstasy. Possibly, I thought, Bob will have actually transcended his suffering by having taken what action he could upon seeing humans, including himself, trapped at such a level below their capacity by state, church, education, media, and their own weaknesses so skillfully observed, caught, and exploited by others, and so skillfully noted, indulged, and refined by themselves when obliged to surrender.

As for myself, the only acceptable justification for my life would be to remember the quintessential, then to select cunningly from that refined memory to create, in conversation and in art, expeditions of meaning for self-chosen comrades to embark upon. I wanted to encounter more real geographers of time and space and more creators of their own history woven upon their own warp and woof. I would go talk to Burroughs. Lilly. Schultes. Coleman. There were others, known and unknown, in the arts and in the sciences.

Princess glided through the beaded door. We both waved to her to sit with us. “I'm so happy you strolled into this magic moment about to become a bewitching memory,” I said.

“Beneath your Hoopoe, the leader of the birds.” Bob added.

“Both of you will have a happy old age,” said Princess, “because you are creating material in yourselves and friends around you, Bob, to carry on conversations, the dance of feelings, creative thoughts to be watched and responded to by audiences in your future, and you Joe, are verifying and registering ecstatic sensations, insights, experiences, and people to write about in stories that will conquer time.”

During this exchange, Mike had brought in three mint teas and set them down, deftly removing the two empty cups. “Fools walking the precipice again,” he laughed in his burly Irish way.

“And you think the hanged man is going to learn more by gazing silently head down into the deepest well,” retorted Bob to Mike.

Mike shot him a keen look from beneath bushy and prognathous eyebrows. “And Princess has become priestess,” he said softly.

We gazed at one another, alive, trembling, not in the mysterium tremendum, but the mysterium fascinans, knowing that we loved beauty, not power, that we trembled at the passing of time, but even more that we trembled because the Hoopoe had just seemed to move. We knew then that we had reached our destination even if for only that moment. And having reached it once, knowing it existed, would find our way back again.

"Have a good afternoon," said Mike, playfully formal, just like we were customers, as he left us, making his trademark quick turnabout.

Seeing The Waves Separate From The Ocean

Before the Farewell to Mr. Hippy scheduled during Seder, I decided to hitchhike to Onsalon in the Big Sur. "The scene actually runs beyond both ends of Haight street, terminating at Landers' garden and carp pool in the Sonoma mountains and the Onsalon hot baths on a Big Sur cliff" I had been told. The coastal redwood ecosystem, of course! Suddenly I saw the eco-system in which The Street nestled. The coastal redwoods needed mild cold weather, fog, and the running streams of mountain valleys so they needed to be by the ocean, on a subsiding coast, therefore with precipices and mountains near the water. In the center of this fresh geology and fresh ecology, drowned estuaries formed San Francisco Bay, the only easy entrance for adventurers of the world to gain access to the fabled 1840's Gold Rush that set the anything goes stage for Haight Ashbury. Before the adventurers the Indians had used the Onsalon hot baths to relax from it all and do their cosmic ceremonies.

Bob, Princess, and Sally had even located their House on Sutter Street, named for the discoverer of gold in California. Redwoods, Indians, hot springs, gold, adventurers, fishermen, lumberjacks, fire, rot and termite-resistant redwood, and therefore strong, beautiful intelligent women, and therefore thinkers, authors, poets, and mystics. An ecology wealthy in natural, human, and historic econiches. Three new social inventions coincided to elevate the Haight Ashbury scene's central action to planetary significance: small group Houses based on Reich's deep de-armoring and liberation of the orgasm and Kropotkin's co-operative economics, a safe cheap quality controllable substance, a few micrograms of which could drastically enlarge the perceptual field of a human with no addictive qualities, and a communication/transport system that could coordinate events occurring in a formerly remote, though distinguished, provincial center with the historic and metaphysical pulse beats of New York, London, Paris, Prague, Tangier, Oaxaca, and Kathmandu.

Add twenty thousand young, healthy, smart people of both sexes applying all they knew and could learn from this wealthy ecology and from the three new inventions with the aim of attaining the maximum experience, insight, ecstasy, and peace. Further add that in that twenty thousand were at least five hundred extremely hip, traveled, educated individuals who put their megalopolis-tested skills to work gaining food, medicine, communications, counseling, and public relations for the community which represented to them the flowering of powerful dreams humanity had been forced so long to keep secret. So now I stood at the edge of Highway One, listening to the surf below, inhaling the salt tang, leisurely arcing my thumb, endeavoring to establish eye-contact with each approaching driver. I had washed my khakis and shirt, trimmed my hair to medium length, and beard to two inches. I set an unscuffed leather suit case borrowed from Princess by my side for wary drivers to appraise.

At Onsalon, I presented a name that got me through the gate. Ned Nolan, a thirtyish black-haired man with eager face and eyes that had seen all they could handle and now, as clearly as if they had been marked by a sign, begged, no more, please, I've had enough. Ned introduced me to his well-breasted slim-waisted girl friend whose body said clearly I'm being laid adequately, nothing different, please, I'm not going to risk what I've got. I liked them. They reminded me of a certain kind of yogi in India that had mastered the forms, but had no interest in advancing to meet the perils on the way to Kali-guarded secrets of the non-independence of all phenomena. Those yogis, however, always clean and disciplined, could operate groups of people as engineers operated chemical systems, releasing them from the stresses and bitter feelings of the bazaar or the bureaucracy so that their reactions could peacefully flow to completion, eliminating unnecessary build-ups of anger and anxiety. I felt a wave of nostalgic happiness meeting these two familiar figures from India now acculturated into at least one American ecosystem.

Ned showed me how to get to the hot baths. "Join us for dinner and then let's talk about your House. Enjoy yourself." Ned sent me on my way with a soft white towel. After showering, I made my way to the outdoor hot baths. Far below, kelp raised and lowered on the shore-hastening waves. Crisp sunlight turned dark green on a cliff above the cliff below which looked down upon us in the hot baths.

Two women and a man sat silent and nude in the baths. The hot sulfurous water had forced them to conserve both their sex and talk energies. Their massage-loosened bodies breathed, perceived, and pulsed as they sat in silent companionable three-dimensioned presence. In a few minutes I reached this realm of body objectification. Bent back from the knees, only my feet touching bottom, I semi-floated, gazing into the deep blueness. I then began to enter deeply the state I had experienced before only briefly. Everything became perfect, not just the sensuously pleasant moment at the bath, but the two women sitting without coquetry or despair with their redundant flesh, the man sprawled lightly without vainglory or servility in strong but untoned muscles needing much more workout than desks, books and television couches could give. Everything became perfect, even the conflicting narratives of my life, left in living pieces around the planet, even my few remaining dollars and soon-to-be ended place at the House and the Sign of the Tarot, my disconnected visions and forgotten dreams, women won or lost, lived with and left or left by, men trusted and distrusted, helped and helped by, deceived and deceived by, worked with and fought against, loved and hated, takings-on and givings-up, the complex operations of living, exuberances, pains, my death stalking me, sleepless nights and afternoon snoozes, ascetic fervors, orgiastic ceremonies . . . the sun that became bigger and hotter in the early afternoon sky. The women rose in slow motion, eyed me like antediluvian giants, dispassionately, sauntering away with temporarily hermetic flesh. The man had grown equal to a walrus, his mustache as natural a phenomena as the mild breeze. . . .

I had found the point for my attention to sit untiringly that produced this state; it metered out the epinephrine and norepinephrine so that the point between fight and flight could produce the equipoise of full attention upon the world-body system, the alert hunter at the sniffing stand-still.

The man rose with the awkward grace of a walrus climbing out of the sea onto rocks, deigning the faintest inclination of his head in signaling full passing on of emotional territorial rights. After a minute, I also rose from the water. If Aphrodite stepped out of the foam, then Apollo stepped out of hot sulfur springs, flashed in my mind. I undulated to the railing to gaze unfocussedly down at the waves lapping into the cove below, onto the small beach covered with black boulders. My heart felt immensely heavy in my heated body which had been semi-floating for nearly an hour, but now had suddenly stood up, subjecting that reliable workhorse to full gravitational force. Drawing in deep breaths, dizzy, I sensed each heavy pulse laboring, the intense effort of the heart not to stop. My heart pounded loudly, drowning the sound of the surf. I could not keep my heart going. I was going to have a heart attack if I kept standing. I refused to stop gazing at the waves. I wanted to see the waves clearly, exactly, more than anything in my life. More than the first woman I had ever seen naked, moving naturally, unaware that I could see her, young and dazzling. More than the first patrol, dangerous, difficult, demanding, exciting as life itself. More than anything human. Only the stars had I ever wanted to see so much. "Where I came from and where I was going," resonated in me.

I felt my body sliding downward at an ever-increasing angle, like a small landslide off a vertical cliff. My body slid slowly downward, quicker and quicker, until it lay on the cement floor like a talus slope. Was it dead? I didn't know or care. I kept an unbroken Himalayan gaze on the waves below as if I were still standing there, my body crumpled below me.

Suddenly, I saw the waves separately from the water. Water went up and down, but waves moved on toward the shore. Finally, deprived of depth, the water lifted by the wave fell over and then inertially flowed on into the sand. The wave disappeared when its material crashed, but a new wave came on behind. The water that lost the wave when the sea became too shallow returned again and again into the sea, the waves continued to come from the far distance and to disappear when their material crashed over into the shallows. A standing wave myself, I saw the pattern of the waves shimmering over the ocean bobbing the water up and down, saw the pattern of the waves being generated by the wind being generated by the sun which I saw as a black solid of matter and energy exploding into light, wind, and waves, moving sea, life, and perceptions, the earth cutting its tunnel through far reaches of the sun's magnetic influence, rotating impacts from that shining energy around its sphere. I saw myself gliding downward and re-entering my body wondering if it were still alive or had it reached its furthest point on life's beach. Must it now withdraw back into the molecular ocean to meet another wave? Was my wave to disappear, having used up its allotted material energy? Where would my body beach through its kinetic energy?

My pounding heart throbbed a little less loudly. I lay there for a couple of minutes longer nursing returning strength. I felt a small chill and sensed someone looking at me, casting a shadow. I tried a deep breath so they wouldn't worry and prematurely rouse me to check if I had a stroke. The sun returned, warming my back. I heard mellow laughter from the hot bath. Soon my heart felt strong, younger than before, powerful again. I had studied enough physiology to know that I had been in striking distance of fibrillation. I thanked Johnny Faraway for having demonstrated to me the heart attention exercise.

A cold shower, invigoration, striding over terraces, strolling a garden green with vegetables, splashed with marigolds for beauty and nematode control, over a clear watered stream, shady from redwoods, down to the sturdy rambling two story house. Ned hugged me on arrival and led me to the fire around which a group of six people, the managers and a couple of massage specialists sat, cross-legged and comfortable.

After a while Sally uncoiled upward, carefully keeping her neck out of the startle position. "I'm going to check the stew." I rose a minute later, "I'll take a look at the kitchen."

In the kitchen Sally and I looked at each other and smiled. I thought that if only she and Ed really understood what they performed so well, Onsalon would become a truly sacred place. It was a sacred place from olden times. The people here now did nothing to bring it down, they kept it up, but they used it for everything but a launch pad toward a deva world above the sea and below the stars. Suddenly I homed in on her gaze and kissed her. She kissed me. I broke away to look at her. She looked at me. "We don't do that here," she said. I watched myself smile, wave offhandedly, and present my easy-going Joe Madison smiling surface. I turned in a friendly way and poodled back to sit by the fireplace. How disappointing that she didn't say, I don't do that, rather than calling on her culture, "we don't do that." On the other hand, that meant on her own she would have. I grinned happily to myself. Don't screw with local tribes' beliefs.

We discussed a bit of Reich, massage, yoga, and the history of the hot baths going back to the Indians the Europeans had found there. We enjoyed testing and prolonging attentively the dinner created from garden produce they had picked that day, the crisp raw carrots, delicious berries, and chewy new baked bread. Ned invited me to join them in their morning meditation.

That night I stood in the center of the small meadow in front of the old house, looking at the stars changing from focus to unfocus to non-effort and back again. I saw the sputnik in its path. Stars put it all in perspective, even the waves. To voyage from star to star in worlds of humanity's own making, until the secret of universe making itself was learned and mastered. Anything short of this led only to the grave meaning only to madness if the full horror of the situation were contemplated. I remembered first seeing the stars between bursts of Roman candles on a warm fourth of July night celebrating Independence. In the dark between the Roman candles, with my family around me, on the grass, at the age of six I had seen the stars.

"What is that?" I asked.

"The Milky Way," my father replied. "The Galaxy. Our Galaxy. The Indians called it Happy Hunting Ground for their great warriors to ride in after they died."

But I wanted it to be my happy hunting ground while alive. I knew even then that going there was not impossible. Somehow it could be done.

Beginning meditation, I crossed my legs comfortably, but everyone else there sat either in the full or half lotus position. Bob had commented he thought dynamic yoga better for adaptability and not to overly perfect static stretch yoga. I could see Ned's straight back emerging like a column from the full lotus. Three or four times in the session I came down, noticed Ned's non-moving posture, and used that to bounce back to the state of reverie punctuated by the first level of sense samadhi, carefully separating word, essence, and knowledge in order to fuse mind with the sense object, my memory of the wave scene.

At the end I leaned over to Ned, "I admired your fantastic state, I had no idea. . . ."

Ned quickly answered with wry depreciation, "Actually, I fell asleep about halfway through and tranced out."

"You certainly maintained a magnificent posture," I said protestingly.

"That's the beauty of the full lotus plus practice. You can lock in. But, "he smiled, winningly modest, "that doesn't mean you stay awake."

I suddenly flash-backed on Landers' dancers, trained to do intentional Lurdyeff dances, appearing totally conscious, but who, when as an experiment, Landers, put up to it by a challenge from Bob, suddenly varied their accustomed musical tempo, collapsed in an undignified bitterly protesting heap on the mat floor.

I also remembered thin white robes on that yogi that Princess had taken me to meet, reclining on his gold-rimmed couch by a large indoor swimming pool, with two white-clad women in attendance. The yogi, after I had been introduced to him, flipped off his white robes to reveal a loin cloth, walked to the wall, deftly laid down a Murphy bed of nails then nonchalantly stretched himself out on the sharp points for three minutes. "I do this for special visitors," the yogi said, "to show them another reality." A polite exchange had followed before Princess and I left. Maybe the yogi had known more, since it would not have been in his interest, living in a foreign county, to have disturbed his wealthy and influential client-students by taking them behind the scenes of phenomenal phenomena.

"Whee," I said to Ned, risking a little, "you know, sleep's considered a higher state than waking if it's done as an exercise." Ned laughed in a friendly way as if he found me a charming diplomat.

"Can you show me an exercise," said Sally.

"Sure." I owed some karma for taking that unasked-for druidic kiss alone under invisible mistletoe.

"Can I watch?" said Ned.

"If you do it unobtrusively." He watched us from a window while we went out under a redwood.

I had her jump up and down for thirty minutes, arms stretched high above her head, something I'd done in the Sudan with a hundred loin-clothed men. I realized why that exercise had "come down" after a while. She needed a good shaking up, and she used the exercise to give herself one. Ned watched between two curtains in a window looking out on the grassy nook.

"Good-bye, I appreciate your hospitality." I did. Hoped I had given back something. I would never forget seeing the waves separate from the ocean. I shook Ned's hand, embraced him, and kissed Sally lightly. Why not stay? By leaving Onsalon I was leaving perhaps my last chance in social life of a place I could truly call home. "I don't want a home," I whispered to myself, headed toward the highway. "It's the open road for me, no, past Whitman, it's off the road, all roads for me, the open seas, mountains, and space for me, come what may for me, an infinite expedition between waves and stars for me. It is humanity's turn at the helm of time in great nature's evolutionary drama, and the biosphere's my true home. Nature is my true love, wilderness my adventure whether on the street or on the cliff or at a base camp, history my recreation, and no philosophy is for me if it's not dancing on my own two feet."

The Future Had Just Been Confirmed

Passover, the night of the Seder to bury Mr. Hippie had arrived. I followed Bob, Princess, and Sally in strolling to the noble three story Victorian mansion selected for the event. This marvelous building was unadorned with any mystic symbols other than its own imperial shape topped by a conical tower. A couple of bearded guys sitting comfortably by the door checked us out. One of them smiled at Bob and gestured us in with a thumb. Fifty people or so had already gathered in the candle-lit main parlor, about thirty feet long and twenty-five feet deep, with twelve foot high ceilings. The dining room lit subtly with blue and red theater lights paced twenty by twenty-five. A roomy library, (with its long polished oak table) beckoned beyond the parlor. Sweet smells of gunja mixed with patchouli in the warm air. Velvet, fine wool, silk, cotton, leather, gold, silver, and turquoise adorned alert bodies in gowns, mini-skirts, earth mother dresses, jeans, jackets, open shirts, vests, boots, moccasins, beaded shoes, and buckled belts.

More people flowed in as I drew on a friendly toke. Even Princess, ordinarily high on her own chemistry, chased the smoke around her mouth for sublingual absorption and to avoid inhaling to the lungs. Bob took a viperish drag as did Sally.

"Hey," Bob said, "the Huckleberries are here, Happening House, Communication Company, some Diggers, that's a Mime actress. It's a party."

The founder of Hare Krishnas was dancing barefooted on a sofa, lightly and happily turning. "Hare Krishna Hare Krishna, Krishna Krishna, Hare Hare, Hare Rama Hare Rama Rama Rama Hare Hare," he chanted softly, eyes sparkling, fitting right into the vibes, adding a soft accentuation to the positive. He had come without followers, by himself, no front, no come-on, a happy fellow, here he was just another guy doing his own thing for his ownself.

"I'll be swoggled," said Bob.

"Whaddaya know, an enlightened guy," I said. "Must be doing the whole Hare Krishna bit as karma yoga, duty work. He gets by on his own perfectly, doesn't need a costumed entourage." They waved knowingly to him and immediately catching the message, he beamed back.

I wandered into the parlor. An erotic flick looped in, playing on one of the darkened walls. A slim young Jewish girl gave thorough and sensuous head to a slim young black guy. Their faces intelligent, their bodies in synch, the straight young phallus tripped off her tongue and lips and then disappeared again. Her fingers stroked his scrotum in a milking motion. His eyes stared straight ahead in erotic trance.

"Oh," one guy said to his girl, "if I had only had that chance at sixteen. I didn't know anything." She drew herself against him. He would get to know anything tonight he had ever missed.

In the second half of the loop the youth's tongue toyed with hers, his wand rolling in and out and around while her slim legs graced his back in feline stroking.

I continued wandering. Upstairs six guys sitting concentratedly around a green-clothed poker table. A fifth of whiskey half-empty at one side under the green-shaded bare electric light. They sat bathed in the naturalistically lucid light radiated from the bare hundred watt bulb and the surrealistic light emanated by the synergistic actions of gunja, whiskey, money, and chance while their attention split into three foci of psychology, cards, and risk.

I drifted onto the screened porch to fuse with the two great tree trunks down by the street lamp at the corner. A long-haired girl stood tripping in the corner off reflections on the screen, in the prophesying trance of Apollo's forms, a Kore.

Back in the parlor, crunching a carrot, I stood with Princess and Sally, grokking the ever-changing pattern of doing your own thing synchronicities when suddenly four couples stood up, each at one corner of the wall-to-wall rug. Wordlessly they shucked off their clothing. Wordlessly they sank, all sturdy mesomorphs, to the floor. The women each lay on her back and opened her legs, knees raised. The men each knelt between the knees and fully embracing the woman's back began the demonstration.

The four women each locked their legs around each man's back. The men's buttocks flashed up and down in regular increasingly rhythmic strokes while the women lay still in rapt concentration. I couldn't take my eyes off this beautiful ritual spectacle. Some people continued their own voyages but others also watched. The ritual splendor spread its golden aura throughout the room. Only the sound of Hare Krishna continued softly.

"The incarnation of Eros," I thought automatically. Krishna and the Gopis. "Eros, that holds all the parts together."

After a satisfying length of time, the men tantrically withdrew, and the couples sat comfortably, nude, each man's arm over the woman's shoulders, almost humbly but like glowing embers, backs against the darkened wall to the rear.

"Never be the same again," Bob came by to whisper. "Anybody who calls himself a hippy after tonight will be known not to have been here, not to have gotten the message. Some will split to the North, Oregon, Washington, Vancouver, some to the East, New Mexico, and Tennessee, New York, some will stay here and blend with the following scene."

"You told me that before."

"Yeah, but it's like an incantation. It needs to be repeated to be understood."

I felt the surging blend of nostalgia, future, and glowing seconds of the present disappearing into memory like flies entering amber, to be preserved as both messages and jewels, ever gaining value as record, power, evocation, and invocation.

When the party ended with preparations finished to take the effigy of Mr. Hippy to bury in the moonlight flooded park, Bob, Princess, Sally, and I left to light-foot it slowly down the hill back toward the Haight together with a slim man of twenty-one, who wore a carefully nondescript set of old jeans, blue shirt, wrangler jacket, scuffed boots, a raggedy beard and sandy sparse mustache. Clearly Princess and Sally thought this guy, Kent, really had something Bob and I should get to know. They had been intensely palavering with him a quarter of an hour before we had all glanced at each other and decided to leave without participating in the ceremony. Bob had joked, "OK, let's start up the new while they're burying the old." We walked silently until reaching an all night coffee joint, each savoring our associations, emotions, and sensations, the pleasure of synching in a small pack on the prowl.

We ordered coffee, then leaned back waiting for the first move. Bob said "We're, that is Princess, Sally, Mike, myself, and a few others splitting for Manhattan to do theater this summer. We're going to do traveling theater for twenty years, around the world, the Theater of All

Time Lines, the Theater combining plots of the West, moods of India, physical precision of the Japanese, the cruelty toward sentimentality of Artaud, and liberating space a la guerrilla theater. "

"I'll be doing the choreography," said Princess.

"And I the stage sets," said Sally.

I sat back, astounded that so much had been decided without involving me in the discussions, but then realized my confronting Bob with narrative and story as primary to theater had led Bob to conclude I was not that much into theater. A bit miffed, I had to admit that Bob had been right. I was more surprised that Princess had not told me. But she was a deep one who didn't like "to mix her monads."

Bob continued with rising enthusiasm. "And our subject matter will be the interplay of human action with the biosphere. For the first time, a theater will be able to do plays from all the great traditions, including our own new ones, without being merely eclectic, because informing the Theater of All Time Lines will be the understanding that all actions have a common element, that they are each a manifestation of nature, the Biosphere, trying to understand itself. So we will also buy a property, or Sally here will, anyhow, since she's the only one with any dough," he laughed, "where we'll do our research as well as prepare the plays. What's beyond acid and Haight, where we've learned so much, is to attain those same states by disciplined exercises plus opening to the impacts of planetary life itself. The challenges of this theater are: aiming to reach the source of the new, the fire, by pushing to the limits the world's paradoxes, the existential dilemma, the conflicts of Death and Eros, of riches and poverty, of oppression and liberation, of vision and darkness."

Kent roused himself from his black coffee. "You're selling technics short," he said. "This government of ours, now taken over by the obscenely rich and powerful can fool nearly all the people nearly all time. When they lose this Vietnam War, it's going to get real mean to prevent its bosses, the oligarchy, the payers off behind the throne, from being exposed as incompetents and reduced to the simple suppliers of market goods that they were till they scared the government by threatening to sabotage the World War II effort unless the New Deal stopped. Then the government had to buy the universities to keep the intelligentsia from exposing the plot. So they're gonna throw many thinkers into jail, or on the street, by their laws against sacred drugs, and those they don't bust because they settle for alcohol and tobacco will find the atmosphere too shut down to really think because there will be that huge taboo topic with all its ramifications they can't afford to open up about. In short, only reductionist-specialists will be left to think for the Bosses and that thinking can only dead-end into more of the same, 'just like' Russia."

"So, what I'm doing, with my friends, is working through physics and technology. We're making light systems, keying them into neuronic response systems, that produce much the same effect as acid. We're heavy into rock, I know Princess here thinks Sun Ra, Cecil Taylor, and Lloyd are where music's at, but that's for the few, who can hear with their emotional intelligence. The people will hear through their body intelligence. We're working out sound that's going to literally vibrate their bodies into trance dance, the trance of Dionysus, one hundred and twenty whacks a minute."

"Don't forget your ninety decibels could deafen them," said Princess mildly.

"Only slightly and they don't dig the fine frequencies anyway," Kent grinned wolfishly. "We're going to shake bodies, put vibrations of higher energy patterns right into the eyeballs, and that's only the beginning. We're hacking the big computers and we're going to put all that info out. We're going to break the information priesthood with their giant calculators in air conditioned nightmares, and put computer power out to the individual. Then information is going to be liberated at such a rate the ordinary human mind is going to be as inundated by overload and forced to pattern think as with acid, but not on archetypal trips that take a classical education to understand, rather zoom directly into contemporary scientific, economic, and sexual facts suddenly bathed in cosmic information energy. Neotypes will emerge, new unions of ideas with the total organism, like androids and cyborgs. The irrelevant, the bullshit, and the treachery is going to be flotsam and jetsam tossed about by that energy. Let's face it, like jazz, acid is for the few, not inherently, but because the repression, the man, the jails, the lousy education produce settings where paranoia is reality and heroin is a solution. But screw them, we don't need it anymore, we know what's there because we went there," Kent knocked on his head and chest, "so knowing what's in here we're experimenting how to turn it on with lights, rock, and information. Screw mass movements, parties, and setting up a few targets, we're gonna network and let it all pour in and out, evolve by interaction. Their power comes from the old boy network, well, we're gonna run so many new kids on the block networks of so many kinds, from electronic to punctuated rendezvous, around the planet, there'll be a total new boy and girl network, more than a network, an organic-technical-info cybersphere which they can't shut down because they can't escape being part of it. It'll be an essential part of their money system."

I watched Princess, nineteen, carefully listening to Bob and Kent. I felt that Bob didn't fully "get" Kent's technotopic vision, Bob believed in the creative few, the catalysts, the change agents, doing it in the flesh in front of an audience of flesh, producing a temporary opening for change, a catharsis. I suddenly knew Bob and Kent were each right each in their own way. I could hardly keep silent sitting there in the midst of such aching poignancy. If the work of Kent and his friends was only ten years more advanced! I had seen the results already adumbrated of Kent's prophecies in the stunned and opened crowds leaving the light spattered Avalon and Fillmore. Producing that mass effect with Jim Morrison still doing a Rimbaud! I still liked Bob enamored, and in many ways so rightly, of the avant garde and the preternatural line of purity established from Lautreamont to Burroughs and Coleman, and in his own way, himself. But Kent had grabbed hold of a truth of immense power. His complex way into psycho-technics the oligarchy would steal, of course, make incredible profits from, and enhance their power for lies and crime for another generation. But to do this the oligarchy itself, because of its mental rigidity, would have to put real technical power and real information into the experience and hands of skilled youth in order to make it work. I had seen the Franz Kline paintings on daubed Moroccan garage walls with the help of majoon, but these new guys would see reality in electrons with the help of money and power, two drugs more penetrating than majoom, and totally legal since they made the laws.

"Bless you both," I said, feeling older than the first shaman and as new as a boy. "I'm too individualistic for action in the theaters of stage and science, and I'm too in love with the subtleties of jazz, ragas, and Berber chants, with alchemy, and simple tools like axes, shovels, and pruning shears which do thicken your fingers, to be able to do delicate dance and electronic things like you guys, but you will also need an observer, not a neutral observer, but a passionate observer, who believes in history, in a possibility for meaningful stories to emerge from this human fracas, a friendly observer you can talk with from time to time over the years to check your inner thoughts and hopes, and I need you to provide the inside scoop lacking which I should become only a hermit living in a mad incomprehensibility of rumors and doctrined reports, 'The trance of the minor poet.' "

We looked closely at each other. Princess broke the silence. "We'll all have a happy old age. We'll have great conversations because whatever happens to us externally, our lives will be rich. I can say this, because I was reared by a Sioux woman who could prophesy. She taught me to know the moment when what is seen will take place in time."

Sally said, "And I'll have some weird scenes to paint and kooky documentaries to edit." Laughing we each ordered our third cup of coffee, sat lingeringly, and joked about fame, disgrace, victory, defeat, and all the shocks that flesh endures. I glowed, knowing the future had just been confirmed, its creation given a few fine strokes, and that all around Haight that night, hundreds of men and women were also doing their utmost to reach insight to the next step. I don't have faith, I thought, and Eros eludes me though appearing from time to time, but I do now have hope, real substantial non-imaginary hope in real people doing real things leading to real futures.

A Strange Formula Entered My Mind

Bob, to the general enthusiasm of the House, had set departure time to New York for June 22, 1968, the day after summer solstice celebration. With a definite time limit on the House's life, with the inner knowledge spreading through The Street of the intentional ending of that epic of consciousness-seeking that carried art out completely in the open, for the first time with no holds barred in the heart of the experience repressive rationalist-theological West, with the end of a sacred hip Kumbha Mela of intelligentsia that lasted over a year in the profane teeth of organized hostility by muscularly armored oligarchs, the steel-armored state and gizmo-armed media, everyone in the know desired to make the most of it. "If you get to it, and don't do it, may you never get to it again," Bob bellowed out one morning. "If you get to it," Princess scatted, "and don't do it," I blued, "may you never get to it again," Sally, folk-songed.

"What is this it?" Princess asked assuming an innocent air.

"That's for me to know and you to find out," Bob sassed back.

"That does it for me," said Sally.

"How long is it going to go on?" said Mike.

"I don't give a she-it!" shouted Doreen, a tall new lady, lean, snaky hipped, about forty with a smokey tone of voice, living in a tent on the roof with her mountaineering boyfriend. In her jazz mystic past of a year previous she had been after Bob to do the 'fuck of the century' with her, but Bob had managed to avoid the final encounter by laughingly agreeing but never showing up.

"The agenbite of with it," I said.

Two guys now lived in the basement, a giant Germanic motorcyclist, Jeff, and a shorter broad shouldered Jewish street philosopher, Henry, from a house that practiced polygamous fidelity, who now understudied Mike as chef at the restaurant. He added a Borscht soup, "from Minsk, or is it Pinsk?", a New York accent, Bronx saltiness, and a passion for Samurai robes and Go. Nine people lived on the second floor, with Sally and Mike in one room, four women in one, two guys in a third, and me in the closet. Doreen and Max lived on the roof, they who had driven stakes in during a moment of euphoria and had to painstakingly fix the leaks, Princess on half the back porch, and Bob on his floor mattress in the library scene-room, made fifteen total. Then Lois moved in with Jeff and Henry in the basement, a sophisticated well-off blonde Jewish girl who "wanted to understand herself and life."

Preparations for the grand solstice celebration became the theme of the House. Sally painted on a fifteen foot mural scrim in the courtyard the main House habitués sprawled or in action around the table each in a characteristic pose, all together making a provocative emblem of humanity at a feast.

Bob, who believed celebratory feasts *were* the utopian society, jovially ruddy, just off center on the table, arm over a girl's shoulder, face alight with a dozen criss-crossing currents of emotionally complex plotted scenes, each a delight that amused him no end. "Who needs TV when they've got a mind," he would chortle, or pointing out some wildness in a corner. "Who needs Tiffany's when they've seen epiphanies!"

Princess, dark eyes shrewdly taking in the scene, storing incidents and metaphors of individual strengths and weaknesses, non-judgmental about her judgments, profoundly intellectual with full access to woman's hormonal intuitions on the meaning of quick chemical changes, gazing delphicly at Bob from across the table. And what she would speak could on occasion be oracular. "It's all moonlight on the pyramids."

I myself, lunar, cool but edgy as if on a hot seat, raised my chin for drinking in the scene, right hand navigating a brimful glass of wine toward my lips, the observer who liked to balance on the brink of action, testing his equilibrium.

Mike, left arm slouched on the table, disdainful of the social hubbub, conscious of his rawbone sinewy strength, diffident about his intellectual and emotional expression, cholerically alert to weakness.

Ed, the saturnine philosopher, for once excitedly puffing his pipe, leaning back, upright, his eyes flashing the dialectics of his Hegelian progressions, his posture rigid from a cynicism about all shifting appearances.

Sally sat stylishly at a corner of the table, aloof, not missing a trick, self-contained, doubtless already conceiving the mural, head amusedly tossed slightly to the left.

Alice, happy with her shoulders lightly under Bob's arm, brown long hair, into herself, sitting with the lissome assurance of a mercurial disciplined free-form dancer who could probably make it in New York or Hollywood with a tad more of worldly ambition and artistic ruthlessness.

Other faces and figures had begun their outlines.

I went to the backyard everyday to look at the next stage of the mural. "Everyone a different type," I said to Sally.

"That's Bob's only criterion," she replied, "Bob only wants people here who are different from each other in some decisive way. You get a cult if there's only one type, and schisms if there's only two or three subgroupings, or so he says."

"By the way," Princess said, "Bobby Kennedy's speaking by the House tonight, the last speech of the campaign, not because of us but because Little Japan is behind us and the Japanese will come at eight o'clock!"

"I'll be there," I cried, without missing a beat. "We're gonna win!"

Hope had spread over the United States. An end to war, a slackening of hatred. One man, young, vigorous, intelligent, who was tough as the frontier, free-thinking (and from the rumors free-fucking as well as a wiry paterfamilias of a gregarious high-spirited Irish family), sensitive to the hopes of the idealists, decisive about crime and its terror, angry about injustice and rip-offs, and realistic and life-educated enough to negotiate from strength an end to the war, a non-inquisitorial type about life styles different from main street hypocrisies and the shopping malls, eloquent, and someone holding real power in the US who occasionally actually talked to artists and writers, this man had launched his campaign at the last moment, but was carrying all before him to become the people's and intelligentsia's nominee for President. Tomorrow it looked as if he would carry California, Oregon, and South Dakota, making his nomination certain. His speech at the corner next to the House would be his last speech of the campaign.

Ten o'clock before he arrived. The crowd of Japanese, of the House and neighboring Houses on Pine Street, a few blocks up from Fillmore Street, stood waiting patiently for the two hours. It was wonder enough to quiet all complaint that he could find any time at all for their tiny neighborhood.

Finally he strode up, no police protection, some big football players by his side, looking like buddies, waving to the audience. I watched his eye take in the crowd composed of two strikingly different components, then flash his big-toothed smile, wave inclusively to all of them, making acknowledgment of expectant emotions.

Then he concentrated on the Japanese. He was there to say he honored them, that they, too, had been one of the groups in the United States made victim by the intolerance of the loud-mouthed minority who had lynched his Irish forebears while proudly calling themselves, accurately, the Know-Nothings. Laughter. He palmed them in his hand. I felt a physical thrill for the first time in my life from a political man. Kennedy had studied rhetoric, history, and himself. This was the grand style of Athens, the Roman Republic, and Jeffersonian America, a true demagogue, a people-teacher, not a rabble-rouser. It was clear he had come to promise no more concentration camps and ghettoes for minorities. Joe remembered the old walled St. Patrick's South and East of the Village. "We had to put up the walls to protect ourselves from the Know-Nothings," an old Irishman had told him.

Kennedy set them laughing. He cracked a joke about how he felt after making a cultural boo-boo at Tokyo University, but the Japanese students had forgiven him. The joke set them up for tears and a look at each other in the audience.

At the end he made a salute "to these beautiful people in their wonderful costumes," and the people of the Houses cheered, and swinging his head, he promised, "Civil rights for each American will be enforced," and finished with a voice-of-truth declaration that the war must first be contained and then brought to an end.

I wandered the streets of San Francisco in a patriotic haze the next day. The nightmares of McCarthyite screams for purges and destruction of free political speech, the incredible inciting of the police and extraordinary penalties for being in demonstrations or taking a substance to explore some part of one's own physiology or mind, substances by and large used by humanity and intelligentsia for millennia, the massive corrupt bureaucracy descending on Washington to plunder the land in the name of fighting poverty, the insane lack of strategic aims and balance in a war on the Asian mainland, all this began to seem like a temporary aberration of the alliance of Texas nabobs and Southern California weapons makers, Wall Street financiers, and Pentagon mad ambitions. Bob would be greater than his brother. The tragedy of that hate-filled assassination must have deepened the formerly aggressive young man immensely.

By evening it became clear that a wave of enthusiasm had caught on in the United States. Not only had Bob won, he had won decisively in each of the three key states. I could hardly believe my organism literally jumping and dancing at intervals in the streets. I strode feverishly to North Beach, Chinatown, Market Street, the Mission, Haight, the peacefully grooving Park. "America, the Beautiful" I sang to myself out loud. People turned their heads. "God shed his Grace on Thee and Crowned Thy Good with Brotherhood from Sea to Shining Sea." I was deliriously happy with the reserves of love for my country welling up with living fountains of memories of soil smells, river gurgles, and soughing cottonwoods.

Bouncing back into the house, late in the night, I saw the light still on in the living room. Bob looked at me, finger rubbing his lower lip. "They shot him," Princess said. Her eyes sent an immense empathy into me to soften the crash.

I ran out, suddenly narrow-shouldered, hands in pockets down the street toward the one coffee shop that would still be open, at the corner of Fillmore and Sutter. Two greyly dressed blacks bent over their coffee. A tired alert waitress walked over. "Coffee."

Suddenly I howled out loud, "Are they going to kill everybody? First, his brother, then King, and now him. It's the end for twenty years or more. They've annihilated all the leaders in a generation or even two! No country can produce more than three great leaders in a generation!"

"Yes. They kills them and lots more," the old man next to me said. "Lots you don't even hear about, before they even get started past their neighborhood."

"And there's nothing we can do about it !" I screamed.

"No, there's nothing we ever been able to do about it," the old man said. The three men steadily sipped their coffee. The waitress refilled their cups without asking.

"We kill them," I said at last, "we kill them by making them our leaders. Because we don't lead on our own, person by person, house by house. And then they kill them because we show them the target."

"A lot of truth to that," the old man said.

"And of course they always claim they didn't do it, there's no conspiracy because they know if they put out enough of their hate-filled rhetoric some nut will do their dirty work for them. All they do is profit by it."

"Happened to lots of our leaders," the old man said.

"The Gracchi, the Gracchi," I howled again, "in ancient Rome, the two brothers who tried to keep Rome from destruction by the rich, they were killed, too. We just lost our Gracchi. Good-bye the Republic!" Why didn't I write something, why didn't I go on to speak, why did I rave in this cheap bare-lighted metal countered cafe to an old man, a drunk sitting it off, and a tired waitress. Because, I said bitterly to myself, this is the only audience you'd dare talk to. An audience so small and helpless nobody would care who said what to them. Free speech reductio ad absurdum. You're scared stiff, and been scared all your life, since you nearly got kicked off the football team in high school for backing the United Nations, and the coach told you some of the team thought you were insulting the American flag. "I'm not against the United Nations myself," the coach said with a creased mechanical grin. "You just have to stay quiet about it, Joe."

"Every country reaches the end of the age of politics!" I shouted. "From that point on it's only the filthy deals of the powerful that count. The structure of decision has been destroyed. Ideas forgotten. Leaders killed. The rest of us terrified! Life becomes an economic calculus for the rich, till the soldiers get tired of dying for them, and take over."

"That's about it," said the old man.

I walked slowly back up the street to my blanket bed in the closet. I had given it all up when I boarded the ship to Tangier in 1963, but all I had given up had been my personal run at the Presidency. Now, in the second Kennedy's murder, I saw why. Nobody would run for President with an idea, passion, and purpose again. And nobody could get by with it if they did. They'd be shot or hounded down to an inch of their lives by smearuendo.

Bob was onto a lot of truth. Creative groups of individuals by creative group of individuals would have to experiment to find new ways. Kent was really right on. High technics and planetary networks were all that could be slipped through the effective blockade to keep the intelligentsia and the people from communicating. Electrons and guerrilla theater rendezvous could move too quickly for the deadly tyrannosauri to hit.

That night lengthened into the bitterest stand of my life. Somehow I had, since beginning to think, assumed, and it had been an extraordinary assumption I saw now, that not only would I ultimately produce of something of great value to my contemporaries, but that my contemporaries would be of a great period, like the Tang dynasty, or Periclean Athens, or Elizabethan London, or Medicean Florence, or the Baghdad of Haroun al-Rashid, and so a myriad of mirrors would reflect each other raising my whole lifetime to an inspiring brilliance, a lighthouse in history's ocean, bringing another audacious expedition safely in to shore, with unexpected treasures from unknown shores.

And no place other than America existed that had even this possibility left. I had traveled the planet and found only debris, debris composed, it's true, of many wondrous found objects but whose only use was to be hauled into a museum of irrelevant associations, a feast of quickly consumed curiosities.

Suddenly I remembered waves, stars, walks with Princess, jungles, deserts, plains, mountains, and the old man who talked so kindly with me at the bare, harshly lit cafe. I remembered how old the world, how ancient the galaxy, how many futures lay ahead, how many pasts forgotten, and all the changing states of consciousness, each revealing a different face of reality, each so glamorous the others disappeared into the shadow, the many-sided diamond itself remaining unsuspected, even undesired.

That was it, I had let myself fall into the realm of the hell-beings, hell did exist. I remembered my father whom I had always felt sorry for as being a non-thinking believer in religion, snarling grimly to me once, “Hell is in a man's own mind, nowhere else,” with a look of grief incomprehensible till now. A strange formula entered my mind, “Hell is one-seventh of Reality and cannot be ignored.”

A Celebratory End

The next day I again walked down to the Fillmore corner, but in a different mood. The fog hung back, low in the West over the hills. Sunlight snappled off surfaces. An esthetics of light transformed utilitarian structures of an economically marginal area, that is, one in which hand labor, including theft and prostitution, predominated, alternating with the queus and shabbiness of unemployment.

At the corner a broadshouldered battered-nosed, knobby-eared man of forty confronted me. The man jabbed the air in front of me, bobbed and weaved, swung air swishing haymakers just in front of my chin. "Okay, fight! Come on, man, fight! I was heavyweight contender for five years. Think you're too good to fight with me? Come on, fight, and let's see who's too good!" The man danced in a ring composed by his mind. The dozen or so gathering people became his crowd. His voice went up. "Come on, fight! You scared? You better be scared. I went eight rounds with the world champion!"

I felt my body go into alert motionlessness. Tranced out, I watched the scene. The man swung his trained fists within an quarter of an inch or less from my nose, from my chin, from my solar plexus. I could see the people gathered around afraid to interfere, afraid something more drastic, probably to them, might happen by interfering. The man danced, jabbed, and taunted. I worked to keep my body relaxed in trance, so that no rigidity or reaction surfaced. I lost my lofty observer status and became one with my body, wondering if I could keep it up till the man quit, or if the man would lose control of the remnant precision of his punches that flickered so closely, so powerfully. One of those jabs full in my belly or against an unprotected chin could hurt me bad.

The man slowly stopped after several minutes, looked at me, shook his head as if waking up, and then grinned before slipping away. Two women let out soft breath they'd been holding some time. "That was the way to handle that," one man said. But I had not handled it until the man had the scene well underway. My body had done it. As it had done so many things beyond my powers of control and foresight.

Just as it had gotten afraid and left the man who pulled the switchblade. Just as it had wailed out its Jeremiad in the cafe.

The day of Solstice arrived. The kitchen, loaded with oranges, strawberries, bananas, figs, dates, peanuts, potatoes, carrots, celery, sweet potatoes, navy beans, onions and shallots, condiments, spices, spreads, dressing, witnessed three chickens being prepared for baking under Sally's supervision, while in the backyard Mike expertly set up an outdoor spit to turn a whole small hog, laughing with Henry who insisted on being his assistant, "to experience the whole Jewish taboo bit."

On the side street, cool as a far-out girl, calmly sat the House's new second hand originally yellow school bus. All the past week the House had enthusiatically painted it over with reds, blues, and yellows to take the Theater of All Time Lines to Manhattan, to play across the country in special spots like Elko, Fort Defiance, Midlands, Dubuque, Normal, Wheeler, and Hoboken. "Let's see America!" said Bob, "Not the superhighways!" "Adventure! Adventure!" he mantramed. A small kitchen had appeared in the back, Bob had half the seats reversed, alternately facing the other half, "so there could be conversations like in Europe". A library lined one side above the seats, a double bunk replaced three seats to spell the driver and navigator on long night drives, a desk-table placed between two facing seats served as office and design place for Princess and Sally, while a toilet waited in the back corner in a six square foot enclosed area, for "emergencies."

They lucked out. Fine weather for the day, a touch of real warmth. "All work stops at noon exactly," Bob said at breakfast. "then we celebrate. Then we sleep." Catcalls. "Then we clean up in the morning from nine to ten, and depart for points East across the continent at ten-thirty en punto!" Cheers. I marveled at Bob's converting retreat from the House into an advance on Manhattan. He had mastered his guerrilla texts.

Kent came over to help. He set up lights and strobes in the living room for the party and the performance. Sally's scrim now hung in front of the windows to Sutter Street to form the backdrop. I humbly helped Kent on the plug-ins. I had mulled it over. Bob would windup an existential failure in all probability after years of exciting and interesting theater adventures. Of course, Bob would evolve into an ever more fascinating character, but could he keep himself from an unhappy poverty-endowed old age? Bob would spread ideas and vibrations, freely "casting his bread upon the waters,"as he liked to call it. Perhaps he would strike it lucky, but I doubted it. His theater was too demanding to be completely pleasurable to more than a few devotees. It could enthrall but to do that it demanded concentrated attention. There would be small turned-on audiences, surely. Just enough to keep going on. And who will buy your novel in twenty years or thirty years or the next century, I asked myself. "The happy few!" Stendhal's audaciously true and bodaciously brash answer sent me higher than a kite. Of course, and those happy few would be the ones who made Bob happy, too. And there I had to hand it to Bob, because Bob would be able to see and meet his happy few. I would have to imagine my future readers, indeed wonder whether they were not fantasy. Anyway, if fantasy, it was the best fantasy I could fantasize.

I felt, however, that in the theater Bob underrated spectacle and plot and thereby overemphasized mood, poetry, gesture, and tempo. That Bob could and should attract the merry many as well as the happy few with not less Dionysus, but with more Apollo, not less Hermes, but more Aphrodite. I felt a bit bookish making that judgment, but esthetics did differentiate itself from ethics by integrating its profound teachings with Reichian surfaces of pleasure instead of Augustinian surfaces of suffering. Humans on the whole drank their pleasure straight and neat when a wondrous spectacle awakened their senses, which then led attention to alight upon whatever inner levels might be aligned with the gorgeous come-on. Only a devoted handful would sip the wine of through lines and emanations by directing attention to rare emotions and development of a theme by gestural and tonal complexities in costume.

Kent, or some rock and roll acid techie like him, would be the big winner the next two decades. Putting objects out that would literally change the space people lived in, objects that people would buy because they carried the cachet of the new, because they could be turned on and off. Because these objects carried information, stimulation that people could directly adjust to their desires, this approach was bound to win, barring a dictatorial level of information control that would openly destroy Freedom of Speech. Kent would probably become personally less interesting as he lost his youth, intellectually ponderous with necessarily carefully described systems, with the speed of logic unable to compete physiologically with Bob's speed of emotional comprehension. But what might his logic do when it donned electronic wings and could circle the planet more quickly than Ariel to contact millions of yearning minds?

And I, Joe Madison? I had already decided to fail existentially back in 1963 when I looked out my window from the top of Number One, Whitehall, watching the Yugoslavian freighter steering past the Statue of Liberty, on out to beckoning worlds of my unknown: Ocean, Africa, and Balkans. I knew in that instantaneous look that I would leave my past future all behind to sail out in two months on the very next Yugoslav freighter, knowing absolutely that letter I'd seen in the Village Voice from a jazz musician I'd grooved on at the Fat Black Pussy Cat, gave out living truth when he wrote: "Come to Tangier now before it's too late. This is the last place in the world you can contact what is being lost."

I had sailed to Tangier. "I sailed to Tangier," I said to myself with fierce emphasis on the I. "I did sail to Tangier and I watched all time lines disappear that afternoon with Terry in the Kief Cafe, above the Medina, watching white clouds in a blue sky with three telephone wires cutting across my vision." In Tangier I had found out how to live in the margins and between the lines. During the Haight I had discovered how to live off the page and away from the entire book. Away from the entire library! I had met Princess who had given me the cues and keys to enter fully this moment-by-moment exquisitely structuring-destructuring emotionally dynamic world. I was now a happy-go-lucky wanderer of worlds, an Odysseus who had turned away from both the sacking of Troy and the return to Ithaca to sail the endless sea. And I wandered time as well as space. As a kid I had admired the hoboes on the Rock Island freight trains that whoo-whooed in the night past my Grandfather's barns and fields. Oklahoma Red. Wenatchee Joe, Snake River Jim. Always some new place to go, things to see, people to meet, until somewhere, somehow, you found yours, and reblended with the whole shooting match. Finally having integrated Odysseus as well as Apollo and Dionysus, I felt breaking into new ground, into new time-space, into new legend to fuel my life, that one true miraculous fig from out of Nowheresville.

Princess would learn all the wondrous madnesses about life and the theater as Bob's essence friend. She would be his artistic Chief of Staff. Who could say what would happen to her? If she were a man, he would predict cultural immortality when she struck out on her own. Being a woman she would meet far more difficulties. He would still bet on her. She never felt satisfied with the completion of an inner vision, like Bob. Princess wanted the costumes, the make-up, the stage lighting, the position of the feet also to be exactly right. She wanted the whole show to jump. To me she exemplified Pallas Athene, woman of wisdom, patroness of Odysseus who kept his craftiness on course.

I snapped back from reverie, realizing Kent had left me sitting there after finishing wiring up the system. He now leisurely paced in and out of the room, darkened by the scrim over the windows and the closing of the sliding door to the library. "Five minutes!" Bob shouted from the kitchen.

They all gathered around the famous "morning table," excited by making a celebratory end to their time at the Haight, trembling with hopes and fears of the future they were going to plunge into intentionally, with no preconceived idea of what would happen when they confronted on the open road the massive inertially momentumed daily check-out for deviations from the world-conquering culture which had stolen the name but lost the glory of that cocky America dedicated to life, liberty, and the pursuit of happiness. They knew their new know-how of energy cascades, montaged impressions, and wild insights reaped from the astounding social experiment and brouhaha they had helped bring off would bring them through whatever befell their voyage.

Sally ladled her special punch into everyone's glass, twenty of them all told. The clock struck. "To the future," Princess toasted, nineteen and radiant. Prayer glided through my entire being as I clinked glasses with her. Prayer was a rare state for me, whose every pulse beat with the frontier selected genes and behavioral units of self-reliance. However, staring at her hope and radiance, knowing full well at twice her age, with rare experience of the world and its literature, how truly fragile were the physical, psychological, social, economic, political, and cultural bases for her accomplishing of her aims, important also to others, maybe even to history, I could not help this organic prayer for her. "Help her, help her, please help her." I did not care a fig where the help came from. I did not give a rat's ass where the help came from. I felt her wise glance pick up on the tear formed at the edge of my right eye. We smiled at each other, joined in vibration, separated by our intentions for the morrow. Her bravery frightened me the way it dared the universe. Her bravery inspired me the way it dared tomorrow.

"To Otter Mongolia," I shouted suddenly. And though only Princess got the meaning, they all got the spirit. "Otter Mongolia!" rose the shout, and the celebration started. "Splash, splash!" said Bob. "Slide, slide," said Sally. "Sparkle, sparkle," said Kent. "Crack the abalone," said Princess. "Float, float," said Mike.

People began to arrive, first among them Pauline in tight chic flaming red dress three inches above her elegant knees with a good-looking bearded guy at her side. She greeted everyone with a bright-eyed challenge, sat down on the sofa, knees crossed, dress pulled back to half-thigh, and clearly settled down for the afternoon. She didn't talk much, but she put out a neutral affect high energy vibration, clearly intending to be both a remembering and remembered part of the party. Bob and she exchanged from time to time high tensile polished glances over which I fancied seeing eye photons shoot, charged with energy brighter than light.

Bob caught my fascinated look. "Well," he said, "energy is the highest form of information, higher than structure or phenomenal content, important as both of these are, because it determines the potentiality of an event. Pauline and I are building energy by absorbing impact, right, Pauline?" She smiled, tossing her head slightly, green eyes dancing invisible emotional structures she rode that day as expertly as the mustangs she had grown up riding alone on high plains with few fences.

By four o'clock about fifty people moved or sprawled or sat in favorite energy postures around the House or in the courtyard. Then Mike carried chest-high into every room the House's bronze bell, there to strike summons to the play to be performed in the living room-library area.

"The Theater of All Possible Time Lines," Bob announced "will present 'a Stranger in Seven Deadly Time Lines'."

Kent's montaged photos began flashing on and off two sheet screens. Vanity, a man with a cock's head and tail, left hand on one hip, the right hand stroking a rose on an elongated stalk leaning forward above his scrotum, on tiptoe peering into a broken mirror; Lust, a man and woman joined rear to rear like dogs, both trying to break apart, the woman to join a rigid phallused silenus, the man to join an ambling nymph, their faces each contorted with hate and excitement. The photos went from close-ups on details to overall views. "Man!" "Wow!" The excitement commenced. Kent, Bob, Sally, and Princess had decided to start off with the visuals.

Then Princess laid down a camouflaged musical trail with "Found Sounds," swishing, stroking, and striking her collection of eight different percussion units from strings to pots to drums to pipes to strips, to bells, to sticks, to rings.

Greed, a tall thin ravenous man with a white goatee, his left hand flung up in a contemptuous rejection of a hungry woman with a child, his right hand counting out factories, offices, mansions, congressmen, dinners, his face with two blind eyes, mouth demonically distorted in unsatisfied grimace, jeering this naive Eve driven into the street.

Sloth, a self-absorbed girl, slouched on her chair, in ungroomed disarray, fingers idly playing with each other, feet crossed at the ankles, head dropped back beneath a spider-webbed ceiling, a sullen pout plumping lazy lips.

Anger, a red-veined bearded face shouting, hands fisted, upraised, his foot caught at the moment of kicking a chair, a frightened woman and young man in front of him, cornered, unable to move, his bulldog beside him in full growl, jaw distended, ready to bite.

Pride, a man, dressed in a tux and white tie, coldly ordering another man, dressed in a blue jeans and long hair, on his knees, with his behind facing his tormentor, to eat from a plate of shit. The man held a whip in his right hand, a handkerchief in his left, sitting upright in a leather chair with lion pawed foot and arm rests, himself shod in soft leather black boots, with a revolver lying on the right arm of his chair.

Gluttony, a woman with a glass of whisky in her left hand, her right gripping a fork piercing a piece of steak entering her mouth, her pushed-up breasts heaving, her face flushed, her shoes unlaced, her stomach swelling and folded beneath a T-shirt, her hair uncombed, dishes mounded with food in front of her on a disordered table, a crow at the window, a rat at the bottom of the table, her eyes somber with focused passion.

Then Alice, Princess, Mike, and Sally began a series of dance scenes that began with the first glimmerings of the full fledged negative emotion in the progress of vanity, the discovery of "me" entranced before mirrors of other people's eyes. The scene then progressed through many a high tempo twist and turn, toward humiliation and impotence, a dandified Mike sitting desperately trying to coax his "wand" up to the scoffing jeers of three hip women that "Dandy" had pursued, each in turn, with every posture at this command, immolated in ever-deepening self-admiration, until his hand was called and the only card he could deliver was a livid joker. Kent bathed each scene in a different overall light. "Dandy," however, could not escape a glaring white spotlight. Bob had the scene build in cross-firing mockery of a combination burlesque show and fashion parade. The flair-filled costumes had all been measured, cut, and sewed at the House. "There will be this one and only showing of the piece," Bob had declared at dinner the evening before.

"But with all this work, it can never pay in one performance, nor will you ever get any rewards," protested Ed the philosopher. "While dedication and integrity are worthy virtues, I don't think this Theater of All Possible Time Lines is actually going to experience anything but the Time Line of hard work, low income, and being forgotten when the few people who've seen your performances grow old and die. You will not even have left a proper paper and film trail so any scholar who might be interested could find his way to you. All your work will die."

"Art is an end in itself," Bob leaned, eyes alight in one of his favorite passions. "Used as a means to an end, any other end, art becomes technics, and techne is not one of the three graces."

"But she is one of the nine muses!"

"Our motto," said Bob, laughing, "is create and run. We shall never perform a piece longer than two weeks anywhere. We give up the "hit," the "stars", the "author". I don't sign the plays, Princess and all aren't featured, and we avoid the hit, on those productions that we might achieve it, by moving on before the hit making apparatus can tune up."

"Great as long as you are young and healthy. What then? And can you take responsibility for the poverty caused by the effects of this esthetic philosophy of ignoring the utilitarian sensationalist profitable categories of your society? Poverty that might embitter eventually the ever-less youthful members of your ensemble who have not yet had a chance to develop their own life-rich philosophy, in other words are influenced highly by you?"

"I don't take responsibility for anyone, and they all know that."

"Can you avoid responsibility? Your engaging presence, the vivacity in presenting your viewpoint, do they get counter-viewpoints? You seduce people, I don't say you intend to, but your presence is a seduction."

"If they don't get counter-viewpoints, it's because they don't pick up books to read, people to rap with, scenes to test viewpoints, and furthermore that kind won't last long in our theater, so they'll get out in time to make a good career."

Ed and Bob both looked around the table, but no one else spoke up. I reflected that I, personally, agreed with Ed. So I was not going with the Theater, but could not criticize Bob. In a way I wished for

Bob's courage, to move out and through the world in the company of artists presenting their visions of being, showing up to the beat of intentional schedules on a definite time, at definite places, to unknown indefinite audiences, building energies for that effort to make Dionysian transformations of old and meaningless into new and significant. I remembered seeing the small off-Broadway production of Albee's Zoo Story and American Dream, leaving in delirious stupor, almost unaware of the beautiful girl beside me, taken there hand in hand with the richest of romantic intentions, my spontaneously jumping up, spinning in the air, and slamming a stop sign with the back of my hand. How I had thought and written the next week, how that intensity had helped build the energy that enabled me to leave my Harvard-Anglo power and privilege spot to seek Tangier. Would I trade that voyage for anything? No, not for anything, that had to be what Bob meant by an end in itself. Just as I would not trade my travels, Bob wouldn't trade what he did, so precious and interesting did Bob find each aspect of his theater, for anything else in the sun's sphere of power. I looked curiously at Ed, tall, grave, serious, desperately unhappy, he said because he didn't have much money, only a few possessions and books, but really because he had no purpose. He clutched his tobacco pipe, his few friends, including Bob, and his copy of C.S. Pierce, because somewhere he had lost his Ph.D. chance to endless ethical equivocations about taking a stand in his thesis, then he had lost his midwest little college job to local moral guardians. Evidently his philosophy was not an end in itself nor did it achieve his utilitarian goals, because he still resented and bemoaned that job loss.

Suppose some or all of the people around Bob left the Theater, fell out with him or whatever, at least they would have followed a hunch, they would have staked a real bet, they wouldn't have subsided in a rut alternating between mud and dust, without having made their bid and showed their cards to the Gambling House of the World where the odds are always less than 50-50. How else could the world expand? At least Bob's table wasn't rigged with cheating that transformed tough odds into certain loss. And Bob did share the pot, whatever it turned out to be. Princess would certainly learn all she needed to strike out on her own as and when she so decided.

You'll Have To Find Your Own Way

The play ended with applause, laughter and silence intermingled, hugs for the players as they re-emerged after removing their makeup and re-changing clothes. Still discussing fine points of the play, people dispersed over the house. Joel and Henry alternated taking the front porch "invitation chair", and I found himself in the garden with Princess looking up at the now sun and fog bleached geometrically adorned banners Bob had strung over the back of the House.

"The geometries of qualitative thought," said I to Princess to draw her out.

"Yes," she said, "each action should be examined from the standpoint of the monad, then the dyad, then each successively more complex structure of qualities to the dodecad if we wish to understand the impossible dimension, the dimension that has no quantitative extensor, but which can accompany not at all, or a little, or totally any given set of existentially vectored dimensions." Ed had told me, "None of us will ever know how smart Princess is. And, unfortunately, she may never realize it, either, because she's not competitive enough." "Maybe she doesn't show it all because she likes to keep something in reserve for herself and intimate friends," I had replied fondly.

I hunkered down on the strong, simple bench Bob and Mike had doweled together out of weathered two inch thick planks they found. The sun still had not quite set that long solstice day, filtering its reds from low in the sky, this shore of earth turning away, resting from the day's production of hundreds of millions of tons of starches which fed tens of millions of tons of new animal flesh, which produced hundreds of pounds of hormones forming dozens of emotions from which a few micrograms emanated between Princess and me energizing our near weightless decision to be friends forever.

"I always knew we would be friends forever," I said.

"And ever," she smiled at me.

"Princess Precious Pearl," I said.

"Playing in Otter Mongolia," she finished.

"No matter what," I said.

"No matter when," she said.

"No matter who," I said.

"No matter why," she said.

Unconquerable rebellion unified the waves of joy and sorrow washing through me like lonely moonlit slopping of a far-off sea. We would prevail in this unity no matter how we got lost in spaces separated in time.

Joel and Henry came laughing by with two colorful girls they had obviously just beckoned in from the street. "This is the Country and Garden," Henry said to them. "These banners, this is their last night. They're, like, pictures of ideas."

"You mean pictograms," said one of the girls flirtatiously.

"And there's the basement room." said Joel. "Want to have a long talk about it?"

"Sure."

They went in, a burst of laughter, then silence. "Everybody's celebrating," I said.

"Each the best way we know how," said Princess.

Back in the living room, I saw Pauline still there, taking it all in, displaying her beauty and pride, her good-looking man devoted to her. Bob and she made eye contact every few minutes, but neither ever made a move to touch.

A young girl, about fifteen or sixteen, bounced in. "This is June," said Princess to Bob and me. "She's bright, bright, bright, and she wanted to see the place so I told her tonight's her last chance. She drove up from Stanford. She's already accepted for next year in marine biology."

Bob gave her warm embrace which she accepted as a gift, then took a swinging look around. "Why don't you show her the House, Joe?" he said. Princess nodded to her. "Great," she said and lightly took my proffered hand.

June turned on to the scene, soaring higher than she'd bounced in. The House undoubtedly at this laid back ecstatic happening culminating its history must have looked to the girl to be the confirmation of all the underground legends of the Haight. Some sat peacefully stoned by acid or contemplation or punch, some talked tranquilly, tracing outlines of memories to share or hopes to reveal, some gazed into each other's eyes, some circulated, butterflies checking out the pollen, always more fragrant in the next flowers. Nobody uptight. Time had become a handsome delivery boy serving up successive intimate and satisfying surprises with promises of more and better to come. People switched roles on subtle cues of inner changes of chemistry and attention. The stoned began to flow like water. The fiery talkers earthed into gazing. One gazer would space out, and his hip partner quickly move away to the dinner table still heaped with garnished foods. Joel and Henry had developed a low key slapstick erotic routine. They brought their third set of girls "on the tour" through the House. The last two times, they came in with their own guys, but Joel and Henry graciously invited the guys to sit down and enjoy themselves in the living room while the girls toured. The guys then toured the characters in the living room with their eyeballs. A small moan had been heard from the basement while the second set toured. Their guys stayed cool. From each according to their own thing, to each according to their cool, I thought.

When I felt June and the scene had synched, I caught her upper arm, and we half-danced out to the garden, then, on impulse climbed the stairs to the top of the roof where Doreen's tent stood, a lone explorers' hut on a frontier of roof tops. A small cool breeze stroked our faces. A few large stars twinkled through San Francisco's semi-luminous sky.

"And you want to - " I said.

"I want to find out what the real score is," she said, furious with some long-suppressed desire for poetry, not only marine biology with its facts, but poetry with metaphors that made the right connections.

"That's why you study pinnipeds, crustacae, and cetacae," I said, feeling sage, a step ahead of her emotional plunge.

"Fuck you," she said. "That's why I'm here tonight, not there. Princess said you guys actually know something here at the House. That it's really different here. What do you know I don't, and don't tell me it's how to make love."

Well, June had laid it on the line. Yes, I supposed that at least a handful of us did know something, had transmuted some lead in the pants to gold dust in the brain. But none of them, certainly not me, was going to trade that gold dust for heaven, hell, high water, leaping flames or a romantic fling with a nubile at her most provocative come-on. That gold dust was to be added to, not spent, until, sealed like a resplendent space ship powering its own motion from captured sun, I could move with the sensations of an immortal, whether or not scientists ridiculed those sensations with the banal indisputable statistical probability of death.

Neither could I send her to Raimondo's fevered high-cost fuck-out and beat-up your conditioned reflexes school, nor to Landers' austere and conscientious yoga, not even to Bob's Dionysian theater, nor could I bring myself to insinuate that dual tantric erotic contact with me would make "the" breakthrough.

But I could stare desperately at her while she stared back her plea and her dare. More than beautiful, raveningly sending out attractive phantoms of total surrender, of super student, of reincarnated goddess in ideal flesh, she pulsed more mysteriously to me than waves or stars. She's teaching me, I thought confounded, at least her changing faces teach my projections as she tries to catch one of them for good. They know more when I reel them back in and that comes from their learning from her. She's using no disguises, only separate realities. Probably on a hundred mikes, whango nubility, sea-swimming body, genius brain, out for a decisive night, wise but naive . . . I felt my body rocking in high voltage contact.

We kissed deeply, thoroughly, quickly, my left hand acknowledged with due admiration the taut fearless breast. We broke cleanly apart.

She had arrived just days too late. The scene was sailing toward its final hours at the House. The Street shutting down with cops, criminals, media unleashed upon its inhabitants to destroy the provocation of their energies. You needed months to live through transmutation, at best. Days to safely start the alchemy. No use starting a voyage if you would drown before crossing the ocean.

"You'll have to find your own way," I said. "I made this scene just in time a year ago. I looked for it all my life. I lucked out. We all lucked out. You lucked out coming by and getting on the vibe so you'll know when you see it when it happens the next time before it's hours to the end. I hope you do make it to the next time. Don't lose it."

She stared at him furious, still in full erotic flush but with a small space that saw. Would she remember? I hoped so. I hoped she wouldn't be too old by the next time.

They climbed slowly down the stairs. I took her back to Princess. "We had a great walk," June said, then sat down and leaned back on the couch lost in an inner vision. A good, a healing trip, but health was only means, not end.

"You did a good job," Princess said.

"I hope I didn't dull her edge," I said.

At ten o'clock in the morning the bronze bell rang through the House. People awoke, refreshed, eager, some with less than four hours sleep. Pancakes, maple syrup, scrambled eggs, toast and honey, oranges, coffee. Packing, loading.

They piled into the bus into their seats and into their new trip to test the powers gained in the old happening. Finally only Kent and I stood on the curb, ready to wave them good-bye. "Off to see the wizard, the wonderful wizard of Iz", sang Bob. Kent and I waved good-bye as long as we could see the bus. I swung up my shoulder bag with an old Navajo rug thrust in crosswise to stay warm at night. Not for me the bloody backpack. I was headed for Mexico. Kent picked up his battered suit case. Kent was headed to Menlo Park. We embraced and split. Kent was nitroglycerine in pure intellect, the very spirit of revolt. Kent was not going explosive, he was going to fuel a decade of warfare to liberate information.

Let the others go, I thought, to the mist enshrouded Northwest, blend in with the sophisticated coffee shops of the Bay Area, or move to Manhattan over the savaged continental superhighways, where bewildered cities gasped for breath between San Francisco's gold rush and Broadway's bum rush, there in the back studios and nightclubs of the world city to up-grade their act with feed-back from audience inebriated spectaculars, or like Kent go into high-tech and hack their way through jungles of malarial corporations to liberate access to undiscovered eldorados of tools, synergies, and computers. I would move around, too, but on my own. I would stop by and see key people from time to time, how they were making out. I'd lend a hand if needed. I kept in mind those creators whose creations came to life a millennium down the pike in the form of new cultural species. If I left any trace of myself to be discovered it would be addressed to those futures. How? I would have to hone a crafty and archeological art.

The jungle war continued. A ruthless oilgarchy controlled both parties, contributing millions both to tweedledum and tweedlehohum now that the Gracchi had been murdered. America now owned, lock (police), stock (money), and barrel (oil), by the rich and fearful. Dictators and religious nuts controlled most of the rest of the world. Liberated areas, some as small as a backpack trail would continue to spring up. History could no longer abide in the capitals, universities, and banks. Information know-how and most importantly a million highly skilled people had escaped. Social selection would eliminate all but the most adaptable mutations of that million. Survivors would evolve rapidly under such severe selection. The Street had made its bid to win by consciously dying and throwing out its seeds upon artistic and technical winds.

I had watched, been a small part of, a new era beginning to live its life out in transparent synchronicities. I knew as before, that genuine organic individual freedom, communal cooperation, and expeditions to explore the oceans and stars would follow this breakthrough, though not the when or where. I would stay in love, on guard, and on watch.

I would play the part of the unknown factor. Bob loved to quote Stanislavsky, "There are no small parts, only small actors." I would ramble, a random element. For the rest of my life I would appear and disappear where a need vibed. Mine would be a guerrilla skirmish in guerrilla wars, a unit of one, though in contact with Time's Operator, my resources located in the invisible. I would even take steps to lose details of memory, so these resources could not be hunted down. I would be at the volunteer service of whoever called on the non-content vibrational network, signaling energy needed, victory near with just a little help in Area A, or escape possible from major defeat with just a little help in Area B, or aid the last survivor from Area C.

Why else had I lived except to make the great escape? To become free, wild again, unknown, able to exist in this freedom around the planet, in most circles, in most countries, at least at the fringes of the center of all skills, to be of some help in the enterprise of creating living futures, of helping to create my own desired life setting of many freedoms.

I sipped café con leche at the Café de la Parroquia. The marimbas played on the wharves just below. Earlier that morning I had stared at the huge Olmec statue, that head sitting on the ground, neckless, nearly twice my height. This head contained my next message, and I had gotten it, and now could enjoy the best café con leche in Mexico.

"Use your head. Keep your head grounded. Without that, nothing will do you or anybody else any good."

The eidolon expanded its message to my tuned ears.

"Connect your head with the cosmos. Your body with the Earth. Then plug your mind in with the Biosphere and look over the horizon at the stars. Then you will know what to do when each place, time, people, and task come together."

"Live in peace."

The message had come straight through from four thousand years ago. The modern Mexicans had built a house around the head. They knew they had to protect it from themselves and tourists and from crazy reactions to the message, but give them credit, they hadn't moved or destroyed it. One day the space would be liberated again, and a plaza created around the Head.

The crowds built up on today's marina and café con leche plaza. Twelve o'clock. Bob, Kent, and Princess walked in just as they had all promised me and each other to do in that last meeting early in the morning of the day the bus left for Manhattan.

Two days from now was Mardi Gras. I had secured a small room, with one cot for Princess, us three guys would split the floor, at the brothel that vacated its premises for the big week. They had done it! My legs leaped about happily, crazily. We embraced in a small huddle, grinning and silent, in a tight hug.

We had kept our word to meet no matter what had happened. Looking at each other's face in turn we saw a lot had happened. One whango of a lot. But we had kept our word. We had not been on a collective fantasy high. We were survivors, ready, willing, and able.

Everything was possible if people kept their word and their decided word came from their dream.

Much could be done. More than could be dreamed.

"You won't believe this café con leche," I said.

Epilogue

Joe Madison had left the United States of America with its greatest and biggest and bestest and boringest for the richest, and hellholes for its melange of the poor, sick, aged, dying, different, tribal, ghettoed, brilliant, crazy and sexy called "minorities" by the small tight-lipped ruling minority, that amongst themselves democratic oligarchy for male European puritans. The unholy name of more-ality had produced, as in democratic, slave-owning, woman hating Athens before, a mighty empire, resentful allies, a power-mad oligarchy, demagogues (in Athens expert in rhetoric, in USA expert in media images), lofty idealists in the universities giving license to the state to lie and to banish poets or embark on world conquest in the name of science, with ever new hits in the latest stagecraft of thrilling murders and sex-crimes, and underground religions for the poor, the women and the artists. These rules only lacked the glorious philosophy, architecture, art, wit, theater, and supple bodies of Athens to be exactly similar.

Joe Madison had "woke up" in 1963, traveled the world by wit and luck and hope, and returned in 1965 to the US of A where his heart turned to a fire that sweated his body at night. He had danced and loved his way in 1967 through Haight Ashbury parks and nights, until that scene fell beneath lies, headlines, police, and prisons. He had escaped in 1969 to a place called Quintana Roo in Mexico.

He had escaped history, ambition, the "only" God, the "Absolute," democracy's terrifying tyranny of the vociferous minority (the 20% who owned the property), the bitter "funded" intellectuals who vilified any member of their subset who created anything that might endanger their privilige. He had escaped the bloodhounds introjected into his own bloodstream, his own breathing, reflexes, associations, muscular blocks, sensations, emotions, moods, passions, yes, even his own will, noticing, attention, even those emanating from the center of his very presence. He had escaped the most comprehensive and clever indoctrination ever known. So slick that those indoctrinated paid and mostly gladly paid to watch and hear their propaganda, knowing it was propaganda, it was so much more fun and sexy than competing indoctrinations.

A movie camera directed with cinema verité point of view would have showed from 1969-1996 a man living most of this time in a one room palapa with a tile floor, a mosquito-netted hammock, a small wood stove, an axe, sitting relaxedly in a rocking chair for morning and evening sun events, dressed in blue jeans, T-shirt, straw hat, sandals for "going out," an occasionally sipped bottle of tequila, a protected stash of marijuana, a clay pipe, two blankets, one for bed in the cool and one for the floor on which he could be seen doing yoga or sitting still for up to two hours a day, and a trunk full of handwritten manuscripts and a supply of clean lined yellow paged pads of paper.

The man would not be found there twice a year, for periods of two to three months. The cinema verité would have shown him in various ceremonial looking affairs with Indians. Mushrooms, peyote, or morning glory seeds would have been noted in some cases. Dance. Or lying in long silences, totally separate looking and totally companioned. Once or twice a year in a famous salon in Mexico City where the freest talk in the world prevailed among handsome people both refined and potent, at home in wilderness and world politics. The man would listen attentively, tell his newest story in return, and early in the morning board a cheap local stop bus back to the rugged limestone and barrier reefed coast. Once a year with a friend in New York's Chelsea district, once a year in the Maraís in Paris, and once a year in a small straw matted room in Kyoto.

In 1993 a beautiful Mexican with impregnable sexual power able to live on her own or with a creative lover of choice called him "Brujo." "Sitting with you in this café, drinking this coffee, you took me to another state of consciousness by only your touch, your gaze, and your words. You are a brujo."

He had listened to the word, heard it sink to his tailbone down the long slide past his breath, and realized that for him it was his "Legion de Honor," his "Fellow of the Royal Society," his "Russian Academician," his "Oscar." Those recognitions had never moved him to exert himself to attain. Brujo he had never strived to attain either. It was far too far above; too magnificent; practically unachievable except for a profound Indian born at the right time, right place, with the right people to put him or her through the experiences, the destructions, the creations, the learning, necessary.

Nothing changed for his behavior, outerly photographed. Innerly, all had changed. He knew he had not attained to what he himself would consider real Brujo being, but neither had most of the Indians who ran great ceremonies. They were mostly curanderos of gift and power. But they were dependent on limited and beleaguered tradition to deal with participants. They carried paraphernalia. They could not create a new culture if that became necessary. "And creating new cultures has become necessary," he said to himself.

December 15, 1996. He strolled out of his palapa toward the beach. Hotels now stretched up and down the white sands deserted only a few years ago. The ocean waves beat low and white against the reef. The trade winds blew a few clouds toward the limestone heads that marked the ends of the long beach, toward the mangroves behind and toward the jungles and Mayan ruins behind the marshes. He could always walk the beach. Mexican law forbade anyone to own the beach. For this one assertion against the power of private property and the market's materialist calculus he would have loved Mexico dearly. This one law alone made life economical, replacing with a daily simplicity set off by cosmic sky and planetary water all the commercial and shriveled details of TV, newspapers, and magazines needed for those in countries penned off from the outdoors by NO TRESPASSING. He could pick up fresh gossip of the human world at a beach café for a dollar cup of coffee, a dollar he seldom had to pay because for the cups of coffee he could exchange the more valuable knowledge of what actually went on locally. Sometimes, his benefactor included a breakfast or even a dinner. And the talk of the vacationing Texans, Italians, Brazilians, Germans, Russians gave him truer information than ABC's sordid one-liners pretending to be factual summings up of a revolution or the Times' ponderous clumsiness, both banging for a buck. Playa Luna played mirror to the world's sun and all the provincial moons coordinated with the World City suns in determining the tides in Earthly affairs.

Suddenly, he stopped. In Tangier so many years ago the world had stopped for him. It once again had stopped for him in Slug's in Manhattan. But now he stopped. He did not try to stop the world, he did not care to and, luckily, he knew no one had the power to stop the world, not even Shiva. The world had to stop itself a microsecond for you to see it. Twice was all you needed.

Now he stopped himself and realized that he would die and that everything he saw or felt or thought would die. He saw clearly as the sunlight's sparkle on the white sand people and states and things and hopes and thoughts dying by uncounted millions, balanced, more than balanced by birthing uncounted millions every second for billions of years. He saw that all this holocaust and all this hullabaloo made up an expanding warp and woof on which life wove a myriad of masterpieces, themselves taken by eternity and decision history during their brief potent phenomenal time, space, and attention to a transcendent-immanent unity of recontactable delight. He saw a dozen cosmic theaters with a thousand authors, ten thousand directors, millions of actors, and billions of audience.

He saw caravans of dreams all headed for someone sometime somewhere someway, many for him still coming, of incredible stuffs, perfumes, characters, costumes, bearing wealth beyond all the fever-ridden riches of the United States of America, that he had plenty, that plenty more remained where that plenty came from, and that the thing was to be ready when one of these caravans arrived because what with immense distances and cataclysms to cross, their exact arrival time and place could never be predicted.

The caravans' inexhaustible surprising goods supplied all the theaters, writers, directors, actors, and audience with all they needed for each new season and these caravans did not care whether a given theater was called Science, or Art, or Politics, or Adventure, or Enlightenment, or Folly, or Tragedy, or Comedy, or Burlesque, or Wisdom, or even All Possibilities.

Somewhere something loaded up all the caravans and he saw that something was called death. That death put on to the caravans all that it could of the thought or hope or person or species or sun which had died that they had not been able to do when existing. He saw every thought or hope or person or species or sun being born or in the onward thrust of its existence off-loading caravans throughout entire realms of exotic beings, aflutter and aglow with all the gifted marvels including eventually the strangest manners of death to pay back all the caravansaries that had helped load these caravans and put them up if they met sandstorms that delayed them along the way.

He saw that his frontier family had been a caravan, Tangier a caravan, Manhattan a caravan, India and Vietnam and Haight Ashbury and Mexico caravans, and that these unforeseen caravans had supplied his wealth and his freedom and his secret delight and that he would be willing to pay his price to keep the caravans rolling until the last one offloaded its splendid offerings to his existence. That last caravan would pleasure his essence in ways more exquisite than imagination's most lovingly worked reveries. No, delight his essence, her dark majesty whose light nudity alone he adored and all the companion essences she had glanced at, recognized, and made alliance with in her deeply hidden net of emanations with all these caravans.

He saw that the first caravan had been his body with its powers to think, to sense, to feel, to move, to dream, to initiate, to act, to react, with its mysteries of apperceptive quality and instantaneous meanings, of magical access to vast libraries, thought-spun mirrors, mood-deepened wells, dancing swords, bottomless cups, voyages to stars, and touching lovely skin to mold pulses of mind/body coordinations in forms inimitable in marble or on screen or canvas.

He saw, he remembered, he observed, he checked and verified, he registered immunely, hormonally and nervely in the two hundred and fifty types of cells, in billions of nerve cells. He tracked a molecule of air, a photon of light, a DNA switch, quantums of twitch building to a dissipative tremor in an eyelid, chaos fractaling uphill in the increasing pressure, temperature, and composition of molecules most rare until the chaos leaped over a dragon energy barrier and fell to rest roaming around a strange attractive valley high above the place he had started out from some epochs previously when he had light-footedly left his palapa for a stroll around the beach before he stopped.

Now he could rest, now he could come back down because he would not ever go back down into that lower valley, the one before Tangier, that isolated valley which believed in . . . almost anything thrown its way, which had to believe in something, work, self-importance, suffering, to fight unceasingly to hold on to, to prolong whatever had been fought for, to keep it as long as it could be kept, a dog snarling over whitening bones, a fight doomed from the very beginning since the inhabitants of that valley were fighting tick-tock time, their own subjective being, themselves, never seeing that toward them came caravan after caravan. They would bewail the lack of caravans as the indifference of . . . whatever name they assigned the unknowable beyond the beyonds. And that "they", he saw, had been his "I" until this day.

"I had to hope and struggle to become a brujo, an abdal, a real man, an arhat, a tulku, a dingelhoofer . . . ." but before he could finish putting down his previous state for its short comings compared to where he now roamed, he saw that his desperate hope and struggle had also been a caravan, a caravan most glorious with gifts of states and earnings of stations, escapes through nothings and returns through everythings, humiliations, that no one could experience without making such foolish, such exalted strivings. The truths he reached at last, at long last!, no one could ever hope to touch except by such total disgrace that would kill that self-deception veiling moments of reality that rendered description useless.

He saw that this new caravan had now stopped in front of his stop. That all that he had seen so far was only the sight of its coming. That he might have missed it entirely had he not stopped. Perhaps it had been looking for him for years but he had not been looking for it, so happy had he been unloading and gazing into and distributing the jewels of 1967, that cosmic caravan which had unloaded biospheres, internets, light shows, karasses, voyages to inner and outer moons, love, theater, and so much more upon those parts of him so needy to receive.

The first sight of this new caravan had been the vision of itself moving toward him. Now, the camels had knelt all around him, hundreds, each loaded, and the caravan master was speaking, standing on the sand, "Also see those ships upon the sea and those spaceships in the sky. Each of these is also filled with gifts. Let us unload them carefully, that you may choose which to pay your debts, which to enjoy, and which to use for your beloved Biosphere, and which to prepare yourself for your next period of existence."

THE END

ABOUT THE AUTHOR

Dolphin, one of the writers to emerge from the '60s Tangiers school, contemplates life from the gutter to the galaxy. Born in Western Oklahoma and reared in the lingering traditions of the frontier, he first left home at age 14 to work in California in the war effort. He became a young itinerate fruit picker, lumberjack and machinist, then scholar, intermittently studying the classics and anthropology at Northwestern, Stanford and Oklahoma Universities. He organized for the Meat Packers Union on the South side of Chicago in the McCarthy period, there encountering two of his heroes, Paul Robeson and W.E.B. Dubois. After the U.S. Army Corp of Engineers, his formal education continued at Colorado School of Mines, where he became a metallurgical engineer specializing in special metals from beryllium to uranium, then a Baker Scholar at Harvard Business School. He worked on overseas projects with David Lilienthal in Iran and Liberia. One day, Dolphin looked outside of his window on Wall Street, and spying a Yugoslav freighter headed for Tangier, decided to launch himself on a two year sojourn around the world. On this trip, he had a painting studio in Fez, met Burroughs' and Gysin's Third Mind in Tangier, Nile magicians, Tibetan Lamas, Special Forces and Buddhist Monks in Vietnam, and many other specialists in rare skills.

Since 1967 Dolphin has continued to travel around the planet, co-founded a theatre company, written three books of poetry, three novels, a compilation of short stories, thirty-five plays and produced and/or directed some eighteen films. He has read at George Whitman's Shakespeare & Company in Paris, in New York accompanied by Ornette Coleman, and at the October Gallery in London with West African musicians, and the Caravan of Dreams in Fort Worth, Texas. His plays have been performed on seven continents, from the ICA in London and Theatre du Soleil in Paris, to villages on the Amazon and streets in California, from Wroclaw to Oshogbo. He now performs several times a year with dancers and musicians as JOHNNY AND THE DOLPHINS.

Johnny Dolphin is the *nom de plume* of John Allen, inventor and co-founder of the Biosphere 2 project — world's largest laboratory for global ecology. An accomplished speaker, he has also written numerous non-fiction books and papers in biospherics, including *Biosphere 2: The Human Experiment* (Penguin).

Many of his books are available through Synergetic Press—
www.synergeticpress.com or through local bookstores.

OTHER BOOKS BY THE AUTHOR

Poetry

Off the Road
Wild
Dream and Drink of Freedom

Fiction

My Many Kisses
Trilogy of the '60s:
39 Blows on a Gone Trumpet (Book 1)
Journey Around an Extraordinary Planet (Book 2)

Drama

Caravan of Dreams Theater Plays:
Gilgamesh, Marouf the Cobbler, Faust (V.1)
Billy the Kid, Metal Woman, Tin Can Man (V.2)

Non-Fiction (J.Allen)

Space Biospheres, with Mark Nelson
Biosphere 2: The Human Experiment (Penguin Books)
Succeed: Handbook of Structuring Managerial Thought
Scientific Papers bibliography at www.biospherics.org

SYNERGETIC PRESS
7 Silver Hills Road, Santa Fe, NM 87505 USA
www.synergeticpress.com